MW00977601

ISLAND LIGHT

ISLAND LIGHT

by
ALEXANDER KEY

Island Light, by Alexander Key

©Reprinted by Forgotten Coast Used and Out of
Print Books www.forgottencoastbooks.com
swolfe@forgottencoastbooks.com in conjunction with
Gambit Publishing www.gambitpublishingonline.com
gailglaser@gambitpublishingonline.com, Chicago,
Illinois. 2011

No part of this book may be excerpted either in print
or by any electronic means without written
permission of the publisher, with the exception of
quotes for publicity purposes. All rights reserved.

Original edition publishing by the Bobbs-Merrill
Company, Inc., 1950.
Original map and title page artwork by Alexander
Key.

Cover design by Kristin Garner, Creative Printing of
Bay County, Inc., www.getcreativepc.com, Panama
City, Florida.

Printed in the United States of America by Lightning
Source, www.lightningsource.com, LaVergne,
Tennessee.

This book is printed on acid-free paper.

ISBN 978-0-9675917-6-6 Hardcover
ISBN 978-0-0675917-5-9 Paperback

To the Memory of
MARSE ROBERT
and
CAPTAIN STEVE

Foreword to the 2011 edition of Alexander Key's *Island Light*

"Oh, wild, bright land, oh, beautiful land of home!"
-- Alexander Key, Island Light

Very few works of regional literature attain the highest public recognition, as measured by numbers of copies sold, awards received or the length of time that they remain "in print." As a result, many titles become lost in the larger and ever evolving panorama of national literature. That snapshot, that sense of time and place, that author's view of human events in a particular time and context, all become lost to later generations of readers.

In the Winter of 2010, a group of like-minded lovers of Florida's Gulf Coast literature and history came together in Apalachicola, Florida to discuss bringing local works back into print. This reprinting of Alexander Key's Island Light resulted from that meeting.

We hope that *Island Light* will be the first of many such titles identified and reprinted.

FC

Regional Literature Worthy of Reprinting

Acknowledgements

There were many steps in the journey of discovery that led
to this reprinting of Alexander Key's Island Light. Several
persons provided support, guidance and encouragement for
the entire journey: Apalachicola Municipal Librarian Caty
Greene, author Dawn Evans Radford, author and publisher
Sue Cronkite, Apalachicola Historical Society president
Tom Daly, Independent Bookseller Dale Julian
(Apalachicola's Downtown Books and Purl), Lighthouse
Keeper Stanley Colvin and Terry Kemp, Board Member of
the Cape St. George Light.

Gambit Publishing's Gail Glaser guided an inexperienced
enthusiast through the publishing process, with help from
Creative Printing owners Sheila and Steven Ruff and dust
jacket/cover designer Kristin Garner. Richard Poole and
Marilyn Hyslop offered helpful suggestions.

Adrienne Love, Esq., and her assistant Whitney Myers,
provided legal support.

Orman House State Park Ranger Mike Kinnett, local
historian Delores Roux, and author and historian Beverly
Mount-Douds provided information and historical insight.

Perienne McKown, my husband Robert Wolfe and my
children, Katie and Andy McConnell, listened patiently to
long discussions of the project and provided
encouragement.

This effort is dedicated to my parents, Louis and Dorothy
Nosco, who, when I was in high school, allowed me to skip
school to stay home and read.

And to my dearest friends, who, after "Hello" and "How
are you?" ask "What are you reading."

Thank you.

Susan Nosco Wolfe

CHAPTER *1*

I

THEY hated this place. Every man within its walls hated it, and they hated everything about it. They hated the heat and the bright and deadly encircling sea, and the loneliness of it, and they hated its terrible remoteness from all those things that make life worth the living. But mostly they hated it because it was no longer a fortress, but a prison.

The officers and men quartered here endured it, with discipline, and existed only for the day when the supply boat from Key West would bring them orders for a change of duty. The prisoners confined here merely existed. Most of them, in one way or another, had fought

9

for the Confederacy, and once they had been important. In their hatred was the bitterness of men who have lost everything and whose victors are unrelenting. A few, who had no hope of pardon, dreamed of escape. But only the mad or the most intrepid ever dared it.

Escape was virtually impossible, for this was the citadel on Garden Key, in that far outcropping of sand and coral in the Gulf of Mexico known to mariners as the Dry Tortugas, and by them carefully avoided. On all the earth there was nothing else like it.

Once, perhaps, there had been a garden here. But the garden was gone now, swallowed, obliterated by this grim immensity of brick that had all but swallowed the key itself and left of it only a barren selvage of scorching sand beyond the south and east bastions. It was impossible and incredible, this place. A monster in the Gulf, a mammoth medieval pile surrounded by a shark-infested moat that could have floated the heaviest vessels of the Federal fleet. Fort Jefferson they called it when they were being proper, though they had other names for it. Even the sea birds shunned it. . . .

Major Roland Gaines was known to his superiors as a good officer, which is to say that he was a man of some principles as well as a martinet, and that he had been persevering under Grant. Six months on Garden Key had thinned him and harshened his features as well as his disposition, and turned his skin a fiery red under its spattering of freckles. He had been homesick before, but never so much as he was here. This afternoon, as he climbed to the upper gun tier and stepped out to inspect the work on the still unfinished terreplein, he was thinking wistfully of the Vermont hills and a girl he wanted to marry, and he was again suddenly re-minded—as always on viewing the Gulf's blue circle—of the long and lonely distance between this spot and the mainland.

He particularly hated this inspection of the ramparts, for it destroyed an illusion that made the rest of the day bearable. Behind him, down in the great hexagon of the fortress where a thousand men could maneuver upon the broad parade ground, it was possible to deceive one's self into thinking that the world was close and that laughter and gay music could be found not too far beyond the limits of the sally port. It was always something of a shock, therefore, to come out upon these heights and be reminded that his microcosm was but a dismal hole of masonry in a boundless sea.

Silently he cursed the place and consigned to particular depths of hell the powers in Washington City who had conceived it. As a fortress it was a monument to stupidity. It had never fired a shot at an enemy, and it never would. Who would want it? Who cared? Even so, he thought, a man might have stomached it with better grace if they hadn't turned it into a damnable gaol for all the rascals and renegades who had schemed against the Union.

Fight for the Union and free the slaves, and what happens to you? You find yourself a gaoler for the former owners of slaves, and practically a prisoner with them. Such was peace!

He glanced at the sun, and realized that he had less than an hour till the evening gun. Then the prisoners—those that were privileged to toil up here—would be secured and the guard changed. After that, while the rascals took their leisure, he could look forward to another night of writing reports. A double dose for the present, for the commandant was down with fever.

Frowning, in no pleasant frame of mind, he straightened and moved with stiff precise steps along the apron. As his eyes probed the little groups of prisoners, on the alert for any small laxity among them, he wondered how much longer he would have to wait for a transfer. What month was this? March? God, it didn't seem like March. But the days and the weeks were all alike down here; they blended into an unending ordeal of heat and routine and stupid reports, with only an occasional day in Key West to see how much rum you could soak into your bones before taking the boat back.

On the southeast bastion he paused a minute to study a distant floating object reported by the sentry. It was to the northward, nearly a half mile away, something barely discernible in the bright silken stillness that stretched to the horizon. Had there been a breath of wind it would have been invisible.

"Well, what do you think it is?" he asked irritably.

"I'm not sure, sir," the sentry replied. "I thought at first it was another one of those big devilfish. There's a lot of 'em around, sir. But it ain't moved none, an' I'm beginning to believe it's an old boat that's half sunk an' adrift."

"H'm. Well, keep an eye on it and report it to your relief."

He shrugged and turned away, doubting the sentry's eyesight. A bit of driftwood, probably, but it was too far off to matter. He swung on around the bastion and instantly forgot the thing as he approached the next detail of prisoners. The guard in charge of them came quickly to attention, but the four prisoners turned their backs and ignored him, and without so much as a glance in his direction went on with their desultory cleaning of the gun emplacements.

Major Gaines stopped. His mouth thinned and his sunbitten face turned a deeper color as his eyes went over the four men. It was their attitude that infuriated him. They had done nothing but ignore him, but their thoughts were as palpable as the heat that radiated from the scorching bricks under his boots.

"Detail, attention!" he snapped. "About face!"

Three of the prisoners turned slowly and straightened. Three gaunt bearded men in faded denims who peered at him sardonically a moment before their eyes slid to the fourth man, who had not turned. The fourth man, who stood upon a gun mount, had merely stopped his pretense of work to lean on his shovel while he continued his absorbed study of the sea. He had, in fact, no legitimate excuse for being where he was, since the emplacement had already been scraped and swept clean of the sand that had blown down into it from the drifts on the terreplein.

"What the devil are you doing there?" the major demanded. "What are you looking at?"

"The sea," the man drawled, turning. "The blessed sea. Or is the sight of it forbidden?" he added harshly.

Roland Gaines eyed him from across a chasm that four years' mortal conflict had left too broad for any small bridge of sympathy or understanding. These men were traitors, convicted of the highest crimes against the Union. Many of them, he felt, should have been hanged. This fellow was patently one of the worst. He'd noticed him before—a tall thin stick of a man with a mane of blue-black hair and a look of suppressed violence about him that marked him for a troublemaker. Defiant and uncompromising. You could thank such rascals for the whole bloody business.

"Get down from that mount," he ordered, "and mind your manners! You're forgetting yourself."

For a moment the fellow's eyes seemed to burn with a glittering blue-green flame in their deep sockets. He was so lean that he appeared taller than he actually was, and his ribs made a broad washboard under the shirt that clung to him in the heat. A straggly black beard covered his gaunt jaws. Like most of the other prisoners he wore ankle irons with a connecting chain.

"I never forget anything," he replied in his slow rasping drawl. "Don't try to force respect from those who feel only contempt."

Roland Gaines straightened. His eyes widened a little until they showed the whites. "When I give an order I'll have instant obedience—and I'll be addressed as sir! It's time something was done to remind you that you're an inmate of a Federal prison! What's your name?"

"Ewing," the man replied, biting out each syllable. "John Maximilian Ewing. *Lieutenant* Ewing, commander of the privateer *St. George*, Confederate States Navy. And may I remind you that I am not a criminal, but a prisoner of war—and may I further remind you that the war has been over these past two years, and that I am being held here contrary to all the fine principles for which you and your damned government supposedly fought!"

To his credit, Major Gaines managed to hold his temper. "You would not be here," he said icily, "if you had not been judged a criminal, and convicted by due process of law."

"Judged and convicted by a jackleg court of vindictive Federalists and scheming thieves! By the Almighty God, if I were in your boots I'd be ashamed to be seen in the uniform of a people so totally devoid of honor!" Ewing spat, and a stream of ropy spittle stained the toes of Roland Gaines's polished boots. One of the other prisoners gave a deep and fervent "Amen!"

Roland Gaines stood speechless a moment, and his freckles were angry spatterings of dark paint on the knots of muscle gathering in his jaws. Suddenly he stepped across the gun mount and struck Ewing sharply with the flat of his hand, first on one cheek and then on the other. Stepping back, he nodded to the guard and ordered hoarsely, "Return these prisoners to their casemate and report to the provost sergeant that all their privileges are canceled. They are to be placed on bread and water until further orders."

Afterward Roland Gaines tried to put the incident from his mind. But it grew upon him and tortured his mess hour so that he left early with his supper barely touched. At his desk that evening he sat awhile dictating to the corporal on duty, but finally thrust his work aside and went over to the window and stood looking out at the parade ground, dim in the starlight. He was still angry, but more now with himself than he had been with the prisoner. He felt he had conducted himself very badly. A word to the guard would have been enough. If he had ignored Ewing and merely given an order to the guard, then the whole thing could have been averted.

Devil take it, the war was over and the issues settled, and it was better to forget about the past. Things were the way they were, and the rebels had to pay. Of course, there were some injustices. Bound to be, with Lincoln murdered on the eve of peace.

Take that doctor who had set the broken leg of the assassinator, Booth. The poor devil hadn't known Booth from Adam—he'd merely done what any other doctor would have done in the circumstances. But yonder he was across the parade ground, in one of those casemates that had never seen a gun; chained with the worst of 'em, sentenced here for life. All because he'd set Booth's leg. A stinking shame.

Roland Gaines touched his cheek and then looked at his hand. He frowned, suddenly troubled. If Lincoln had lived, no doubt a lot of things would be different these days. Certainly that doctor would be free. Probably a great many of the other prisoners would be in their homes. There had been injustices. Sometimes they didn't make you any too proud. . . .

He swore and turned back to his desk, and became aware that his corporal, waiting with pad and pencil, was regarding him curiously.

"Jordan," he said, "bring me the record for the prisoner named Ewing, John Maximilian."

"Yes, sir. Isn't he that Captain Ewing who had a privateer?"

"Eh? You know anything about him?"

"I've heard of him, sir." The corporal thumbed through a file and lifted one of the records. He placed it on the desk. "A man of some reputation, sir."

"A lot of rascals here are men who once had reputations."

"Yes, sir. What I mean, sir, is that when I was stationed in upper Florida with the occupation forces, I heard a lot about him. He's an Apalachicola man."

"Where's that?"

"Straight up the Gulf from here, sir. East of Pensacola. Used to be a big cotton port. I had duty there a few months. Captain Ewing is from an old shipping family there. Very wealthy people, once."

"No doubt what you heard about him up there was very much in his favor."

The corporal smiled. "It wasn't what you'd call derogatory, sir. I guess he really was a little hard on our shipping. Anyway, those rebels seem to think we've dealt very unfairly with him."

"They would."

Roland Gaines peered at the record. His lips pursed. *Ewing, John Maximilian. Piracy and treason.* A blanket charge, probably, by which they'd handled a lot of these rebellious seamen. Well, the courts looked on them as criminals, and they'd been out for blood. *Twenty years.* A bit rough, that. Captured in '64 and held a couple years in Fortress Monroe. Brought down here last March. Former navy officer, eh? Annapolis man. Well!

He leaned back in his chair, frowning. These prison records told so little. All the details on Ewing, John Maximilian, were probably filed away somewhere in Washington City, forgotten. *Piracy and treason. Twenty years.* The courts that had handled these war cases had been a little free with their phraseology, and naturally they'd had their daggers out for Annapolis men. Still, twenty years . . .

I am not a criminal, but a prisoner of war. . . . Convicted by a jackleg court of vindictive Federalists . . .

Roland Gaines touched his cheek again and looked at his hand, suddenly wishing that he had not slapped the face of Ewing, John Maximilian.

II

Sometimes they hardly spoke for days, these four men in the corner casemate. At other times they would have puerile outbursts that belied their years and education, or they would talk quietly far into the night, blanketing the present and the future with little fragments of the past. Dawson, who was sixty and who had owned many thousands of acres and hundreds of slaves, could speak gracefully and even lyrically of subjects that might have come forth as crudities from other mouths, so that when you heard him you thought tenderly of certain reels you had danced and women you had loved. But Dawson, when bitter, could rant like a schoolboy. McInness, the colonel who had lost a hand at Antietam, was an irascible man, yet he had read widely and could quote long passages from Milton and Shakespeare. Meriwether, the pale scholar who had given up his researches for espionage, had fits of brooding, though he could take you with him to far places and make you see the Nile and the Euphrates and the works of ancients crumbling in the sand. Ewing was the most taciturn. They could seldom guess what was in his mind, so that when he spoke it often came as a surprise.

This evening, after the gratings had been locked upon them, Ewing lifted one of the loose bricks in the casemate floor and from the enlarged cavity under it that held such treasures as a pencil, checkers made of fragments of sea shells, and an almost indecipherable deck of playing cards, he retrieved a sharp-pointed bronze marlinespike he had stolen from a carpenter's kit. Without a word he sat down cross-legged in the shaft of light angling through the barred port, and began studying the chain connecting his ankles. The end links were weaker than the others, for repeated applications of sea water from the brine barrel—used in sluicing down the latrine in the corner—had pitted them with rust. Finally he thrust the marlinespike into one of the end links and twisted it experimentally. He was preoccupied and grim.

The others watched him silently, a little curiously. The marlinespike had long ago ceased to interest them. Chains, undoubtedly, could be broken with it, just as bricks and bars could be loosened. In fact, one of the bars in the casemate port could now be moved at will— but what did it avail them? Suppose a man actually ventured to swim the moat and managed to reach the spit of sand on the other side. What then? Where could he go?

Their thoughts boiled around the incident on the ramparts. Presently McInness, the colonel who had lost a hand, swore with feeling. "The freckled bastard! The goddamned freckled Yankee bastard! But you put him in his place, Max. Good for you!"

Max Ewing shook his head. "I should have kept my damned mouth shut."

"Bah!" said McInness. "They can't do any more to us than they've done already."

The elderly Dawson said, "They can hardly take from us what we haven't got. I've never considered it a privilege to toil in the sun. As for bread and water——" He shrugged. "The bread is palatable, but I'd have been ashamed to feed the rest of the slop to my field hands. In fact, they wouldn't have eaten it."

Again they were silent as they watched Ewing picking at the rusty link. There was something unfathomable in the man that held all three of them. Each secretly admired him for a different quality: Dawson because he considered him a gentleman, McInness because he looked upon him as a fire-eater, and Meriwether because he had come to think of Ewing as his only friend.

It was Meriwether who asked finally, "Max, what were you really looking at up there when Freckles came snorting by?"

"A boat adrift," he answered, without glancing up.

The three peered at him sharply, suddenly intent, curious, speculative. A boat adrift. Their imaginations reached toward the unseen boat, exploring its possibilities. But they watched him silently and asked questions only with their eyes.

"It was just a skiff," he said slowly. "A turtler's skiff, maybe. I couldn't make it out very well. It was full of water, and it was nearly a half mile north of Bush Key."

"Oh."

With knowledge of the boat's location the spark went out of them. They were very well aware that Bush Key, a sand bar covered with a sparse growth of knee-high scrub, lay a hundred yards beyond the eastern corner of the moat. Those hundred yards made even the key almost inaccessible. Anything in the deep water beyond it might as well be in another hemisphere.

Max Ewing strained with the marlinespike, and Meriwether said, "What's the use of breaking it, Max? They'll just put a heavier one on you."

McInness cursed. "Chains," he said hoarsely. "Blast their souls! Is it insolence or stupidity that makes them keep us chained in a place like this?"

"Insolence," replied the elderly Dawson. "And fear, too. Have you ever thought what could happen if we had a real riot in here?" He got up stiffly and shuffled over to the latrine in the angle of the bastion, and presently they heard him slosh water from the barrel into the open drain that ran out to the moat. He came back and sat down again on the brick floor. There were no chairs in here nor even a table, for, insolence or not, such articles could become dangerous weapons in the hands of irate men. The sole furnishings other than the brine barrel were three flimsy cots, a pail of tepid cistern water in which wiggle-tails were always active and a tin cup. Once this casemate had held a dozen cots, but they had been taken out one by one as their occupants died. The last to die had been a lad named Miller who, crazed with homesickness, had made a mad leap into the moat and been shot. Miller was often in their minds, but they seldom spoke of him.

From a distant casemate, in stubborn defiance of the commandant's orders, they heard discordant voices rising hoarsely with the words of "The Bonnie Blue Flag." For a moment the old song that had carried many a footsore company through the bitter red years to Appomattox, sounded pathetic and forlorn. Then suddenly scores of voices caught it up and the great hexagon roared with the sound of it. McInness rose and shouted. "You Texans! If we had a few more of you in here, by God, we'd tear this bloody hole apart!"

Sometimes one of these outbursts would grow and develop into a near riot with the prisoners shouting their defiance at the guards half the night. But this evening they quieted abruptly, and in the silence they sat brooding of home. Max Ewing's mind reached across the long sea miles to the upper Gulf, to the port at the river's end. He closed his eyes and saw again the familiar white houses fronting the bronze bay, the shell streets leading down to the harbor, the great saw-grass reaches beyond the river's mouth. At this hour the ibis would be winging across those marshes to their rookeries in the swamps. Ah, there was a country for you! From the black swamps behind the town to the islands in front of it with their miles of white beaches, it had a wildness and a beauty that men like Dawson and Meriwether could never comprehend. They were Virginians. Yet he knew how they felt when they spoke of the oak hills of Sussex and the redbud that was now coming into bloom. Their hearts were in Virginia, and the soil of it was the stuff that had made their very blood and marrow. He thought, wherever you are and whatever you are, you remain an inextricable part of the land that bred you; it's the soul of you, and there's no ache like the ache of wanting to go back to it, just to taste it and smell it and feel it again before you die, because it's home.

Viciously he twisted the marlinespike, and the link broke. He thrust the spike into the other end link and turned it violently, so that the leg iron cut into his ankle. The chain fell free.

The others stared at him, and Meriwether whispered, "My God, Max, what are you up to?"

"I'm getting ready to leave," he ground out, and pressed the marlinespike into Meriwether's hands.

"Here, get busy with it! When you get tired I'll help. We're all going to get out of here tonight!"

"You're crazy, Max! There isn't a chance!"

"There's a chance if you're willing to take it."

"What sort of a chance?"

"That drifting boat I told you about."

Meriwether looked at the others. McInness mumbled something into his beard and the fingers of his remaining hand touched the stump of his forearm. Dawson shook his head. "But, Max, I understood you to say that the boat was a half mile beyond Bush Key."

"I said it was a half mile *north* of the key. When I saw it the tide was beginning to ebb. Down here the tides run north and south. Ever since I spotted the boat I've been trying to calculate where it will be at slack tide. If there's no wind between now and eleven o'clock, I'm almost certain we'll find it in the shallows on the north side of the key. But it won't be there long. The minute the tide turns it'll start northward again, and it'll go fast. The inshore current turns northward here. It's pretty strong."

For long seconds they were silent, thinking of the boat and what would be required of a man to reach it. Then Meriwether began testing his chain with the marlinespike.

Dawson said, "It's quite a drop from here to the moat. Twenty feet, maybe. And the damned thing must be seventy feet across." He paused, and they thought of the sharks in the moat, attracted there by the garbage thrown to them daily; and they thought of the sentries who would be watching. But Dawson did not mention these things. "After the moat is crossed," he went on, "there'll be a run of at least five hundred feet along the edge of the sand before anyone can reach the channel to Bush Key. That channel must be four hundred feet wide. It will take time to cross it and find the boat and dump the water out of it. But let us say the thing is accomplished. What then? What are the chances in an open boat? Where would it drift?"

"It depends on the weather," Max Ewing said. "Ordinarily, with the winds the way they've been, it would drift to sea, to the edge of the Gulf Stream. It swings around out yonder about twenty miles. The Cuban fishermen go there to catch red snapper. There's a possibility of being picked up by one of them. On the other hand, at this season, we could have a nor'wester. That would take us back toward the reefs, somewhere around Key West. Anything can happen. I—I'd rather die at sea than go on rotting here. When ten-thirty comes I'm taking to the moat."

Dawson looked away. "To reach the boat you've got to be fast. If I had it in me to swim seventy feet, run five hundred and then swim four hundred more, I'd be with you." His voice broke. "It's worth the risk. But I haven't got it in me. I'd only be a danger to the rest of you." He turned to McInness. "How about you, Colonel?"

McInness considered his stump of a forearm. "I can't swim," he whispered.

Meriwether said quietly, "Give me a hand with this chain, Max."

They waited quietly in the dark, listening for the faint all-is-well cries of the sentries that sounded hourly from the terreplein. Once Meriwether said, "If we're lucky enough to reach the coast, Max, what are you going to do?"

"Depends. We'll have to take things as they come."

"I wasn't thinking of that. I—I was looking farther ahead. I mean, well, the world that we knew no longer exists. Everything has changed. If we were safe ashore now, I—I wouldn't know what to do or where to go. My wife is dead. My property has been confiscated. My relatives and friends are all scattered or dead. I—I haven't a penny. You see what I mean? When I had money I thought nothing of going to some of the most dangerous places. I had my researches. . . . But now, when I think of actually being away from here and free, I—I'm terrified. There's no place for me."

"What do you want to do most?"

"There's an oak grove back of the house at home. I'd just like to walk through it once again. After that . . . "

"How old are you?"

"Thirty."

"I'm thirty-three. We're still young. There's a devil of a lot for fellows like us to do."

"That's what I asked you about at first, Max. It will take a while for us to get our bearings. But you're in the same position I'm in. To go where you're known is to be recognized and recaptured. You can't go home."

"I'm going home. I'm going to make it there if it's the last damned thing I ever do."

"What will you do when you get there?"

"Mother's there. I'll see her first. We won't be able to stay in town, of course—but I have friends, and a little money hidden away. If Branch Clabo is alive— and I'm sure he is—we'll be well taken care of while we're resting up and making our plans."

"Plans for what?"

"You don't think for one instant, do you," he said, peering at Meriwether's dark form beside him, "that I'm going to let the scoundrels get away with what they've done to us? I've a long score to settle. And I've had a long, long time to think it over."

"I've often wondered what you were thinking about when you were sitting here, saying nothing."

"Well, you know now."

"The war's over, Max. We're beaten. There's nothing left to do anything with. Of course, even if I were free, I wouldn't live under their damnable rule. I believe I'd rather go to Mexico, as so many have done."

"I won't go to Mexico unless I'm driven there, or unless I have to use it as a base. I'm not beaten. They'll never beat me! I fought honorably for what I considered my rights—and they attacked me in a neutral harbor, killed my brother and convicted me as a criminal. Very well, I'll be a criminal. I'll give the scoundrels a taste of something they never dreamed of."

"How?"

"It'll take time, money. But I think I can get the money. There are ways. But first I want to go home."

He was silent again, thinking of home, and now it was sharper and brighter in his mind than it had been in all the years he had been away from it; and so clearly did he see it that he did not hear the others when they spoke or speculated or offered their little crumbs of hope or advice. Had he permitted himself to examine their chances coldly he would have said that they had no chance tonight, and that even if they gained the boat and found it serviceable, it would be but to drift in it on the open sea until they died. He was a practical and reasoning man who loved Euclid and believed in logic—but he would have been no seaman if he had not believed in signs and in many things beyond logic. The boat itself was a sign. Even the weather—the lack of wind when there should have been a wind—was a sign. And all day he'd been thinking of certain people at home, of his mother and the servants and of the family lawyer, and of his friend Branch Clabo across the bay, and of Bella Tacon. And the clarity of their faces was a sign.

He wondered suddenly, as he had often come to wonder, if his mother knew of Bella. Perhaps not, unless Bella had had a baby. But it seemed unlikely, for there had been not even a mention of her in those few early letters that had managed to come through to him. His mother's last letter was months old and it had been sent to Fortress Monroe. As soon as it was allowed he'd written to her of the change, and he'd also written Cassius Drew, but there'd been no answer. No doubt things were in a mess outside. And, of course, the powers that be didn't give a damn about prisoners' mail. Probably they destroyed most of it.

He was not aware of the faint voices of the sentries outside until McInness, somewhere in the close dark beyond him, said, "Ten o'clock. You'd better be getting that bar loose. I'll be counting the minutes for you."

He moved to the patch of starlight coming through the port, and used the marlinespike to pry out the bricks that had already been loosened. Meriwether hunched beside him and placed the bricks on the floor. Then they put their weight on the exposed end of the bar and heaved until there was enough space for a man to slip through.

It was now that Dawson brought the bucket and the

tin cup. "You'd better drink your fill," he advised. "I'd
drink until I couldn't hold another drop."

"If I drink too much," said Meriwether, "I won't be
able to run."

"Don't worry about the running," Max Ewing told
him. "Just drink, and be thankful for the wiggle-tails.
But maybe we'd better squeeze through the bars first
and do our drinking on the other side."

They forced their flat bodies through the opening and
crouched facing each other in the narrowing space just
beyond. He reached back and filled the cup from the
bucket and drained it, and filled it again and passed it to
Meriwether. They drank slowly, passing the cup back
and forth, silent and more remote now from the others,
their eyes on the patch of starlight where freedom lay.

He visioned Bella, and the vision became a revitalizing
force flowing through him. It was a force that had kept
him alive when others had died. A man can long for
home, but the longing can become only a destructive
sickness as deadly as those winters at Fortress Monroe,
as vicious as the fever here. He had survived those things
with the memory of Bella's warmth and her laughter and
the eternal promise of her strong vital body. He had
never questioned whether or not he loved her. From the
instant of their meeting there had been a flame between
them that had never needed words. Had there been time
in those hurried days he would have married her, but of
course there hadn't been time. Not that it really mattered. The flame was there, and it would be there when
he returned, unquenched by years or distance. He knew
that as certainly as he knew the stars beyond the port.

In the darkness behind him he heard McInness say,

in a voice unusually gentle, "I guess it's about time, Max."

He turned and groped through the bars for McInness' hand, and then found Dawson's hand and heard him say, "God be with you, son. I'll be praying for you." And it was suddenly very hard to tell these men good-by, for they had been closer than brothers to him.

He crawled on through to the ledge and hunched there, peering down at the broad moat until Meriwether came up beside him.

Meriwether said, "You'd better go first. Shall we take off our shoes?"

"No, there's cactus all over the sand. Keep your shoes on till we reach the channel. You won't need 'em after that. Can you swim under water?"

"Fairly well."

"Then go as far as you can before you surface. Take a quick breath and go under again. If anything happens to me, just keep going and try to reach the boat." He paused and took a quick look at the moonless star-flung sky, and listened to the whisper of the sea on the spit of sand. "Well, here goes. Count ten and follow me."

He swung his feet over the ledge, took a deep breath and dropped.

III

There were times when he had wondered if fate were a fan, with many paths from which to choose, so that in a sense a man was largely master of his own destiny . . . or were all things ordained to follow an inexorable pattern of cause and effect and circumstance, so that no matter what the choice and the path, it was written thus in the beginning? Can a man choose his father and mother, and his place and hour of birth? Can he alter any particle of the past? If he cannot, then surely the past is fixed, and thus the present is the unchangeable sum of it. And what is the future but the present a moment or an hour hence? Does it not fall into the exact and unalterable pattern of all that has preceded it?

Or is fate only what is haply woven from moment to moment with the threads of chance?

Long after he had gained the boat he was to wonder how it might have been if he had dropped into the moat a second earlier or a second later. Perhaps the time would have had no effect whatever on what was to happen. Perhaps the happenings of this night were fixed, and as utterly beyond change as what had happened that time more than three years ago in the Bay of Cárdenas. He had chosen his course there, and by all the laws of neutrality he should have been left unmolested when the enemy found him. Had he been in British waters the enemy would not have dared such a highhanded action. But Cuban waters are not British waters, and the enemy, as contemptuous of neutrality as they were of the rights of man, had been out to stop him at any cost. Well, they'd done it—for three years . . .

In the moat he had to come up twice for air, and he was all but exhausted when he pulled himself over the lip on the far side. His clothing and the ankle irons, of course, had not made it any easier. Even so, his weakness worried him. I'm not even half a man any more, he thought, and lay gasping for breath while he tried to pick the best course along the sand ahead.

The cry of a sentry and the sudden sharp crack of a

rifle from the nearer bastion brought him to his feet, running. He ran bent over, trying to conserve his strength, letting the weight of his body help swing his long thin legs over the lumpy sand. He glanced back twice before he saw Meriwether, more than twenty yards behind. Almost at the same time he heard the dull boom of the signal gun over in the parade ground.

The run seemed interminable, for though every step carried him nearer the channel, his course for most of the way was almost parallel with the eastern ramparts. Actually, he knew, he and Meriwether were in far less danger of being hit by a rifle bullet than of being attacked by a shark or a barracuda in the channel. A moving object makes a poor target in the starlight, without a moon to cast shadows. Just the same he was immensely thankful when he reached the water. He went splashing out and threw himself into it, and did not stop to wrench off his shoes until he was well away from the beach.

Finally he turned on his back and floated, resting with only his face out of the water while he watched Meriwether gain the beach and follow him in. So far, so good. But their margin of time was running swiftly out, for already he could hear the rattle of the chains lowering the drawbridge, reminding him that a search detail would soon be coming on the double. There would be some delay, of course, before they got around to launching the commandant's yawl drawn up on the sand opposite the sally port. And there would be more delay while the thing was being manned with oarsmen. He counted on their clumsiness in such matters to give him and Meriwether the extra minutes needed to drift out of sight in the derelict boat.

As soon as his ragged breathing steadied, he rolled on his side and began to swim. Over his shoulder, far behind, he could make out the spot of movement that was Meriwether's head. Occasionally he saw a little geyser of white flipped up by a bullet, but at last the firing ceased as they neared the key. Finally his dragging feet touched sand.

He crawled out and lay resting for precious seconds until Meriwether reached the safety of the shallows, then he got up and ran at a crouch along the north side of the key, searching for the boat. It took minutes to find it. Already it was beginning to float away in the tide, and when he reached it, far down at the other end of the key, it was fifty feet out and on the edge of the deep water. The precious boat. He drew it back toward the stumbling Meriwether and searched quickly for some means of bailing it.

It was a turtler's skiff, badly battered but apparently seaworthy. His hands, exploring under the thwarts for a bailing bucket, encountered nothing but a pair of rough spars lashed to a slimy piece of canvas. A sail? He had not even hoped for such luck. But how was he to get the water out of the thing?

He drew the boat back until the bottom scraped sand, then got his fingers under the chine and tried to raise it. A little water spilled over the opposite gunwale. It was beyond his strength to lift it higher. He turned and saw Meriwether sloshing toward him.

"Hurry!" he gasped to Meriwether. "Give me a hand—we've got to tip the water out of it."

Meriwether, breathing with a rasping whistle through his teeth, slumped to his knees beside him. Together they tugged, strained, fought and finally, with a desperate burst of effort, managed to lift the starboard gunwale high enough for most of the water to drain out. Then Meriwether collapsed.

He got aboard and feebly dragged Meriwether in beside him. For a long time afterward he lay motionless, exhausted, conscious only that the boat was drifting. When at last he roused himself and peered over the side he realized that the night had darkened and that a light breeze was coming out of the east. He could no longer see the fort.

He touched Meriwether and said, "We've won, Jim! They'll never find us now!"

Meriwether did not answer, and he touched him again. "Are you all right, Jim?"

"I—I'm hit," came the faint reply. "They got me in the back."

"Oh, my God! Why didn't you tell me?"

"There wasn't time. We had to get away. Besides, it didn't hurt much. It just felt numb."

"Here—let me have a look at it. I can stop the bleeding. Maybe it's just a flesh wound."

"No—no. Don't bother. It won't do any good. It's not even bleeding. It's way in me, deep—deep." Meriwether sighed and closed his eyes. Presently he opened them and said quietly, "I don't mind. I'm glad, really. It's been bad without Juana. Very bad. We used to go everywhere together. Everywhere . . ."

"Jim—isn't there anything I can do for you?"

"No, I'm quite comfortable. I don't feel a thing, really. Just a numbness . . . It's creeping over me . . . like a blanket. Let's talk, Max, while there's time."

"All right. What would you like to talk about, Jim?"

"Life. It's so short, Max. So damned short . . ."

"Yes."

"I can see now there's no time in it for bitterness. It's a waste, Max. Life should be spent for other things. . . ."

"Maybe. It depends what life does to you."

"No. . . . You're seeing it from the wrong end of the glass, Max. You're bitter. It's been eating in you like an acid. It'll destroy you if you let it. You mustn't let it do that to you."

"I can't help how I feel. Those self-righteous scoundrels . . ."

"It's all over, Max. They've wrecked what we were. You can't bring it back. I've thought about it a long time. . . ."

"So have I. And I'm not going to let them get by with what they've done to us."

"Don't be vindictive, Max. You can't build anything new by being vindictive."

"My God, Jim, they're the vindictive ones! They——"

"I know. And that's why you can't afford to be. You've got to be smart in other ways. . . . If you don't, you'll be twice the loser. Were you ever in North Africa, Max? In old Carthage?"

"No. I didn't know the Romans left anything of it?"

"They didn't. Not a stone. They were very vindictive people. . . ."

"But what happened then hardly applies to us now."

"Perhaps not. . . . But Rome and Carthage had once been brothers—and they fought once too often. Anyway, I was speaking figuratively. . . . I was thinking, if you could be a little bigger, see it a little more clearly when you go home . . ."

"Yes, Jim?"

Then he realized that Meriwether was through, and had said all that he was ever going to say.

He sat staring bleakly at Meriwether while something clutched inside him and turned slowly hard and cold, and it was like that other night in the Bay of Cárdenas when young Randy had died.

For a minute his lips moved and trembled without sound. Then he grasped the thwart and stood up, and shook his fists in the direction of the invisible fort. The cords in his neck grew taut and his whole body trembled as he cursed.

CHAPTER 2

_I_

HE COULD take no accounting of the miles and the days
behind him, the hundreds of slow miles and the dragging
days of heat and thirst and fever. They were lost behind
him, lost in time. There were only points of memory,
like the memory of Meriwether, and the uncertain in-
terval in the turtler's skiff when he had barely managed
to reach Key West. There was the search for food, and
the furtive, hurried search for a better craft—anything
seaworthy. The rest had not been so bad. Just a matter
of enduring, of sailing on, following the green coast
northward and around.

He was almost home. All this was home country.

36

Max Ewing crawled to the weather side of the sloop and drew his gaunt body upright. He rubbed his sunken eyes and peered reverently up the long broad reach of St. George Sound. Everything here was different, blessedly different and familiar. It gave him strength just to see the change in the water and the higher look of the land. The hated mangroves were gone, and in their place to leeward were the tall pines and the white dunes of the upper Gulf. No sign of a habitation yet—but here were landmarks he had known all his life: a dead tree supporting a monstrous eagle's nest, and a dune like a schooner's topsail. On the nearer beach were a few stray cattle—probably some of Branch Clabo's herd.

Oh, wild bright land, oh, beautiful land of home! He wanted to shout and laugh. He wanted to lean over the side and dip his hands into the faintly bronzing water. For the past hour the water had been changing color, and far ahead he could see the vague bands of bronze creeping down with the tide from the distant bay.

Three pelicans crossed his bow, flapping lazily and then gliding low, heading seaward for the dark line of St. George Island. His eyes followed the island's endless line until it vanished in the sun's glare ahead. There, dead ahead, the sound broadened and became a great glittering bay. There was only the glitter of it in the distance, but in his mind's eye he could see across it and look down upon the cotton port at the river's mouth, a promise beyond the horizon. Home!

But he couldn't go home yet. His first destination would have to be Clabo's, on this side of the bay.

He could almost see Clabo's. Yonder where the bay and the sound met, and the mainland seemed to come to an end, was the point of land where Branch Clabo's

father had built his trading post and tavern. The point
was still miles away and even the cedar grove where the
tavern lay might have been indistinguishable if he had
not known the place so well and if the thought of reaching it had not been uppermost in his mind for an eternity.

He lay with his head above the cockpit coaming, his
eyes on his goal. As it grew slowly larger on the bow his
thin body tightened and shook with a sudden spasm of
trembling born of eagerness, weakness and all the little
uncertainties he had refused to consider until this moment. But finally, seeing the dark rectangle of the tavern among the cedars, seeing the familiar sameness of
the point and the trees, the present and the future were
for a little while banished by the past.

He might have been a boy again, sailing over from the
city with his servant Janus to go hunting with young
Branch and little Hermes. It had been an odd friend-
ship in a way, for he and Branch had been born poles
apart, but in those days they'd been like a pair of In-
dians together, taking any excuse to get out of doors
and range the coast.

Clabo's! What a wild place that had been! Stuck
yonder on the isolated point and patronized in the past
almost entirely by sailormen, it had always been noisy
with drunken crews from the vessels that had once
crowded the outer anchorage. Those had been the great
years before the coming of the railroads, when uncounted
ships had put into the bay to load the cotton that came
pouring down the muddy river from the new plantation
lands of Georgia and Alabama. At that time the name
Clabo was as familiar on the high seas as the port across

the bay. Probably it still had a special culinary con-
notation.

Every vessel that entered port had depended on the
elder Clabo for pickled beef. That beef, butchered by
his black boys and put up in casks of brine, came from
the scrawny palmetto-eating Spanish cattle that ran wild
all over the coast. Incomparable forecastle fare! And
of such redoubtable qualities that a slice of it was said
to be good for three crossings to London, since it took
that much time for a man to chew it.

Well, the big days and the wild days were long gone
now, and old man Clabo—a violent old brute thoroughly
hated by his blacks and his family—was long gone too,
and the money he had made was probably gone also, for
certainly Branch had searched everywhere for it.

Poor Branch! What a shy, awkward, miserable youth
he had been—at least around strangers. But that,
mainly, was because of the clubfoot. Actually, the clubfoot had never bothered him, for he was as quick as a
panther and hardly anyone could keep up with him in
the woods. You couldn't expect him to care much for
trading. And he'd hated his father so much that he'd
shunned the tavern even long after the old man was
dead. His mother and one of the yellow girls had had
to run the place.

It had taken secession and war to make a change in
Branch. Aye, it had really done something to him. He'd
overcome some of his shyness, having grown into a powerful fellow with a barrel chest; and now suddenly he
became a figure of importance as the war made demands
on means and talents that no other in the area possessed.
Knowing Branch, and realizing his painful awareness
of his shortcomings, one could almost believe that Branch

had taken the war as a chance to reach beyond the limitation of his birth.

Max Ewing eased the helm and studied the distant landing. He thought of his last visit to Clabo's, and remembered how the city across the bay, asleep for a decade, had been stung to wakefulness and had suddenly begun to seethe as it found itself again important as a port. Overnight, it seemed, blockading gunboats had taken up positions off the island passes. But there were too many passes for the Federals to watch—and too many blockade runners slipped through the net. So it became necessary for the enemy to make occasional forays into the unguarded city, much to the embarrassment and annoyance of Cassius Drew and all the others charged with sending such desperately needed items as kegs of English powder and cases of Enfield rifles to the armies far up the river. Branch, however, soon became adept in the handling of contraband. Moreover his establishment, located with deep water to his door and a bewildering world of tidal morass and river tangles stretching away at the rear, seemed to have been contrived by nature for the sort of traffic that now passed through it. Even so, in hands less cunning, this great flow of goods would have come to a swift and disastrous termination. For the watchful Federals were everywhere in those days, suspicious of everyone. Many times they landed at the Clabo place, to spread out and go tramping through the tavern and the outbuildings and the palmetto thickets and leaving—so they thought— not a cranny or a cask unplumbed. But always they found only the same emptiness and air of indolence and look of run-down poverty that had come to characterize the spot.

All that, of course, was years ago. Since then a great deal had happened. Aye, a great deal . . .

II

Branch Clabo limped across the shell ridge along which the tavern and the other buildings sprawled, and moved down through the cedar grove toward the distant point. Normally he walked with his right foot dragging awkwardly, but this afternoon the limp was barely noticeable. He achieved this effect with considerable muscular strain and much discomfort, and stopped frequently to rest and take short practice steps in an effort to train the unwilling foot. He was a towheaded man with quick observing slate eyes in a rather flat impassive face, and there was a sort of sly quietness about him often found in those who have always lived close to nature. Today being Saturday, he was freshly shaved and was wearing a clean linen shirt, a pair of sailcloth trousers and new cowhide sandals he had made himself. On other days he was less particular about his toilet as well as his limp. But once every two weeks, when Captain Lassaphene and his family at the lighthouse sailed over here to lay in supplies, he was at great pains to be at his best.

At the tip of the palmetto-covered point dividing the sound from the upper bay, he stopped and stood squinting at the vast sweep of water that lay about him. To his right, where the distant port of Apalachicola was a smear and a smudge of smoke against the sun, the water was a bright clay-red from the muddy river whose dozen mouths spewed their color into the bay. But in front of him the color was changing with the tide. It swirled in bands around the point, and long paling bronze fingers were thinning in the bright blue of the sound. His eyes, searching for a sail, lifted hopefully to the miles-off barrier of St. George Island that crawled like a ragged pen line across the entire southern horizon. For a moment his attention focused on the approximate location of the lighthouse, out of sight near the island's western extremity, then he followed the hazy tracery of dunes and pine tops until he made out a sloop well to the eastward.

The sloop, seen bow-on, was only a narrow slash of gray sail in the distance. He studied it for several minutes. Sometimes the lighthouse keeper took a long beat to windward, hugging the lee of the island before coming about in order to make it easy for Mrs. Lassaphene, who was a poor sailor. Then he realized that the mainsail was patched, and that the craft was smaller than the lighthouse boat. Some fisherman, probably.

The Lassaphenes, he decided, must have gone to the city today.

He turned reluctantly, snapping his fingers, and started back to the tavern, limping heavily now.

At the long veranda running across the front of the place, connecting the post and its adjoining taproom to the main building, he paused, suddenly lost. He thought wistfully of Lassaphene's niece, young Mrs. Maynard, whom he had expected to see today. Then, because she was an ideal as yet unattainable, he thought of hidden money and the various possible locations of it. He wanted badly to be out hunting it, but he hated to leave the post. What little business there was these days came mainly on Saturdays, and he could no longer afford to lose any of it. He frowned, thinking of his mother who had died during the winter. For the first time he missed her keenly. She had been an old busybody, but at least she'd always been here to keep an eye on matters. Now there were only little Hermes and himself, and Lily Bright—who did a little too much managing at times— and a couple of the old Negroes who were too broken down to leave or to do much. The rest had all drifted into the city, and wouldn't work for hell so long as they thought they had something coming from the Government. Damned devils!

He spat, and saw Lily Bright standing in the doorway of the post with a glass of whisky in her hand. She was a buxom and attractive mulatto woman several years younger than he. She was barefooted and wore a white apron over a checkered cotton dress that had once belonged to his mother.

Her full lips twitched in a suggestion of a smirk. "You might jes' as well take off them clothes I works so hard ironin' an' save 'em till next time," she said. "Dey ain't a-comin'."

"You think I dress up jest for a bunch o' Yankees?" he grumbled. "Don't you reckon a man wants to be clean oncet in a while?"

"Only thing ever makes you put on clean britches is somethin' in skirts." She made a face and added knowingly, "I got eyes. I knows who you gits dandified up for. But she ain't never gonna warm yo' bed."

Branch studied her a moment without expression, tempted to go over and slap her face. Then he shrugged. Lily Bright was still pretty, and in these days of new freedoms he had learned to accept certain liberties from her in return for liberties granted. He had always been fond of her. She had been born on the place, and was part of it, and with matters as they were he could hardly afford to be without her.

"You drink too damn much likker," he said finally.

She lifted a rounded shoulder. "Might as well drink it. Us got it, more'n us kin sell, an' I don't see nobody buyin' much of it. An' hit cheap as water."

She could swill it by the quart, he knew, and hardly show it except that it made her talkative. In the old days he'd always been afraid that she might talk too much when the Yankees came around, but she never had. She'd always frozen up and acted dumb as little Hermes.

"Seen Hermes around?" he asked.

She smiled and motioned with her head, and he saw Hermes come out of the shed at the other end of the long veranda and start down to the pier with a pair of oyster tongs over his shoulder. Hermes, a man of thirty now, had stopped growing at seven.

Branch grinned suddenly and called, "Hey there, Herm, you fixin' to git us a mess of oysters?"

Hermes glanced back at them and nodded vigorously, his mass of wiry yellow hair flopping like a fuzzy mop across his large head. He had very short arms that seemed at first glance to be without elbows, and tiny bowed legs encased in little cotton pantaloons that would have fitted a child. He waddled out on the pier like a puppet on strings, determined and full of business, and scrambled into one of the skiffs tied up beside the family's old catboat.

"Oysters," said Lily Bright, and they both chuckled, for there was no telling what Hermes might or might not bring back when he started out with a pair of tongs. Rocks maybe, old bottles and whelks, but never oysters. Let him go to shoot ducks, thought Branch, and sure as

the world he'd bring in a bag of jaybirds or a brace of
buzzards. But the little fellow could handle a boat. Aye,
man! Black night, fog or high wind, and there wasn't a
soul could touch him at the tiller. "Li'l coot," he said
indulgently. "Damn li'l piddlin' coot."

Lily Bright finished her drink. "Ole Hettie's boy
Pinchy come round whilst you was out. Bought hisself
some likker."

"That sneaky varmint. Hope you didn't give 'im
credit."

"Didn't ask fo' no credit. Paid cash."

"Where'd he git cash?"

"Man like Pinchy kin always git a li'l cash these
days—if'n he hangs round the right places." She raised
her eyes to his. "Pinchy, he left word that Mr. Dau wants
to see you next time you sails over to town."

"So that's it, eh? Pinchy's got 'is hand out at that
Freedmen's Bureau." Then, suddenly uneasy, he asked,
"What 'ave I done that would make Dau want to see
me?"

"You ain't done nothin'. Pinchy talked like Mr. Dau
jes' had some business to do with you."

"What sort o' business?"

"Why don't you go to town an' find out?" She smiled
at him slyly and went inside, adding over her shoulder,
"Mr. Dau, he's a mighty nice man. You had ought to
keep on the good side o' him."

"That bastard," he mumbled. Frowning, he followed
her in and sat down on an empty flour barrel whose contents, thirty months ago, had fetched a small fortune.
The trading post, though it was now a wing of the tavern,
still had its original rough log interior. There were two
heavily barred windows on one side and a counter and a

row of shelves and cases on the other. At one time the place had overflowed with goods of every description, but there was little here now save a few necessities and some odds and ends of hardware for the scattered settlers on this side of the bay. In the adjoining taproom, however, were ample stocks of whisky for the crews of sailing vessels that still occasionally dropped anchor off the point.

Lily Bright padded into the taproom and returned presently with a glass of whisky in each hand. She gave one glass to Branch, then sat down on the counter and began sipping her drink slowly, curling her long yellow toes with pleasure.

"Like I say," she went on, "he's a mighty nice man to know."

"You mean he's a nice man for you to know."

She rolled her eyes at him. "I can't help it if'n yo' ma was white, an' mine was mo' favored."

"Aw, shut up."

"I been good to you," she said. "You better be good to me."

He scowled at his whisky and drank half of it at a gulp. He said nothing, and she went on quietly, "You wants to keep dis place, don't you?"

He stared at her. "What d'you mean keep it? Sure I want to keep it! Hit's mine, ain't it?"

"I reckon—unless somebody slaps his eyes on it an' has a talk with Mr. Dau, an' you gits yo taxes raised."

"They can't do nothin' to me. I didn't fight against the Union."

"You done other things."

"What of it? They can't prove nothin'."

"You still got some things hid away."

"What if I have? They don't have to find out about it."

"Mebbe dey done found out." Then at his sudden sharp glance she added hastily, "Don't gimme no hard looks. I ain't never opened my trap to nobody, an' you knows hit. An' you knows how I feel about you, too. My eyes don't never stray." She took a sip of whisky and her long smooth yellow hand tightened on the glass. "If'n yo' eyes strays a little, I don't pay it no mind. I wants you to have what's due you. I—I jes' hope you gits it, 'cause I feels like I does about you."

She stopped a moment and looked down at him, and her eyes were suddenly soft. She had large fine eyes of a limpid brown; they could glow or darken or flash fire or narrow to slyness, so that it was not always easy to know what was in her mind. But when her eyes softened like this her rather full oval face became beautiful and she spoke what was in her heart.

"Branch—" she never addressed him thus except in close intimacy—"you's a mighty smart man in a heap o' ways, but in other ways you's blind. You jes' don't know what's goin' on. Me, I keeps an ear in town, an' I hears a heap o' things you never hear. Look, this is a Sat'day. You know how much money us took in today?"

He shook his head, frowning.

"Less'n six dollahs us took in. A few more peoples is due to come around by dark, but dey ain't gonna fill the money box."

"We can't help that," he said. "No one has any money. What's goin' on in town that I don't know about?"

"Heap o' things. Dey's fixin' to raise taxes."

"They can't do that! Folks won't stand for it."

"Folks won't have nothin' to say about hit."

"We can still vote, can't we?"

"Mebbe. Them that's allowed. But all the cullud folks kin vote—an' there's a heap of 'em."

"They'd better vote right, or there'll be trouble."

"Dey'll vote like Mr. Dau tells 'em to vote. An' if'n you ain't got tax money when the times comes, you's gonna be sleepin' on the beach."

"Yeah?" He spat on the floor in sudden anger. "Let 'em try anything like that, an' there'll be some real trouble around here."

She was silent a moment. In her eyes was a shadow of fear. "I'm jes' tellin' you, Branch. There's things goin' on. I sees trouble already."

He shook his head. "This place ain't got the value it used to have. Who'd want it?"

She shook her head. "I don't know. But you got a heap o' land, an' peoples is gittin' land-hungry. That's how come I say you'd better git next to Mr. Dau. The other Yankees goes to him when dey wants somethin'. He ain't no better'n the rest of 'em, but hit makes 'im a mighty good man to know."

"I don't want no truck with 'im."

"You wants money, don't you?"

"Yeah."

"Well, he's doin the fiddlin', honey. Hit might pay you to dance to his tune."

Branch looked down at his twisted foot and absently studied the unhappy shape of it. Though he did not fully realize it, the foot symbolized a heritage that he hated. In the shape of it was a constant reminder of the grossness of his father, of the blood taint that had produced little Hermes and himself, and of a status that was well beyond the fringes of social acceptability. Only one person of consequence had ever sought his company and become his friend. To all the others he was merely old Hermes Clabo's son, and not even the great leveler of war had changed his status in the least.

Had his foresight equaled his slyness in handling contraband, he at least would have been a wealthy man at the war's end. But it had not occurred to him until too late that the Confederacy might collapse. When it was over he had, in fact, a great deal of money hidden away, but unfortunately it did not happen to be in currency recognized by the Union.

He got up and limped over to a huge scarred safe in the corner behind the counter, opened it and took out a wooden box packed tight with Confederate notes. His long sturdy fingers slid across the edges of the notes, spreading them and showing their large denominations. His wide mouth thinned. Abruptly he tossed the box into the safe and closed the door.

Lily Bright took his empty whisky glass and slid into the taproom and filled it. Returning, she handed it to him silently.

Branch limped to the window. He peered out across a tangle of palmettos toward his tumble-down barn and drank the whisky in little gulps. In his mind the thought of money was a mountain that overshadowed all other thoughts. He did not value it for the reasons that others valued it. But money, like his twisted foot, had come to be a symbol. The fact that two fortunes, so to speak, had slipped through his fingers, made him more determined than ever to lay his hands upon wealth. His longing for it was at times a physical hurt, a cramping hunger. For illogically it seemed that to possess money, a vast sum of money, would be to possess a magic that would wipe out the heritage of the twisted foot and bring him the respect of all other men.

He decided that Lily Bright was right. He'd better go over and kind of play along with Ramsey Dau. Probably there wouldn't be any profit in the deal, but at least ,it would put him on the right side. If he got caught on the wrong side now, and lost the place, he'd be in a hell of a fix.

He was considering the ramifications of Dau and the Freedmen's Bureau when his eyes, following the curving path beyond the barn, made out the distant figures of two Negroes approaching. He did not recognize the man at once, but the girl lived over in the quarters near the bay. The man carried a cane and moved jauntily with that new step of cocky assurance which too many of the freedmen had acquired. He wore a red silk shirt and a wide panama pulled down to his eyes.

Lily Bright said, "That's Pinchy comin' back. Bet he's bringin' that girl here to git her likkered."

Branch squinted at the former slave who had run away from him at the beginning of the war. Old Hettie, Pinchy's mother, was a good woman, but Pinchy wasn't worth cutting up for shark bait.

"Where'd that sneaky varmint git the money to dress up like that?"

"I done tole you where he gits it."

"From Dau? Hell, there ain't a Yankee alive that kin make that bastard work."

"Pinchy don't have to work. He's in with the Bureau. I'd mind what I say around 'im."

"Let 'im git sassy with me an' I'll kick his damn britches off."

"You better not," Lily Bright said quietly. "Shoe's on t'other foot now."

"Huh?"

"Like I tole you, you jes' don't know what's goin' on. Start kickin' that Pinchy; an' you'll have Mr. Dau an' the hull Bureau after you, An' mind what you say."

"You think he peddles what he hears?"

"Course he does! If'n ary thing is knowed about you that you don't want knowed, hit come from Pinchy. I bet you."

Branch turned away from the window in slow wrath and limped to the door. He stopped in the doorway, momentarily forgetting Pinchy, for little Hermes was trotting up from the pier where a man was bent over making fast the lines of a small sloop on the other side of the catboat.

For a hopeful instant before his eyes could adjust to the glaring sunlight on the pier he thought it was Lassaphene, then he realized that this was impossible. The sloop, very small and battered, was probably the one he'd seen with the patched mainsail. While he studied it Hermes ran up on the veranda and seized his arm and tugged, dancing and giving little goatlike bleats as he pointed to the man on the pier. Lily Bright pressed into the doorway beside him and stared.

The man on the pier straightened and looked uneasily up and down the beach, then peered up at them.

Lily Bright whispered, "Oh, holy me!"

"Who is it?" he asked.

"Hit's Cap'n Max!"

"No," he muttered in disbelief. "It can't be. They've got 'im in prison. They'd never let 'im go."

"Then he musta busted out, 'cause that's him! That's him sure as the world! Skin an' bones an' barefooted, but I'd know 'im anywhere with that black hair an' beard, an' him so tall. What's that on his ankles?"

"Must be irons. They musta had 'im chained. Christ, you're right! That's Johnny Max." He whistled softly. "By God, he's escaped!"

They stood silent a moment in the doorway, each suddenly apprehensive.

All at once she said, "That damn Pinchy's comin'. What us gonna do?"

"Keep quiet," he told her. "Don't let on nothin' to nobody. I'll go an' keep Johnny Max out o' sight till Pinchy's gone. If'n he asks you anything, jest let on hit's some feller from Carrabelle mebbe stoppin' by lookin' for work."

He swung quickly off the veranda and started down to the pier. Then, with a glance over his shoulder, he slowed and followed Hermes with apparent unconcern.

CHAPTER 3

===========================

I

MAX EWING looked thankfully at Branch Clabo across the centerboard casing. It was good just to lie here in the tiny cabin of the sloop and look at Branch and listen to him, and to see the sun on the cedars beyond the hatchway. Garden Key and the Key West passage, and the bleak coast and the long miles, they were forever behind him. Just to be here suddenly had the nature of a miracle.

And part of the miracle was that everything seemed the same. The red bay and the grove, the weather-beaten tavern and the old catboat at the pier, and even little Hermes. They'd hardly changed. Only Branch and he himself had changed. Time and circumstance had dealt unfavorably with them both, and there was much that was gone forever. But nothing could obliterate the memories of a shared boyhood. They'd fished and hunted and ranged this whole upper coast together, and once they'd been like brothers. For a moment he felt as if he'd slipped back into his youth and that nothing had happened.

Then as they talked he became aware of little differences that had turned Branch into a stranger. But in his weariness he could not define the differences. He could only sense them and wonder.

"You're not like yourself," he said. "You look sort of worried—or perplexed, maybe. Or is it just my sudden appearance?"

"I reckon everybody's both perplexed an' worried these days, Johnny Max. But you sure did give me a turn. Before God, I never thought I'd see you alive again!"

"Well, I wasn't going to die in prison—and I knew if I could get out that I'd make it here."

Branch shook his head. "You look like you jest barely made it. You look plumb beat out."

"Oh, I feel a little better now. Just being here . . ."

"Hell, you're sick. Soon's that nosy black varmint up there leaves I'm puttin' you to bed. Jesus, what all's happened to you since you broke away?"

"Very little. Been living on wild limes and oysters— and fighting off chills and dysentery."

"Christ!"

"I hope you've got plenty of quinine."

"I'll fix you up."

Branch thrust his head briefly above the narrow hatch

and looked at the tavern. "Damned bastard!" he muttered, settling back. "He's jest sittin' up there with his girl like he owned the place. We gotta be mighty careful with him around. Fact is, we gotta be careful with everybody. You're too easy to recognize. Lily Bright, she knowed you right off."

"Maybe it was just seeing the ankle irons. I hardly believe——"

"Oh, you look a heap more pindlin' than you did— but you're the same old gangleshanked devil you always was. You can't change the way you're built."

"Perhaps not. But when you've changed inside you get to thinking you've changed outside to go with it."

He peered beyond Branch's shoulder at the patch of red water astern, wanting to go out and dip his hands into that water and wishing he could cross the bay tonight and slip into town. His mind touched questioningly on home and his mother, and on Bella Tacon, and he wondered if Branch knew anything of Bella. He had never mentioned her to Branch, and he hesitated to ask about her now. Three years. Suddenly he was fearful of what those three years might have done.

"The last time I put in here was at night. Remember?"

"I'll say! Blowin' like hell, an' you with all them rifles for Atlanta."

"Too bad I didn't have more. They might have stopped Sherman."

"They didn't have no chance with Sherman. I still got the damn things."

"*What?*"

Branch shrugged. "Couldn't help it. Everything went to hell after that. Wasn't no way for me to git 'em up the river."

"Plague and the devil! After all that effort . . ."

"Forgit it. Hit's over now."

"I can't forget it."

"You might as well, Johnny Max. Hit's all over an' done."

"It's not over for me."

"I reckon I know how you feel. Sure, an' we all feel that way, but it ain't no use. We got to figger on what's happenin' now, an' what to do with you." Branch looked curiously around the cramped cubbyhole of the cabin. "Where'd you find this leaky li'l beat-up packet?"

"Key West."

"Huh?" Branch eyed him blankly. "Thought they was holdin' you in Fortress Monroe."

"They did, for two years. But I spent the last year in Fort Jefferson, down on Garden Key."

"Great God! You mean to say you escaped out o' that hole—an' came all the way up here in this wormy li'l bucket?"

"Not exactly. Found a turtler's skiff and managed to reach Key West one night, by the grace of God. The skiff was much worse than this. Barely made it there. Then I had to steal the first thing I could lay my hands on, and get away fast."

Branch glanced around the cabin again and peered out at the cockpit. "I don't see how you made it this far," he said in his quiet and almost mumbling way of speech. "You ain't got nothin'—not e'en a blanket."

"Oh, I've fared worse, though it was a little rough. There was nothing on board but some fishing lines and a scuttle butt of water. I used the lines for mending the rigging. There was no use trying to catch fish, for I didn't have a lucifer to light a fire. All I had was a marlinespike. But that fed me. I used it to open oysters. I suppose I could have picked up a few things by going ashore at some settlement. But I hated to risk it in my state of health, and with these damned irons on me. The Yankees seem to be everywhere. So I headed for here as fast as I could make it."

"Lord, Lord!" Branch sat back and rubbed the tips of his fingers along the broad flat squareness of his jaws. He was immensely strong and the least movement brought a little rippling of muscles under his skin, which seemed to fit him too tightly. His skin, much darker than his sun-bleached hair, bound his flesh without the least softening vestige of fat.

"Soon's I git you to bed," he said, "I'll take a hack saw to them ankle irons. An' when you feel like shavin', you'd better git rid o' that damn black beard."

"Why the beard?"

"Hell, you been wearin' it ever since you come home from the Navy, when your pa died. Folks are used to it. But I'd leave the mustache. You never wore just a mustache before." He glanced briefly out at the tavern again and grumbled, "That damn Pinchy an' his gal are still there. Them rascals, they don't none of 'em know their place no more—an' I got to swallow their sass 'cause I need their trade." He spat out of the hatch and swore softly. "If'n I was you, Johnny Max, you know what I'd do?"

"What's that?"

"Soon's I got on my feet again I'd either fix up this bucket, or git me a better craft, an' then I'd sail slap on around the coast to Mexico."

"I can't do that."

"You can't afford not to do it. If'n you was jest any-

body, hit wouldn't matter. But you used to draw a heap
o' water on this coast, an' everybody knows about you.
You're marked. There's troops in town, an' I'll bet my
last plugged penny they've been ordered to be on the
watch for you."

"I can't help it. I've got things to do here. I'll keep
out of sight."

"I sure wouldn't go near town."

"Plague and the devil, man, I've got to go over and
see my mother!" Then, at the odd look in Branch's eyes,
he asked quickly, "Is she all right? She's not sick, is
she?"

Branch turned away and frowned down at his twisted
foot. "I'm sorry, Johnny Max. I thought you knowed.
Ain't neither of us got any folks left now. Your ma, she
passed away about six months ago."

Max swallowed, suddenly beyond speech.

Somehow he had not even considered that she might
be gone. He'd always imagined her as he'd seen her last,
a proud little gray person with something indomitable
and seemingly indestructible about her that time had
never touched. The liveliest, busiest person in town.
He'd never known her to be ill. How could she be gone?

He closed his eyes and sagged against the bulkhead.

Presently Branch said, "Might as well tell you the
rest of it. You ain't got nothin' left. Not a damn thing."

"What happened?" he mumbled.

"They confiscated everything."

"The house too?"

"Yeah."

He opened his eyes and struggled upright. "You—
you mean to say they took it away from her, put her
out?"

"Almost. I mean, well, the first year after the war hit

warn't too bad. Folks sort of took up where they'd left off, or tried to. Then the niggers was told they could vote, an' the Yankees started comin' in an' runnin' things. Hit's been gittin' worse ever since. Last year they gobbled up a lot o' property, mostly from them who'd fought. They took your house, I understand, an' tried to put your ma out. She was sick at the time. Fever, I think it was. Ole man Drew, he tried to help her, but she died before anything come to a head."

"It was her house," he said unsteadily. "They had no right to touch it. No right whatever." Suddenly he was shaking with an uncontrollable fury. God damn them! he thought. God damn them through all eternity! God damn their mothers and their sons and all their dirty grasping kind to the ends of hell!

Branch murmured, "Ain't no use in gittin' worked up about it now. Hit's done, an' there ain't nothin' you kin do about it."

"I'll do something about it. I'll do a great deal about it."

"Might as well luff up, Johnny Max. You can't do nothin'."

"Don't tell me to luff up. Who got the house?"

"Feller named Dau. But you better not monkey with 'im."

Max looked stonily toward the hatch and said nothing.

"No," said Branch. "Anything happen to Dau an' there'll be hell to pay. He runs the Freedmen's Bureau."

"What's that?"

"Hit's something the Yankees cooked up to help the niggers, but all they do with it is use it to help themselves. Anything the Freedmen's Bureau tells you to do, you'd better do it fast."

"Hasn't anyone any rights at all?"

Branch laughed. "Sure—if'n you're black." He shrugged. "Over on this side o' the bay they don't bother me too much. I didn't fight, an' they ain't got nothin' on me. But I'm gittin' worried. Things is shapin' up bad. I own a heap o' land, an' if'n hit warn't for hopin' I could hang on to it, I'd git out."

He stopped a moment and studied his twisted foot, and then reached down and pressed on it with his strong hands as if he would straighten it. "That's why I say," he continued slowly, "if'n I was you I'd keep right on movin' west. Ain't nobody gonna bother you in Texas or Mexico."

"No. I've laid my course. I'm staying here."

"You can't do nothin' here. 'Tain't only that you're broke. You're a marked man."

"They haven't begun to mark me yet. I'll give them something to think about before I'm through."

"You'll jest be puttin' a rope around your neck."

"I'll take that chance."

"What about money? You can't do nothin' without money."

"I've a little hidden away. I can get more."

"There ain't no money around here."

"Oh, yes, there is."

Branch leaned back, and his restless eyes were suddenly focused and intent. He touched the tips of his fingers to his lower lip. "Where would that be?" he murmured.

"You know where. We spent enough time poking around for it when we were boys."

"Oh." Branch wet his lips. "That damn business on the island. Well, I know one thing. There's a heap o' sand over there."

II

During those first few days he hardly stirred from his bed. Later he began rising in the afternoons, to come down and spend a few hours puttering about the place and, when customers appeared, slipping away unobtrusively and working on the boat. Bereft of beard and anklets and wearing an old gray shirt and a pair of army trousers that Lily Bright had carefully patched and lengthened, he attracted only casual attention. Even now, so long after Appomattox, veterans were still drifting homeward or, homeless, were merely adrift without course or means of livelihood. He automatically became one of these latter. To any chance inquiry Branch would say, "Yeah, jest another one with no place to roost. One o' Gordon's men from up in Georgia. Call, his name is. Cap'n Call."

The name came easily to Max, for his mother had been a Call.

Once, during the second week, he walked down to the end of the point to test his legs, and stood there a little while peering earnestly across the six bronze miles separating him from home. He wanted badly to have a talk with Cassius Drew. It was important, although there was really no hurry about it. Nothing Cassius had to tell him would alter things in the slightest. Nor could he afford to rush his plans. They would take time and care. But Bella was another matter. It was suddenly galling to know that she was so close, but still as remote from him as ever.

He walked slowly back to the tavern, thinking of her and clenching his hands in the long-denied and mounting need of her. Had his sloop been in any condition for use he might have ignored the risk and set out immediately across the bay. But both the leaky sloop and the catboat had been run up to the beach and careened for repairs.

Impatiently he threw himself into the task of readying the catboat, which needed only a cleaning and a coat of bottom paint. Branch, coming out to help, protested. "Ain't no use in wearin' yourself to a frazzle," he said. "You ain't hardly got your strength back yet. Me an' Hermes kin finish up. Some night next week, when the wind's right, I'll run you over to town—if'n that's what's botherin' you."

"I'd like to go before that," he told Branch. "And it would be much better if I went alone. I may have to stay several days."

Branch shook his head. "You'd be crazy to stay over."

"Plague and the devil, I have to take chances."

"You ain't fitten to take chances yet. You don't know what it's like over there with them nosy troops watchin' everybody in the place. Hell, I hate to go there myself. I—I had to go over last week whilst you was laid up, an' damned if they didn't stop me twice before I could git done with my business."

"They've got their nerve!"

"Hit's like I tell you. Things ain't what they used to be."

"Why didn't you let me know you were going over last week? I'd have had you take a couple of messages along. I've been wanting badly to get in touch with Drew."

"I'm jest as glad you didn't know," Branch replied. "Ole Cassius, he ain't popular with the sort o' people you got to honey up to these days. I'd rather not be seen callin' on 'im.''

Max looked hard at Branch and said testily, "That's a damned funny attitude for you to take. What's Cassius up to that you don't want to be seen associating with him?"

"Hell," Branch grumbled, "I don't know what he's up to. I don't want to know. I got me to think about. All I aim to do is mind my own business an' keep out o' trouble."

"You don't have to turn Yankee to do that."

"Huh? Who said I was turnin' Yankee?"

"I'm going by what you've told me."

"Goddammit, Max, all I said was that I was keepin' shy o' Cassius. You got to be careful who you take up with these days. Jest suppose, f'r instance, that hit got out about you bein' over here. Ever think what'd happen to me?"

"If it worries you, Branch, I won't waste any time leaving."

"Aw, hell an' dingbats, there you go again! Christ, Johnny Max, a feller can't say nothin' without you rarin' up an' spittin' like a lit fuse. All I'm tryin' to do is tell you how it is these days. We got Yankees. Mebbe we don't like 'em, but we got 'em, an' all we kin do is put up with 'em an' make the best of it. Hit's like a dog gittin' fleas. Mebbe he don't love 'em either, but there ain't no gittin' rid of 'em oncet he's got 'em. So he jest scratches a bit an' makes the best of it."

Max looked at him without smiling. He thought of his mother, and of Meriwether, and he thought of young Randy that night on the Bay of Cárdenas, and of other things that had eaten deep with the years.

"Maybe I am like a lit fuse," he said in a voice that rasped a little. "As for making the best of it, that's exactly what I intend to do, and with everything in my power—but not in quite the way you mean. I'm going to blow up one of these days, Branch. Soon. Just as soon as I can get things ready. But before it happens I want to know where you stand. Are you going to be on my side—or are you going to stay over in the corner scratching your damned fleas?"

Branch gaped at him a moment. "Aw, hell," he growled. He turned away and spat. "Ain't no use in talkin' to you now. Wait till you've been to town. Jest don't forgit, Johnny Max, that we've always been friends."

Silently, a little grimly, they went to work on the catboat.

By the following afternoon the craft had been scraped down and the seams puttied and made ready for painting. Then a brig hove to off the point and the brig's yawl came ashore for a load of beef. For three interminable days the catboat lay untouched. While Branch and all available help plunged into a furious orgy of butchering, the brig's crew lolled in the taproom and hourly became noisier as Lily Bright dispensed liquor. When it was over the tavern was filthy and everyone was exhausted.

Branch, in spite of the unexpected and badly needed revenue, was glad to see the men leave. "If'n they'd come earlier in the week," he said as they were cleaning up, "I wouldn'ta rushed so to finish an' git rid of 'em. But tomorrow's Saturday."

"What's that got to do with it?" Max asked. "Are you expecting a big day tomorrow?"

Lily Bright, mopping the stained floor, raised her oval face and sniffed. "He sho' is," she said sweetly. "Tomorrow's lighthouse Sat'day."

Branch gave her a flat stare. "Cap'n Lassaphene an' his family, they come over here twice a month to trade. They missed comin' last time. So I'm countin' on seein' 'em for sure tomorrow. I wouldn't want no drunk foc's'le hands around with them wemmin folks here."

"Dey's ladies," said Lily Bright with a saccharin lilt. "Dey's *so* refined. That skinny Miz Maynard, she———"

"Shut up," growled Branch. "You ain't got no call to talk like that. They're good people."

"Yankees," she said.

"They ain't Yankees. They're Marylanders."

"Hit's the same thing."

"No, it ain't. There's a heap o' difference."

Max said, "I don't care what they are. I'll keep out of sight tomorrow."

"You don't have to worry about 'em," Branch grumbled. "They don't know nothin' about you, an' wouldn't care nohow. Lassaphene, he ain't been at the light more'n a year. He don't hardly ever go to the city. He don't like it there. He does nearly all his buyin' over here."

"What about that Mrs. Maynard? Is she the assistant keeper's wife?"

"No, the assistant keeper is a feller named Haik. He's a new man too, but he's from Alabama. Mrs. Maynard, she's Cap'n Lassaphene's niece. She—she's right nice."

Branch turned away. His broad face was a trifle pink under its tan.

CHAPTER *4*

I

IN THE night's stillness there came a faint rushing of
wind and a sudden beating of rain on the roof. It became a furious drumming that ceased abruptly as the
squall passed on, moving inland. Then there was only a
soft dripping from the eaves and the cedar boughs, and
stillness again. Beyond the windows the night grayed.
A vireo began to trill a prelude to the dawn chorus.

Max lay watching the seaward window, waiting for a
flush of crimson. He thought, as always, the best of day
is dawn. It is the world reborn, with everything created
anew. Night may be a grave for the day, but every dawn
is promise.

66

He thought of his plans. They were complete now, and he felt compelled to action. He had been here two weeks. That was long enough to gain his strength. Tonight he must see Cassius Drew.

A spear of color touched the window. He swung out of bed and rubbed the stiffness from his long body, and slowly drew on the clothing Lily Bright had altered for him. Once, as he fumbled with the laces of the cowhide sandals Branch had made for him, he had a momentary vision of his old self and his other life. Because the sandals were rough and ill-fitting, his memory narrowed on a pair of fine English boots of which he had been very fond. He had worn them for years. Now he thought of them wistfully, for they were part and parcel of all the things he had once accepted and taken for granted—the comfort and the simple grace of those days, the respect he had had for himself and the institutions of his kind, and the ready respect of strangers. As he flexed his feet in the uncomfortable sandals he was suddenly irked by the reminder that he was no one, that he had nothing whatever save a single pocket piece he'd managed to hide while in prison.

There was the possibility, of course, that Cassius had managed to save part of the money he'd left with his mother. He'd given careful instructions about the money. Surely Cassius would know of it.

I'll see him tonight, he thought, if I have to cross the bay in a skiff.

He slipped down to the kitchen wing and warmed up the dregs of last evening's coffee in the fireplace, and gulped it black while he munched a cold hoecake. Then he went out and studied the tide.

The tide was in and lapping under the catboat's

cradle, but it was not yet at full flood. There was time to paint the boat and launch it if he worked fast. He hurried to mix a bucket of copper compound, and before sunup was busy applying it to the keel.

There is the oddity of but one tide a day in this area, and he raced with it, paying no attention to anything else and quite forgetting that the Lassaphenes were expected. By midmorning he was through. But now the tide had turned, and he needed assistance quickly if he hoped to get the boat into the water. He was about to go up to the tavern for help when he saw Branch coming down the path.

Branch was carefully dressed in white and, except for a slight stiffness, was walking with only a trace of a limp. He considered Branch's gait a moment, mildly curious about it but not immediately comprehending.

"Can you give me a hand?" he asked. "There's enough tide to float her, but we won't have it long."

"Huh? Oh, yeah. Sure. In a few minutes." Branch did not stop. "Lassaphene's coming."

Max crawled around the bow of the catboat and for the first time saw the lighthouse sloop, hardly a cable's length from the pier. It was a rebuilt oysterman's boat with a tiny cabin aft and a large midship hatch for carrying supplies. He watched it approvingly while it came about and dropped sail and drifted neatly into the weather side of the pier.

Branch was waiting to make the lines fast and assist the women up to the pier. There were two women in dark dresses and sunbonnets. The man with them was spare and scholarly; he had a gray goatee and wore a sailing master's cap, a light pea jacket and shiny but carefully pressed serge trousers. Max frowned at them a moment, looked curiously at the women, then turned away. The women had their backs to him, and in their long plain dark dresses they seemed as impersonal and as neuter as nuns. He retreated around the catboat and pretended to be busy while they went up the path to the tavern.

When they were gone he waded out to the stern and knocked away the supporting chocks, leaving the catboat half afloat.

Impatiently he waited, expecting Branch to return and help. Hermes would have been useless, for the task needed brawn. Finally he got a pole and tried to pry the bow free alone. Failing, he stood swearing awhile, then dropped the pole and started reluctantly up the path.

Captain Lassaphene, with cap and pea jacket in one hand and his suspenders gleaming a startling crimson against his white shirt, was slowly pacing the long veranda. He might have been any age from his middle fifties on, for his face, though very thin and aesthetic, was tanned and weathered and crisscrossed by many fine wrinkles. He had one of those restless and protruding lower lips that seem ever to be testing unspoken syllables. Max, approaching him, managed a perfunctory "Good morning, sir," but was acknowledged only by an absent nod. The man continued his slow pacing, his eyes directed on the distant island while his free hand twitched nervously at his side. Max passed him and went on to the end of the veranda where he could hear Branch and one of the women talking in the trading post. He was not offended. Just another lighthouse keeper, he thought.

He entered the post and stopped by the end of the counter, for Branch was ingratiatingly busy with the two women. He had never known Branch so talkative, so eager to please. The counter was littered with seed packets and he was speaking of gardening, of which he knew practically nothing, and though only the elder woman seemed to be listening, it was obvious that most of this dubious wisdom was for the benefit of the younger one.

Max stood scowling at her. She had removed her bonnet and was standing biting her lower lip while she looked out of the corner window toward the sea. She was rather plain, with pale reddish-brown hair and features as thin and sensitive as Lassaphene's. Though he saw nothing particularly attractive in her, he could not help staring, for she was the first white woman he had seen in over a year, and, in fact, the first he had observed except from a remote distance in more than three years. But even she, so close, contrived to be frigid and remote.

As if suddenly aware of his attention, and coldly resenting it, she turned her head and went quickly around him and out the door. On the veranda he heard her say in a low tone to the passing Lassaphene, "I'm beginning to hate to come over here. Some of these people ..."

And he heard Lassaphene murmur, "It's better than the city."

Damned supercilious female, he thought, and said irritably to Branch, "Pardon me, but you'd better lend me a hand while we still have the tide."

"Uh?" said Branch vaguely, a little flustered. "Oh, yeah, the boat. Aw, forgit it. We kin put it over tomorrow."

"No, it's much better while the copper paint is still wet. Anyway, I want to use it this evening."

"Do go and help him, Mr. Clabo," said the older

woman, turning from her inspection of the seed packets.
"We've all day. And don't mind the captain—you know
how he is." Her voice was sharp but not unpleasant.
She was a comfortable person of middle age with a shiny
red skin that refused to tan and intensely bright blue
eyes that peered with all-seeing curiosity from under
her bonnet. She glanced toward the veranda where Lassaphene and his niece were standing. "Those two, they're
just alike. Never want to leave the reservation, and can't
wait to get back to it. But I'm not stirring from here
until my stomach settles. Salt water always does that
to me. It just gathers me into a knot."

As if happy to have another listener, whom she exam-
ined with quick searching sweeps while she talked, she
rattled on for nearly a minute about the bay, the reservation, their gardening difficulties, and the various
bunglings of the assistant keeper whom evidently she
held in very low esteem. She was finally interrupted by
Lily Bright coming in from the taproom.

"Miz Lassaphene, would y'all like to have some fish
chowdah for dinnah?"

"Why, yes, Lily, if I can retain anything it will be
chowder. It may settle me. But no tomatoes, please.
I simply cannot abide tomatoes, and neither can the
captain. Now Charlotte—Mrs. Maynard—has a taste
for the things. She's even trying to grow some over
there in the sand. But I wouldn't give a Davis dollar, if
you'll pardon me, for all the peppers and tomatoes——"

"Us ain't got any," Lily Bright told her a little grimly.
"An' don't pay no mind to what Marse Branch says
about making a garden, 'cause he ain't never raised so
much as a wormy turnip in all his bawn days."

Branch, unhappy and beginning to purple, eased from

behind the counter and followed Max through the door and down toward the catboat.

"You didn't have to come bustin' in like that," he grumbled.

"There's the matter of the tide," Max told him.

"Goddammit, you coulda waited."

"I've been waiting, but the tide hasn't. It's very inconsiderate. Perhaps, if it could have heard your enlightening discourse——"

"Aw, hell! Them folks, they don't come over very often. An' Mrs. Maynard, she's different from other people. If'n you knowed her better——"

"I don't care to know her, or anyone connected with her. I'll eat with Lily in the kitchen and leave you the whole field to cultivate."

"Aw, hell an' dingbats, there ain't no cause for you to git all riled up." They had reached the boat, and now Branch seized the pole and angrily thrust it under the bow. With one powerful heave he freed the bow and sent the catboat sliding out to the end of its hawser. He tossed the pole aside and started back to the tavern, unmindful of his limp. "You'd better think twice if'n you're goin' to town tonight," he growled. "You're jest headin' for trouble."

"Oh, no, my friend. There'll be no trouble till I'm ready for it."

II

He stayed well out in the bay until nearly sundown, then headed in as the breeze was dying and crossed the swift current in the channel leading from the river's mouth, and eased over into the shallows south of town.

A quarter of a mile from the beach he hove to and dropped anchor. Unhurriedly he went about making things secure. Finally he got into the skiff he had towed astern and rowed slowly in to the little pier in front of Cassius Drew's cottage.

Night had come, a starry night with a half-moon so bright that he could clearly make out the details of the picket fences and galleried houses peeping from the tangles of palms and coastal oaks along the densely overgrown shore. Up above the beach, where a long boardwalk curved around the bay front, undulating with the different levels of the low sand-and-shell bluff, the picket fences made broken patterns of white in the black umbra of the trees. There were big oaks along the street end where the Drew cottage lay, so that the place was invisible save for a bit of white railing around the roof. But far to the right, where the boardwalk curved toward the river, he could distinctly see the long roof and upper gallery of his own house. It stood higher than the others, in the most prominent spot in town.

He crouched on the pier, looking at the house and biting his lips while his gaze traveled along the fences, stopping at each remembered gate—the English consul's with its coral vine and honeysuckle, the Loring place and the old Wentworth house, and the smaller homes of retired seamen, and old Dr. St. John's little mansion in minature. There was a tightness in his chest that made his breath come painfully. It seemed incredible, suddenly, that he couldn't stride boldly ashore and go up to any of those houses and cry out, *"Ahoy there, folks! I'm back! This is Max Ewing. I've come home!"*

A dog began to bark, and he saw a man cross a patch

of moonlight on the walk. The man moved furtively, hurrying, and vanished in the blackness under the trees.

He swore and sat very still, listening, waiting for the dog to stop barking. From the region of the river far around on the eastern face of town he heard the low bellow of a paddle wheeler, and to his nostrils, mixing with the nearer scents of jasmine and honeysuckle, came the familiar and somehow pleasant reek of rotting shell and gurry from the fishhouses. He remembered the roisterous days of cotton—he'd been only a small boy at the time—when his father had grown wealthy and everyone had had money, and the town had been a blustering place, wild and gay and dangerous and not a little pompous. In those days the great Mansion House, always crowded and aglitter every night till dawn, had dominated the town and been a beacon that could be seen far out on the bay. Then the railroads had crept inland and drained the cotton to other ports; the Mansion House had burned and the bluster and the wealth had vanished, and the paint had begun to peel from most of the houses. But the town had become a happier place. It had settled back and found time for the fun of living.

Then war had come. It had struck like a hornet's sting and set everything whirring with its early madness. It had destroyed the idyll.

Now, tonight, the town was quiet again. But it was not an indolent quiet, or a happy one. Hardly a light showed along the entire bay front, and the few sounds of activity came from the Negro section far over near the river. And this was a Saturday.

The dog had stopped barking. He could see no one.

His lips thinned and he moved swiftly along the pier and climbed to the boardwalk. In the shadow of Cassius Drew's oaks he hesitated, knowing that it might be better to leave some things to memory, but in spite of it he turned right and warily followed the curving walk until he reached his own gate.

His hand touched the gate and lingered there. It was a mistake to come here, as he realized instantly, for it was like death to stand here and be unable to open the gate and go running up the short walk to the steps. He backed away from it and leaned against a palm his father had planted years ago, and studied the house, searching for every little familiar detail.

Every sailor on the coast knew this house, for it was the first building you could see after entering the island pass and heading across the bay. No pretense had gone into the building of it, but much honesty had, for it had been put together by shipwrights for a plain man who had loved the sea. From the upper gallery you could look out across a little park and take in every bit of the harbor as well as the whole vast sweep of water that stretched from the distant swamps to the far islands. His father had died up there on that gallery; died peacefully in his favorite rocker, with his spyglass in his lap and one of his fleet of schooners coming up the channel to load lumber for the eastern ports.

Max closed his eyes, remembering. He'd been an ensign on the old *Albany* at the time, and he'd resigned immediately and come home. Someone had to run things. Young Randy had been only a kid in school. Poor Randy, he thought; you loved it here so, and you grew up with so much promise. Why did I ever let you wheedle me

into taking you along on the *St. George?* You were only
seventeen. You were too young for what happened. If
only I'd left you here with Mother! . . .

He locked his hands together in a silent and bitter
anguish, and for the moment he was oblivious of the faint
scrape of boots in the park behind him. Nor was he aware
of a movement on the upper gallery until a spark, falling
from the railing above him, glowed briefly and caught
his attention. Now he made out the form of a man
standing in the shadow by his father's old hickory rocker.
The moonlight touched only upon an outstretched hand
with a cigar, so that the hand seemed detached and sus-
pended.

"You down there!" came a voice, brusque and a little
querulous. "What do you want?"

Max wiped his palms over his eyes. A spasm shook
him. It seemed a sacrilege that this interloper should be
occupying his father's favorite spot on the gallery. But
his emotion left him no capacity for violence. He could
see his mother's jade plant in its big Chinese urn by the
steps—it was the finest one in town and she'd been so
proud of it—and there to the right of it was the trellis
Randy had built for her climbing rose. Everywhere he
looked he found a reminder, and it was these little things
that sharpened memory, and hurt.

So to the voice he could say nothing. He wanted only
to flee. He turned to retreat along the boardwalk, and
only now did he notice the two figures in uniform coming
from the park.

The man on the gallery called loudly, "Hey there, you
men! Stop that fellow!"

Max ran. There was nothing for it but to dodge and
run and hide like a petty thief. It sickened him. Then

anger came and knotted into his vitals with black hands
and he trembled with a fury that was all the worse because it was helpless. Finally it left him, bleak and
shaken and overcome with a gnawing loneliness, so that
when he crawled at last from his thicket near the beach
he sped through the shadows as if drawn by something
tensive and unfathomable to the one source that promised comfort.

It was a small weathered cottage far out on the bay
road and set a block back from the beach. Before he got
there he saw it in his mind's eye as it had been, with its
neat board fence and vegetable garden on one side and
its sprawling fig trees and wisteria bower on the other.
Almost within sight of it he stopped, aware of the rich
pervading scent of the wisteria in bloom. Then his chest
contracted with the sudden fear of what the years might
have done. Would she know him without his beard and
in these clothes? He touched his mustache and ran his
fingers through his scraggly hair. He went on, and his
heart began to pound, but the stifling contraction remained in his chest.

He heard a woman's low vibrant laugh. Could that be
Bella? It sounded a little like her. There was something
warm and earthy in Bella, and she'd always accepted
things as they came, with a shrug or a chuckle. He'd
never known her to be moody.

In the shadow of the pines at the corner of the yard
he came to a frozen halt. The house had changed. The
board fence was gone. Two Negroes sat on the front
steps, and a third, a woman, stood in the darkness of the
doorway, laughing softly.

He walked slowly up to where the gate had been, and
saw now that the fence had fallen over and lay rotting in

the weeds. The laughter died abruptly. The three Negroes stared at him in silence. In the bright night their faces seemed unfriendly.

"I'm looking for some people named Tacon," he said. "They used to live here."

He stood waiting for an answer, conscious of a deliberate scrutiny—it amounted almost to effrontery—that had never been a part of the old order. Presently the woman said, "Don't no Tacon live here. Ain't never heard o' no Tacon."

"They lived here during the war," he said. "They owned this house."

"Dey don't own it now," she told him shortly. "Us owns it."

It was dismissal. He would get nothing more out of them. As he turned and started back he could feel their eyes following him, cold from their new height, and uncomprehending.

He was a little sick. The contraction in his chest had crept down and was gathering his stomach into a knot of coldness.

What had happened to the Tacons? How could he find them?

There had been only the two of them, old Nolly and his daughter, and they'd come here just before the war, from somewhere around Mobile. Maybe they'd been forced to return. Maybe there'd been no help for it. Nolly Tacon was more than a shipwright. The man was a designer, and a good one. About the best he'd ever known. He'd planned, when the war was over, to have Nolly design and build him a new schooner. He'd even set the money aside for it, for he'd seen in time how the war would go. Only, he hadn't dreamed it would go quite so badly. He'd expected a sort of compromise, with hard times afterward—but not this utter collapse of everything.

With matters as they were, a man like Nolly would have to seek elsewhere for work. But what of Bella? Surely, he thought, she wouldn't go away without somehow leaving word for me. But whom would she leave it with? Whom do I know that Bella knew?

Suddenly he realized that they had no friend in common. Their worlds had never touched. The Tacons had come here strangers, and bought a little place. He'd employed Nolly to help fit out the old *St. George,* and he'd met Bella only by accident.

But maybe, he thought, Cassius will know about them. Certainly he can find out about them.

He became increasingly cautious as he came down a back street and approached the Drew cottage from the rear. Once, in the quiet, he heard the slow tread of men on patrol, and he slipped behind an oak and waited until he was sure they had reached the far corner and turned away through town. He cursed them, no longer in anger but with a presentimental coldness, then went on and very carefully crossed the street to the oleander thickets behind the Drew place, and eased through the creaky gate.

There was a growl and a quick scurrying behind the lattice on the back porch, and a brown water spaniel erupted from the shadow and hurtled toward him barking furiously.

"Easy, Teal! Quiet!" he ordered in a half whisper. "Don't you know me, boy?"

The spaniel whined and in an instant was all over him in an ecstasy of greeting. He crouched and held the aging pet he had given Cassius long ago. Behind the lattice the back door opened quietly, and a figure in a light cotton dressing robe materialized near the cistern and appeared at the head of the steps.

Max straightened. "Hello, Cassius," he said simply.

CHAPTER 5

I

THOUGH he sometimes referred to him as old Cassius, he had never thought of him as an old man, at least in years. Cassius, after reaching an indefinite sixty, had merely remained that way, perennially the same, neither young nor old, a soft-spoken and distinguished man of medium height with very fine silky hair so pale that it had always seemed white. With his white hair and his lean Roman features and his deliberation of manner, it was said that Cassius had been born middle-aged, for his contemporaries had never marked any change in him from youth to maturity. Max, in fact, had hardly considered him as more than middle-aged, for Cassius had

81

always lived with his mother, whose indubitable presence had somehow blanketed the passing years.

But now Cassius was old. It was a shock to see this outer change in him. Here in the littered study, by the light of the sputtering nubbin of a candle on the dusty table, Cassius was gaunt, wasted, bent, with deep hollows in his face and with that look about him of a tree that has been lashed by a hurricane. Even his dressing robe reflected this impression, for it was torn and frayed and out at both elbows and had but a single button, which hung by a thread.

But more startling was the inner change in Cassius. He had always been a mild man. In the past he had served a term or two in the legislature, but had turned his back on it in distaste, having no heart for political wrangling and chicanery. "If I cannot be a statesman," he had said, "I'll stay home and remain a lawyer, and stay sober. In the stench of our present-day politics I find it too difficult to maintain sobriety."

That had been long ago. Tonight the aging Cassius was cold sober, grim and, for the first time in his life, full of fight. His voice was firmer, if a little harsher, and there was a sort of repressed fury about him that reminded Max of an indignant old eagle.

"I knew you would escape sooner or later," he said, after Max had given a brief account of himself. "I've been expecting you for months, Maximilian."

"I'd have managed it sooner if I hadn't got 'sick in Monroe. Then they shipped me down to Garden Key . . ."

"That place! I've heard about it." Cassius swore in a manner unusual for him. "Oddly, it was only a week ago that I managed to find out you were there. I almost lost hope for you then. Getting out of there was a miracle." He shook his head. "Oh, I've been busy, Maximilian. I've been writing everywhere, trying to do what I could. . . . Anyway, my boy, I knew 'twas you the moment Teal acted the way he did. He'll not let a stranger in the yard. Only certain people come here, and I've had to teach him not to make a fuss. I'm very much suspect these days."

"So Branch Clabo told me."

Cassius snorted. "Clabo's well off, comparatively, and he's been playing it cozy. Very cozy. Anyway, I have to be careful. I suppose he warned you about the town being patrolled."

"Oh, yes, but I had a little brush with the rascals even so."

"I remember hearing a shot. Was that intended for you?"

Max nodded. "Patrols," he muttered. "Imagine it!" He wiped his hand over his face and frowned around at the dingy study. It was close in here, for the shutters were fastened and Cassius had carefully drawn the curtains before lighting the candle. In the dusty clutter of this place his eyes noted things that were not immediately comprehended. "Barbarians!" he spat out. "They're not content with winning. They've got to roll over us and smash us down and take everything we've got. They treat us like a conquered people!"

"Well, aren't we?" Cassius said dryly.

"Aye, we surely are, from the way they treat us. But suppose it had been the other way around. Suppose *we* had won. Can you imagine *us* rolling over the North, utterly wrecking them and then keeping *patrols* over them afterward?" His hands gripped the arms of his chair and he leaned forward, his voice rising. "I ask you, Cassius: Can you imagine us doing anything like that?"

"Hardly. But we were a different sort of people, with quite a different set of values. Probably that's why we lost. But all that is beside the point. The thing is that we lost. We're beaten. We're down. We're——"

"By heaven, we don't have to stay down! There are thousands of us——"

Cassius, who had been looking at him intently, suddenly held up a warning finger. "Don't wake Mother," he cautioned. "You know how she is."

"Eh? Your mother? She——" The leaping flame in him died down. It seemed incredible, considering Cassius, that old Mrs. Drew was still alive. "How is she now?" he asked lamely.

"Beginning to fail a little—but otherwise just the same. Just the same." The repetition of the phrase brought to Max a vision of a crinkled little waxen shadow of a woman in rustling black. She had been a great lady, and she still wore the gowns and thought the thoughts that belonged to a day long past. "She's back in her New Orleans period now," said Cassius, smiling thinly. "If she gets up, she'll probably mistake you for General Jackson and want to make a social event of it. And it'll upset her to find there's no wine in the house, and no servant to pour it. The main change is that the last six years hardly exist in her reckoning—which makes it rather difficult at times. By the way, my boy, you must be hungry. Allow me to fix something for you."

"I—no, thank you. I brought a lunch over from Clabo's. I couldn't eat a bite, really."

He had hardly touched the things Lily Bright had packed for him and he was beginning to be hungry. But it had suddenly occurred to Max that Cassius might have very little in the house to eat. His poverty was all at once overwhelmingly evident. There was the nubbin of the candle, which in the past Cassius would have disdained to use. There was the lack of wine, and Cassius had always loved his wine. There were other evidences, including Cassius himself.

"I see you have all your law library here," he said, peering at the dusty books and papers piled helter-skelter all around the room. "What have the rascals been doing to you, man?"

"They've done everything but disbar me!" Cassius snapped. "I've no doubt they'll arrange that in time. They wanted my property downtown for government use, so they just took it over and ran me out. They've taken everything from all of us that they could lay their hands on, and with hardly a pretense of legality. The thieves even took my chickens! Yes, sir! My prize layers! Wrung their necks for a damned chicken dinner! If the bay didn't have fish and oysters in it, Maximilian, a lot of us wouldn't be eating."

Cassius stopped. For a moment he sat glaring ferociously at the candle. "Maximilian," he began slowly, "we've got a fight on our hands. We've got a harder fight than we had before, and it's going to last longer."

"I came back to fight, Cassius. I don't know how much I can do, but at least I can even a few scores. I'm determined to do that."

"What's this? Even a few scores?"

"Aye, and right a few wrongs. That's one reason I've been wanting so badly to see you. I'll need your help. I've got to raise funds, organize, get men together. And of course I'll have to have vessels."

"Eh? Vessels? Hell's mischief, boy, what are you talking about?"

"Weren't we both talking about fighting?"

"Yes," said Cassius slowly. "But I'm afraid we weren't thinking in the same terms. I'm fighting for self-preservation. You're thinking mainly of revenge."

"And why not? What else is there left for me?"

"Now wait a minute, boy. There's a great deal left. It's all in what you value and how you look at it."

"How do you mean?"

Cassius sighed. "We're all bitter, Maximilian. All of us who gave what we had, and lost. And it's going to be very hard not to be bitter all of our days. For we're a conquered people, in every sense of the word. We can never go back—and don't ever think we can. And we can't even go forward. Things are bad enough now. But the terrible part of it is that our situation is bound to become more and more desperate for years."

"You really believe that?"

"Believe it?" the other said hoarsely. "I know it! They've taken the yoke from the blacks and put it on us. Their intention is to grind us down until there's absolutely nothing left of us! That's what we've got to fight, my boy! Our enemy is no longer the Stars and Stripes—but an army of ghouls who've taken advantage of the upheaval and wormed their way into power everywhere. Washington is full of them—they're hand in glove with that turncoat Johnson. And they've taken the South. They've got a strangle hold on us. Sherman himself wasn't more ruthless or vindictive. I could stomach him in preference to these carpetbaggers. They're going to keep the yoke on us as long as they can stay in power. And that's *how* they'll stay in power. Do you see?"

"Good Lord, sir, can't you manage to shoulder them out? Haven't the people any rights as citizens?"

"Rights?" snarled Cassius. "What rights? Those who bore arms have no rights whatever! No returned soldier can vote or hold office—and soon the rascals will have disfranchised every white person. The machinery's already in motion. They've just tossed out our new state government. We're under military rule again. Only the ignorant African can vote. Now do you see what's in store for us?"

"I'm getting an idea."

"It's going to be the worst kind of hell, Maximilian. We're going to have the Negro crammed down our throats—and disgraceful laws crammed down with him, and if we disobey we'll risk being hanged. They're absolutely determined to grind this generation into the dust. As a little illustration of what I mean: an order has just been given to destroy every grove of fruit trees in the state."

"Oh, my God!"

Cassius spread his hands. "They're out now with troops, whacking down the orange groves. It's senseless, but there it is. I wanted you to have the picture. It's a hard one to face. It'll try any man. Somehow, in the face of what they're doing, we've got to maintain honor and respectability if we would avoid degradation—and at the same time fight them with every weapon left to us."

Max got up. He paced the narrow room with its clutter of books. It used to be a neat little room, more of a

private parlor than a study, for Cassius had spent most
of his time in his big office downtown. In those days the
room had been as precise and orderly as Cassius himself
had been, as bright and well arranged as life had been.
But now the room was an embattled place, a microcosm
of the appalling disorder of the present. He went to the
window and briefly parted the curtains. Through a
broken shutter he could see the moonlight glinting on a
few ragged cabbages where formerly there had been
flowers. He wondered what had happened to old Cynthy
who had once kept the house spotless and the vases filled
with roses.

He turned back and carefully pinched out the sputtering candle flame. "No use wasting it," he said. "We've
seen each other."

"Yes, we've seen each other," Cassius repeated sadly.

Max went to the window again and drew back the
curtains and partially opened one shutter, letting in a
thin shaft of moonlight with the cool night air. He stood
with his hands bunched in his pockets a moment while
he sniffed a trace of wisteria, then returned and slumped
in the chair.

He felt unutterably weary and depressed. "Where's
Cynthy?" he asked abstractedly.

"Dead, poor soul. Peace be with her. We have Bethsheba now, after a fashion."

"Eh? Our old Bethsheba?" He sat up, staring at
Cassius in the shadow.

"Yes, your Bethsheba. She came here after your
mother died. Refused to have anything to do with that
fellow Dau. I expect Branch Clabo told you about him."

"He told me enough."

Cassius sighed. "Then I won't go into details. I'll

just say that the government—which means people like
Dau and his friends—took everything. Oh, there are a
couple parcels of land—the island area and that bit
down the coast—they overlooked. Mainly because they
have no immediate cash value, and nobody's thought to
search through the tax records to see who owns 'em.
Bethsheba and I did manage to retrieve a few personal
articles from the house. She has them hidden out back."

"She's living out there in Cynthy's quarters?"

"Yes. She cooks for us and helps Mother, and takes in
washings on the side. Before God, I don't know what
I'd do without the old battle-ax."

"I've got to see her before I go."

"She'll want to see you."

"Cassius, I—I left Mother a lot of cash when I was
here last. It was in gold."

"I remember you said you were going to leave her
some money. You had me convert everything available
to gold."

"Yes, and I added some to it. It came to better than
ten thousand. I was worried, you know, with the way
things were going."

"I remember."

"Well, I told Mother to use what she needed of it, and
to keep the rest hidden in a safe place. She—she told me
that if anything happened, I was to see you about it."

Cassius had been sitting hunched in the shadow. Now
he turned, and the moonlight sharply etched his nose
and made a long silver curve down the locks that fell to
his shoulders. It gave him more than ever the look of a
brooding old eagle, fierce and implacable. But when he
spoke his voice was soft.

"Your mother had fever, Maximilian. It came upon

her suddenly, and she was delirious most of the time. She was too ill to tell me anything."

"Do—do you think the money's still in the house?"

"I doubt it—if there was any of it left. I'm sure she knew she was going to lose the place before she got sick."

"Maybe Bethsheba knows about it."

"Possibly."

"Then let's go and see her."

"Presently. First, let's talk about your plans."

"But my plans will depend largely on the money."

"Very well. Suppose you had all your money now. What would you do with it?"

Max took a folded piece of paper from his pocket. "I have here a list of men I'd want you to communicate with. That's the first thing. Some are my old crew members. Others are friends scattered about."

"Who are some of them?"

"Well, there's Andrew McLane, Tim Eastman and the Weatherby boys. And there's Julius Carmichael and Billy Marsh——"

"Both Julius and Billy are dead," Cassius interrupted soberly. "The Weatherby boys are in Egypt or someplace, in foreign service. Tim Eastman is missing. I don't know what happened to Andrew McLane."

Max was silent a moment. He shook his head. "God, we've lost a lot!"

"Yes, we've lost too much. Those are the sort of men the South needs today."

"They're the sort that *I* need. Anyway, I have a long list. There'll be a few around, and I can probably find all the extras I'll need in Mexico. A great many men went there, I understand. I'll have to go there myself. To Vera Cruz. I'll get in touch with our old agent there. He'll help me find a suitable vessel and fit it out."

"Fit it out for what?"

"To take Garden Key."

Cassius stiffened. He started to raise his hand, then lowered it. "Go on," he whispered.

"I see you don't approve," said Max. "You don't even believe I can take Garden Key."

Cassius said nothing for a moment. Then he moved, and his eyes seemed to burn in the moonlight. "Why waste yourself in such madness?"

"It's not madness! I can do it, by heaven! I could have done it during the war if I'd known there was only one serviceable cannon in the place! And do you call it a waste for me to liberate all those poor devils who are rotting and dying there for no more reason than that they fought on the losing side?"

• "Maximilian, listen to me! Use your head, boy. The war is over. You can't——"

"The war will never be over for me until I've done something to even the score—and the one thing that will do it will be to take Garden Key! I'd rather do that than anything else on this earth. I know exactly how I'd do it, down to the last detail. With the right crew and equipment I could manage it without losing a man. I don't care what it costs, or what happens afterward. All that matters is that I take the place and put an end to the crime of it, and get those men away from there."

"And just how far do you think a few thousand dollars would go in such a scheme?"

"Not far, I'll admit. But cost is no object. I'll raise the money somehow. If I can't get it in donations I'll dig it out of the sand."

"Are you talking about the island?"

"Certainly. There's money over there. You know that." He took out the pocket piece he had carried for years and held it in the moonlight. "I found this when I was a kid. I know where the rest of it is now. I've had three years to figure it out——"

"You've had three years to get steamed up," Cassius interrupted harshly. "You're all steamed up and full of hell's mischief. I knew that the moment I saw you tonight."

"And why shouldn't I be?" he spat out. "By heaven——"

"Maximilian, you're stark mad."

"Mad, am I?" he cried, rising. "Have you ever been in prison? Do you know what it's like to be chained in a damned casement week after week, month after month, for years, eating your goddamned heart out for just a sight of home and knowing that time is turning every hope and dream you ever had to dust? And it's not just yourself. It's others like you, hundreds of others. Did you ever hear a man cry because he couldn't see his babies? Or go out of his head and try to claw through a wall because he didn't know what had happened to his family? I can't tell you about those things. There aren't words to tell you. You'd have to know men like Dawson or Meriwether, live with them, see them die . . ." His voice broke. He sank trembling in his chair.

Cassius got up. He came over soundlessly and touched Max on the shoulder, then went to the window and stood looking into the garden while he flexed his long thin hands.

The knowledge of his own helplessness made it hard, at that moment, for Cassius to know what to do. He had been deeply affected. Of all those who had left this area to go to war, comparatively few had managed to return.

Those who had come back had been bitter men, disheartened and broken. He had pitied them and done what he could for them; but now he realized that they had been lucky men, for without exception they had had somewhere to go. A home of some sort, and a family. That made all the difference. They could walk abroad by day and speak openly with friends, and at night they had sanctuary, however humble, and the sense of being needed and wanted. A man had to have that to cure the sickness which war leaves in him.

He wished with all his heart that he could offer his home to this man whom he had looked on almost as a son. But he had only words to give. And what are words when a man needs the balm of time and peace to counteract the acid of his sickness and change the look of violence in his eyes? It was that look which frightened Cassius. He knew what could result from it, and it moved him to a greater pity.

"I know how you feel, son," he murmured, turning from the window. "I don't blame you in the least for wanting to strike back at an enemy who has been so unjust. And God knows I'd like to see those prisoners freed—but freeing them by force, at a time like this, would cause incalculable harm. You'd bring the wrath of our enemies upon innocent people. I've explained to you how things are. Remember: our old enemies no longer exist as such. We've a new set of enemies, and an entirely different sort of fight to make."

"Why tell me that? What help can I give you? Don't forget that I'm an escaped criminal, probably with a price on my head. I can't even show my face in public."

"So far," said Cassius, "there's been no mention of your having escaped. I don't know why. But just suppose you managed to get a pardon. Wouldn't you like to stay here and help us?"

"Hell, they'll never pardon me!"

"Suppose I told you that I've been working for nearly two years to get you a pardon?"

"You—you have?"

"Yes. I have a few friends scattered about who have a little influence in the right places. I'm not saying they can do much these days, but there's always the chance."

Max stood up. He walked around the table and plucked uncertainly at a pile of papers. Suddenly he looked up and said angrily, "Why should I belittle myself to accept the pardon of a bunch of thieving rascals, a government without honor? Run by the scum of the earth! Damned if I'll stoop to accept favors from such people! I'm free now and I'll do as I please—and if I can raise the funds——"

"No," said Cassius. "Stop thinking emotionally. It's a trap for logic. You were always a clear thinker in the past. It was one of the things I admired about you. Sit down. I want to tell you something."

Max took his chair. "What is it?"

"Just this. We need you here. Someone who can formulate plans and carry them out. As I told you, so few of our men came home. And I can do so little, alone," Cassius added sadly. "I'm getting old. It's a horrible thing to be slowed and dulled at such a time as this when there's so much to do, when you need double your strength and wits. It makes me doubly afraid. And I'm afraid, Maximilian. I can see what's going to happen. The country is full of strangers. Most of 'em are vultures, the backwash of war. And there are scads of new

Negroes in town. Poor ignorant devils, they don't know they're being used. They frighten me. They're potentially very dangerous, for if anyone should fill them with wild talk and whisky, and give them arms . . ." Cassius shook his head. "You must have noticed how quiet the place was tonight when you came ashore. That's because of the troops stationed with us. We may hate them, may hate the patrols that are keeping the streets clear, but we can thank God for them! There's been talk of their being ordered away—but I've quietly been doing everything in my power to keep them here."

He stopped and waved a thin hand, and went on earnestly, "Now do you see how it is? Don't you think it's worth swallowing a little pride if it will place you in a position to do some real good?"

"There's no use thinking about it. I haven't got a pardon, and they'll never give me one."

"There's a possibility of it. I'm expecting some news almost any day. Will you wait until I hear about it before you commit yourself to a course of action you're bound to regret?"

"I—I don't know. I can't do much without funds. Let's go out and see Bethsheba."

"In a moment. First promise me you'll wait."

"I can't just sit around doing nothing. I'd go crazy, thinking about things. I've got to do something."

"Yes, but not what you're planning to do. You need to do something that will help bring back your perspective. I wish you could stay over here with me."

"Thanks for the wish, but that's out of the question."

"I know. But you're not safe even at Clabo's. In fact, you're not safe anywhere along this coast—you're too well known, and too easily recognized."

Max frowned. "I was rather thinking about sailing over to Mobile for a little while."

"The place is full of troops. I wouldn't attempt it. Anyhow, why Mobile?"

"I—I'd like to locate Nolly Tacon. Remember him?"

"Vaguely. But the man's dead, Maximilian. He died here over a year ago."

Max closed his eyes. Presently he said, "Nolly had a daughter. Do you know what happened to her?"

"No. I've never seen her. Possibly Bethsheba knows."

"Then let's go and see her."

"First, are you going to give me your word to wait and not do anything foolish until I've heard about the pardon?"

"All right. You have my word."

Cassius went to the door. He hesitated. "Perhaps I'd better go ahead and wake her, and tell her you're here. She talks about you all the time, and if you appeared suddenly she might forget herself. You know how excitable she is." He opened the door and tiptoed out into the black hallway.

CHAPTER 6

I

THE moon had gone down when Max returned to the boat, but the night was still clear and luminous with starlight. By the position of the Dipper it was long after midnight. He went below, got a blanket and the basket of lunch Lily Bright had packed and sat on deck with the blanket about him while he finished the hoecake and the hunks of beef. Then he drew toward him a heavy leather bag that Bethsheba had helped him pack. It was an old rawhide traveling bag that had belonged to his father. He ran his hand over it fondly, and suddenly impatient to see again some of the treasures Bethsheba had saved, he opened it and began pawing through its contents.

97

Long ago, when he was only a small boy, he had been almost in terror of Bethsheba. She was so big and strong, and so fearfully black in the way that a carved idol is fearful, and so ominously belligerent. But as he grew older he had learned that her belligerence was only that of a jealous and proud watchdog to whom the family was everything. When he had graduated from Annapolis and come home on leave, she had been immensely proud. "Jes' look at you!" she'd beamed. "Whar'd you be if'n I hadn't laid de law down an' chastized you when you needed hit? But hyar you is, growed up plumb decent an' come back nigh as fine a man as yo' pa!" Then she'd thrown her big arms about him and cried.

Tonight she'd held him like that and cried again. "Jes' us two left," she'd mumbled over and over. "Jes' us two!"

They had talked for a long time. She and Cassius had managed to save a few portraits, his mother's little box of jewels and most of the silver, some of the family books and keepsakes and odds and ends, and Bethsheba had saved a trunk of clothing.

"I knowed you was comin' back," she said. "I knowed all along you was comin'. I says to myself, They can't hold my boy. With God's help he's bound to git away. He'll be comin' home one o' these days wi' nothin' but de rags on his back. He won't have nothin'. We'd jes' laid yo' po' ma away, an' I was all broke up, but them peoples was comin' in de mawnin' to claim de house, an' I knowed I had to work fast. So I went quick around grabbin' an' snatchin' things, tryin' to figger what you'd want an' what you'd need. . . ."

That which he had been most concerned about, Bethsheba did not have. But it helped to get the clothing and the other things. From the trunk of miscellaneous apparel she had saved he had selected a few articles he might need in the immediate future—boots, shirts, spare trousers, a jacket and a light suit—and she had packed them in the bag. He thumbed through them now, and suddenly drew out the boots and studied them in the starlight. They were fine English boots, his favorite pair. He tore off the sandals Branch had made and tried to pull on the boots, but they pinched badly. He worked them with his hands until the leather felt soft, then tried them on again. Still they pinched. It was impossible to walk in them.

"Oh, the devil!" he muttered, and put them aside, frowning. It was a little unsettling to discover that he could no longer wear them. It gave him the odd feeling of having lost his identity.

He thrust the boots from his mind as his exploring hand went through the bag and brought out familiar and reassuring objects from the past. He placed them close around him on deck: a brier pipe, a small folding tooled-leather case containing daguerreotypes of his father and mother, a pocket-size copy of *Hamlet* that various Ewings had carried for a century, an old jackknife, a pouch of moldy tobacco, a razor and a shaving kit, a tinderbox and a flat wooden case holding a pair of ornate silver-mounted pistols that had belonged to his father.

The knife and the tinderbox went into his pockets. The other possessions, one by one, were returned to the bag. All save the pipe and the tobacco pouch which he toyed with a while, wondering what it would be like to smoke again. In prison tobacco had been a luxury beyond his reach, and he had convinced himself that he no longer cared for it. Now tentatively he sniffed the moldy stuff in the pouch, then dumped it over the side. But he thrust the pipe between his teeth.

He was tired out, but it was impossible to sleep. For a long time he lay on deck with the blanket wrapped around him, chewing on the empty pipe while he watched the constellation of Scorpio rising in the southeast like a blown umbrella. Almost he wished he had not come over here tonight. Save for the clothing and these few possessions, the visit had brought only disappointment and a sharper bitterness.

Bethsheba had said, "Them folks named Tacon, I jes' barely recollects 'em. I 'members de ole man dyin'."

"Do you know what became of his daughter, Miss Bella?"

"What'd she look like?"

"A rather large young woman, not heavy exactly. She had dark hair. . . ." Odd, but in trying to describe Bella he'd been at a sudden loss. He remembered the quality of her, the way she laughed and spoke, and particularly the smell of her skin. She wasn't what you'd call a beautiful woman, perhaps, but certainly she was attractive. A very vital sort of person, full-blown—although he'd been careful not to describe her that way. For no reason at all he'd had the sudden feeling that old Bethsheba, had she known Bella, would not have wholly approved of her. Bethsheba had very rigid ideas about what constituted a lady.

But Bethsheba had no memory of her. "If'n you wants," she'd said, "I kin find out about 'er. Jes' give me a few days."

Of the money he had left with his mother, Bethsheba knew little. "Mebbe she jes' used hit all, Marse Max.

Hit took a bar'l o' money to run things whilst you was gone. Many's de time she'd put a double eagle in my hand an' send me out to hunt up a few vittles. Hit wouldn't hardly buy nothin'."

"Did she always give you gold?"

"Mighty near always. Couldn't buy *nothin'* with dat paper. You ain't got no idea. An' later when de fightin' was over an' all de new peoples come ter town hit was jes' as bad." She told him about the other servants who had stayed on and helped until the past year, when his mother had insisted that they take advantage of better employment. One by one they had drifted away under the promises of the new order, all save his man Janus who had acquired a boat of sorts and taken to the bay. "He keeps us in fish an' oysters," Bethsheba admitted. "Ev'ry time he comes he wants to know has we heard from you. Hit's gonna be hard to face 'im, me knowin' you're back an' him wantin' so bad to see you."

"I'd certainly like to see him again."

"Sho, but 'twouldn't be safe. Janus, he's got a boy workin' with 'im what ain't too good, an' somethin' might slip." She shook her head. "You got to be mighty careful. I hates to think o' you over there at Clabo's. You had ought to be off somewheres a-layin' low till Marse Cass'us gits de pardon. Sho, he'll git it somehow. Jes' give 'im time."

That was ridiculous, of course. It was too late for a pardon now. Escape had ruined whatever chance he might have had. Not that it mattered.

He lay thinking of Bella, and of Cassius and the promise he had made, and of the money. He should have realized that there would be no money left. After all, he'd been gone a long time. And what were a few thousand dollars in those terrible years? Just so many leaves in a whirlwind.

What should he do now?

He tried to plan, to think, but depression weighed on him. In his mind there was only confusion.

He drifted away into sleep, and awoke abruptly with the raw edge of the morning sun slicing into his eyes. He sat up, groggy and unrested, and saw the sun burst furiously from the sea in sudden flaming brilliance. He felt as if he had slept but a minute or two.

A few hundred yards to the east a pair of shrimp trawlers, with sails dyed a rusty red from many soakings in the river water, were running out from the inner harbor into the bay. Nearer, in the shallows along the beach, several Negro boys were cast-netting for mullet. A church bell tolled, and at the same time there came four impatient little toots from an unseen steamer somewhere beyond the brick warehouses lining the river. All at once aware of his proximity to the waking town, Max went forward and drew up the anchor and made sail.

Far out in the bay he dropped sail and anchored, and went below. He was asleep almost the moment he stretched on the hard bunk.

He awoke late in the morning and crawled on deck, refreshed and hungrier than he had been in days. The lunch basket was empty; but the boat, like most small craft in the region, was equipped with poles, tongs, hand lines, a dip net and other gear. It was only a matter of minutes before the net, tossed over the stern and dragged carefully along the bottom, produced enough small crabs and shrimp to bait several of the hand lines. These presently yielded a spotted trout and a pair of redfish which he broiled on deck over a charcoal brazier.

He ate slowly, relishing the fish, the bright spring day, the shimmering bands of color over the miles of familiar water, and feeling for the moment a strong primal satisfaction in being here, sufficient in his known element and alone with it. He had always felt a certain contempt and pity for landsmen, especially those in cities. They are like people lost, he thought, without knowing they are lost. Their minds travel in cramped narrow orbits because their lives are cramped and their horizons limited. Ashore, in a city, a man lives within walls, and looks out of a window and sees not space but the boundaries of streets and the walls of his neighbors. And never, never, night or day, can he escape his neighbors, or remove his mind from the busy insistence of them save by retreating to a forest or climbing to a mountaintop. A man can close his door against other men, but their little thoughts intrude and the insistent sounds of them come in. Busy, busy, always busy with their little thoughts even when they are doing nothing, clamorously busy doing nothing, circling all their lives in mortal conflict, one against another.

Aye, you can escape it in the forest, but you become lowly and feral in the forest without horizons; and you can escape it on the mountain, but the height beguiles you with the illusion of omnipotence, so that you forget your smallness in the scheme of things and feel greater than the mountain because you stand on top of it. But it is not that way at sea.

At sea a man never forgets his smallness. The sea is too mighty to allow him any illusions. If you are a seaman you love the sea and you fear it, and above all you respect it. And only here, in this freedom of space where mountains can be seen as trifles, can your mind be wholly free.

Today, looking toward the distant mainland, he suddenly resented the land for all the tangling emotional holds it had on him. It was a place of bitterness and hate. For an instant he wished he could up anchor and turn his back on it and forever feel released from it. But his love for it bound him. Its bitterness and its hate were his own, and made him a prisoner to it. He could never leave it until he had fought his fight and achieved some sort of peace within himself.

Cassius had understood this. *You need to do something that will help bring back your perspective.* Only, Cassius hadn't known Meriwether; nor had he been on the Bay of Cárdenas or lain in the black rotting silence of a casemate. Perspective, he thought. Oh, hell!

He thought of the boots that no longer fitted him, and frowned down at his feet. Around either ankle the skin was rough and red from the long chafing of the irons. He rubbed his fingers over the chafed spots, wondering how long it would take for the redness to go away. Maybe the boots would fit him then.

Suddenly he hated to return to Clabo's. He wished there were a spot back in time, back in his own life, a somewhere that was remote in time and space that he could return to and find it untouched and unchanged, so that he could go there and take up his thoughts afresh while he waited. At the moment he was like a man trying to decide what to do after a hurricane. You couldn't just prop up the walls of a house that had blown down. You had to clear out the rubble and get down to something solid that hadn't been touched. All the old symbols and the old values were gone. His mind was full of rubble.

Until this morning it had seemed entirely feasible and logical, if he couldn't raise funds any other way, to go to the island and find what scores of others had long sought in vain. "It's there," he told Cassius. "You know it's there. Why, even you and Father used to go over there and look for it."

"Oh, possibly it is there," Cassius had replied. "I'd hate to think it isn't. Surely *something* is there, but I'm glad we never found it."

"How's that?"

"If we'd found it, that would have been the end of it."

"I see what you mean. But I'm not being romantic about this. I'm being entirely objective. I have a purpose."

"I decry the purpose. And as long as you're being objective, I'll remind you that after all it's only an old story."

"Old stories always have some truth in them. And don't forget that I've actually found something."

"I've found things too, my boy. I picked up seventeen pieces of French silver right down yonder on my own beach one morning after a storm. They were in a broken jar. After all, we've had a very turbulent past. One rather expects to stumble across things occasionally. But to be factual and practical, what you found doesn't prove there's any truth in the story that people have built around three cannon on the island. We know that three cannon are over there, for they've been seen—but no one man has ever seen more than two of them. The mystery of the missing one adds a touch of fey to what might be only another tale. Now, don't mistake me. I'm not trying to dispel an illusion. I'm only trying to show you that illusions have their proper place. God knows, we need them! But in your damnable objectiveness you refuse to see illusion, and you've completely lost sight of matters fey."

Last night the thing that Cassius had tried to tell him had seemed obscure. But this morning it was clear enough. Certainly he had lost something. Maybe, sifted down, it was simply youth. There was a taste of ashes in his mouth when he thought of what had once given him pleasure.

But knowing his loss didn't help any. It solved nothing.

The wind was beginning to haul a little and freshen. He studied it, undecided what his next move should be. It was time he started back for Clabo's; but he delayed, trying to put it off as long as possible by making things shipshape. Finally he stripped down and plunged over the side.

He wished he did not have to see Branch again. Cassius had said, "I used to like the fellow, in spite of his limitations. But I've had no use for him ever since he took advantage of his situation when times got bad."

He had been surprised at this. It seemed entirely out of character.

"It was during the blockade," Cassius had explained. "He dealt with a lot of vessels, and handled a great deal more than supplies for our men. All kinds of frivolities and nonsense—which a lot of fools wanted. They were willing to pay any kind of money for the trash. And later, when conditions were terrible and it took everything we had just for food and medicine, Branch supplied that—for a price. Hell's mischief, how that rascal charged!"

"I wouldn't have believed it."

"Well, I'm just telling you. He surprised me. I'd never thought of Branch as greedy. It still doesn't seem like him—although his father was that way. Anyhow, he didn't gain a thing. All his good money had to go for buying his stocks. He saved only Confederate notes."

"Serves him right!"

"Anyway, Maximilian, it's something you should know about him. He's a simple man—but sometimes simple people have capacities that we overlook. Right now, incidentally, he's playing up to the powers that be. He shies away from the rest of us. Maybe he's just afraid. But I don't like his attitude."

Damned bastard! he thought, as he crawled on deck. I can't stay there any longer. He helped me when I needed help, and Lord knows I appreciate it. But it's time to leave.

He stood up and shook the water from his face and glanced in the direction of Clabo's, several miles away. A sloop had appeared from behind the distant point. It was too far off for recognition, but it looked a little like the lighthouse boat. He watched it while he slapped himself dry. It was probably a fisherman. Surely Lassaphene would not have gone back over there today.

He got out his kit and shaved, and put on clean shirt and trousers. It was good to have these personal things again, for in a sense they made him independent. The small matter of being forced to use another man's razor had bothered him more than having to accept almost any other favor. But he no longer had to lean on Branch for anything. He could return and put his own boat in repair so that he could live aboard it, then pick out one of the sheltered coves along the island and stay there for the time being. There were a few articles he would need, but he could buy them from Branch and pay for them later after Cassius had disposed of some of his mother's jewelry. Most of the money from the jewelry he intended giving to Cassius and Bethsheba. Cassius was desperately poor; and Bethsheba was old—far too old to be taking in washings.

The sun was reaching past noon when he started back. The day had turned hot and white continents of clouds were steaming upward with a summer intensity from the cauldrons of the swamps, and drifting seaward. He studied the sloop that had come from Clabo's. It was off to starboard now, passing in the distance, running swiftly down the long brilliant reach of the bay on a course toward the almost invisible lower end of the island. It was unquestionably the lighthouse boat.

II

Little Hermes met him on the pier and made the lines fast, then as usual scrambled aboard to rearrange all the gear to a preconceived and just-so order. It was as if he had been created as a diminutive afterthought for Branch, who was lax and untidy and kept nothing in repair.

For a moment Max looked clinically at the mute little man, viewing him no longer as part of the familiar pattern of his youth, but as an evidence of something he had overlooked in Branch. For the first time even the weather-beaten tavern and the moldy and sagging outbuildings affected him unpleasantly. Everything here was decadant.

Branch came limping down from the tavern.

"Well," he said. "Well. You got back early. Wasn't hardly lookin' for you till tomorrow. How'd you make out?"

"Oh, all right."

"No trouble?"

"Nothing to speak of." He could see that Branch had something on his mind. His flat face was expressionless, if evasive, and he was slowly snapping the fingers of one hand across his thumb.

Branch said, "Glad you didn't make it here no sooner. That varmint Pinchy showed up a little while ago. First time I've seen 'im since the day you come back."

"Where is he now?"

"Gone over to the quarters. He's liable to be around a couple days. You better lay low till he's gone back to town."

"Branch, I was planning to leave as soon as I can get my boat in shape. Tomorrow if possible."

"Yeah? Where you figgerin' on goin'?"

"Oh, I don't know. No particular place. I just think it would be better if I left."

Branch peered at him sharply and looked away. "I don't want you to feel you ain't welcome. You're welcome to stay as long as you please. I jest want you to be safe." He stopped and peered up at him again. "However, as long as you're aimin' to leave, I got an idea for you. You know, Lassaphene was here today."

"I saw his boat heading back for the island. Is anything wrong over there?"

"Yeah. That feller Haik."

"The assistant keeper?"

"Yeah. Had a fall an' broke 'is leg."

Max frowned. "But why did Lassaphene come over here? Didn't Haik need a doctor?"

"Oh, I reckon hit warn't too bad a break. Lassaphene set it himself. He's pretty clever that way. Trouble is, it kind of messes things up at the lighthouse. They're doin' some repair work over there, an' it leaves 'em short-handed."

"I see." Max chewed thoughtfully on his pipe. He saw clearly what was coming, and he wanted nothing to do with it.

Branch said, "I promised Lassaphene I'd bring 'im a man to help out."

"Hmm. Why didn't he go to town to find someone?"

"Not him! If'n he went to town, they'd make 'im hire a colored feller. He may be a Yankee, but he don't want no Negro over there. Anyhow, them Haiks wouldn't stand for it. They'd have to board 'im. Lassaphene, he wanted me to come over an' work."

"Then why didn't you go?"

Branch sat down on the pier. He watched Hermes scuttling about the catboat, fussy as a woman. "I'd sure like to work over there," he admitted. "I'd like to mighty bad. But I'd have to stay over there quite a spell, an' I couldn't very well leave things here for long. I got a heap to do."

"What have you got to do that's so important?"

"Oh, a heap o' things. You jest don't know how it is with me. So I told Lassaphene I'd send you over."

"Oh, no." He shook his head emphatically. "Absolutely no, Branch."

"You crazy, Johnny Max?"

"Devil take Lassaphene! I have other plans."

"Yeah? Thought you'd been wantin' to git over on the island. Here's your chancet—with pay an' board to go with it. An' you'll be safe in the bargain. You sure as hell ain't safe over here. But who'd bother you over there? Now I ask you, don't it look like a smart move?"

"Possibly. What's the pay?"

"Seventy-five cents a day and found."

"My, my, what would I do with so much money?"

"Aw, hell an' dingbats, that's a heap these days. An' you're broke, ain't you?"

Max shrugged. "I've little need for money at the moment. And I most certainly don't care to earn any by working for a man like Lassaphene."

"You won't hardly ever see Lassaphene, either him or the women. You'll be staying with the Haiks, an' them two families don't have nothin' to do with each other. Not a damn thing. But them Haiks, they ain't such bad people. They'll treat you nice an' feed you well."

"What are they like?"

"Ben, he's a big redheaded feller. A mite steamy, but he's all right when you git to know 'im. Alabama man. An' Bella, she's dark-complected an' sort of a looker. Right personable. She sure knows how to cook."

"Bella?" Max bit down on his pipe. "Where's she from?"

"From the same place as Ben, I reckon. All I know about 'er is that her pa was a shipwright."

Max turned away and looked out over the sound. It was shimmering with a sickly brightness in the afternoon heat. There were bands of brightness that seemed to undulate and slide one into the other, so that looking at it gave him a feeling of vertigo.

Oh, God, he thought.

But almost casually he managed to ask, "Was her father named Tacon?"

"I don't recollect," Branch replied. "Why, do you think you know 'er?"

Max fumbled in his pocket and touched his tobacco pouch. He took it out and looked at it, and cursed it. He felt a smouldering helpless rage. "I want a smoke," he rasped. "Plague and the devil, I haven't had a smoke in damned near three years! I think I'll go up and get me a twist of that mixed leaf. I'll pay you for it later, Branch."

"Forget it," Branch said. "I reckon I owe it to you. What about that job with Lassaphene? He wants somebody right away."

Max thrust the pouch into his pocket. He tried to think, but thought was impossible. He could only vision the torment of being over there, being forced to see Bella every day, at every meal, being inescapably with her and yet distant from her.

Then, as if the decision had already been made by another part of him over which he had no control, he found himself saying, "Very well. I'll take the damned job. Will I have time to patch up that boat of mine so I can sail it over?"

"No, you'd better leave it here. I'll have Hermes do a little calkin' on it, an' you kin git it later. Lassaphene wants you in the mornin'. If'n we start over there right away, we ought to make it before dark."

CHAPTER 7

I

MANY a man has claimed the island, but no man has really owned it, for it belongs to the sea. It is entirely the sea's handiwork. For more than seven leagues it parallels the coast, a gleaming white-and-green pine-covered barrier enclosing the bay and the sound, a wall of dunes cast up by the sea in sullen resentment against the spreading red of the river. Occasionally, at the whim of hurricanes, it becomes two islands, and sometimes three, but always when the wrath is past the sea hastens to repair these breaches and make it whole again.

Races of unknown ancients have left their bones and their crumbling shell middens along its leeward shores;

113

freebooters have used it for a rendezvous, and French, Spanish and English adventurers have claimed it for themselves or their kings, and built their fortifications on it. But always their tenure has been brief. Time and intolerant tides and winds have wiped out all their works, and the sea has strewed the wreckage of their ships from one end of the long narrow island to the other, and buried the bleached remains in its sands. Only the lighthouse has endured.

The lighthouse, flanked by the stealthy dunes, rises tall and white above the cape where the island makes its far southwestern curve. Every brick in the powerful rocketing tower was firmly set down and mortared with a tenacious British stubbornness to defy the sea and the centuries, and it is the oldest standing work of man in all the region that it serves and dominates. But tempests have left their mark in its masonry, and the sea is forever fingering its foundation or casually reaching in and toppling a retaining wall. The sea, at will, has taken other such structures in the vicinity. It is in no hurry.

From Clabo's place, on the eastern point of the mainland opposite the city, it was a fourteen-mile run down the main portion of the bay to the lighthouse pier, which was on the island's leeward side. A visitor, unless he was met by one of the keepers with the reservation's mule and wagon, was still remote from his destination, for ahead lay a two-mile tramp along a sandy road that wound across the widest part of the island—the densely wooded and almost detached extremity that is known locally as Little St. George.

This afternoon the catboat, with a light breeze on the quarter, ran for nearly three hours before the lighthouse pier became visible in the far distance. For some time now, while they had been drawing gradually nearer the main island, Max had been aware of the low rumbling explosions of the surf on the outer beach, all of two miles away. Not in many months had he heard such a sound, for in the whole great length of mangrove-bordered coast from Key West to the upper Gulf there is no surf worthy of the name. Suddenly restless, he went forward by the cabin and stood listening to it, remembering nights as a child when he had gone out on the gallery at home and heard, clearly across the vast reach of the bay, that thunder on St. George. Sometimes it had been very loud, a beating of mighty drums that seemed to shake the earth. "De ole war drums," Bethsheba had always called it.

He glanced briefly at the sun, a churning radiance smothering in the western clouds, and studied the pier on Little St. George. The pier was a mere scratch in the haze. His eyes turned to larboard where hundreds of egrets were clouding over a fringe of marsh. All at once he had a craving to be ashore; he had an inexplicable hunger for the feel of the island and the sight of the beach.

"Put the helm over," he called to Hermes, who was hunched in the stern sheets with one tiny foot braced against the tiller.

Branch, sprawled across the fantail, sat up with a blank stare. "What's the matter? You aimin' to go ashore here?"

"Yes, I'd like to."

"You're makin' a hell of a long walk for yourself."

"It's not so far along the beach. Anyway, we'd be till dark reaching the pier, and I'd still have a walk ahead of me."

"Suit yourself."

They ran in close and anchored, and Branch poled him ashore in the skiff. Briefly they shook hands. He knew that Branch was relieved to be rid of him.

"Thanks for everything," he told Branch. "I've hated to put you to so much trouble."

"Hit's all right, Johnny Max. Hit ain't been no trouble."

They peered at each other uncertainly a moment, then looked away. Accident had brought them together as boys, but they had matured in their different molds, and their ways had long since parted.

"Well, Branch, I'll see you in time."

"Sure, take care o' yourself."

II

Bella was suddenly a torment in his mind as he started across the narrow island. I'll see her soon enough, he thought. What will be, will be. Maybe it's all for a reason. . . .

Once, after entering the belt of pines, he glanced back, but the bay was hidden behind the palms and the dense forest growth. He pressed on toward the dunes and the rumbling surf. The pines became dwarfed and twisted, and gave way to low tortured oaks. The oaks dwindled to mere shrubs, torn, battered, raked and pressed backward, clinging to one another like children in mortal terror, turned violently away from the sea in frozen flight. It was difficult to force his way through them and reach the final ramparts of the dunes. Here the perennial sea oats grew untroubled, thick and waist-high, and below them the lush goatsfoot vine crept cool and green over the hot white sand. The vine reached toward the sea, eager for its caress.

He dropped his bag and drew a deep satisfying breath. His mind cleared; he felt suddenly reborn. The sun had gone down, leaving its spilled brilliance across the sky. The Gulf spread a deep silken richness before him, surging with stealthy movement, alive with half the colors of the spectrum. A long lazy ground swell was sweeping in, rising high and creaming, and abruptly crashing with a great smother of white. The sound of it was the contented but ever-watchful rumbling of some mighty animal.

He shouted to it, greeting an old friend he was able to love without trusting, and sat down to rest and watch it until the swift dusk drove him to his feet. With the bag over his shoulder he descended the dune and set out along the damp hard-packed sand of the beach. The lighthouse was a star low on the horizon.

Night came with a tropic brightness, so that there was scarcely a change from dusk to dark. He stopped to rest, trudged on and stopped again. The bag became heavier, his stops more frequent. Sand crabs raced ahead of him in the moonlight, pale little ghosts casting moving shadows that seemed to come from nowhere. Once he circled warily around a large wild hog with glinting tusks. It stood black and evil in his path, refusing to retreat.

His pace slowed. It seemed that he had been walking for hours, but the lighthouse was still a star low on the horizon. The bag had become an enormous weight.

He reached a trickle of brackish water that ran across the beach, and got down on his knees and drank thirstily.

When he straightened he saw by the Dipper that it was nearly ten o'clock. It was ridiculous to go on at this hour.

He studied the dunes. The island here seemed more familiar. The dunes were lower and rolling, and there was a break in the pines beyond them. Now he realized that he was close by the narrow marshy neck connecting the main body of the island with Little St. George.

Wearily he picked up his bag and went floundering over the soft dry hillocks to the edge of the pines. A small herd of dozing goats sprang up and fanned away on his right, then turned and stared at him curiously. He went on and found a sheltered spot where several pines grew close together, and dragged up a few dead branches and kindled a fire. He opened his bag and found his jacket and drew it on. At last he filled his pipe and stretched out with his head propped against the bag to smoke away his sudden hunger before going to sleep.

As he thought of the goats he wondered if they were his own. But undoubtedly they were, for there had been no goats on the island until he had brought a load of them over a few years before the war. He had brought them here, he remembered, soon after buying part of the island. In fact, he was probably camping on his own land tonight, for his holdings started somewhere along here and took in all of Little St. George except the light-house reservation.

He was rather amazed at himself, looking back. To think that he'd bought this island property, and stocked it with goats! Why? For what? It seemed so out of character with his present self. But of course he'd been different then, and everything in life had been different. If you wanted to look at it commercially, the place was worthless. It was just a wild, pretty stretch of island.

Beautiful, really, and delightfully remote. It was land without having the clutter and the ties of the land, and it didn't smell of man and his works. It was all of the sea.

But why the goats? Somehow it had needed them. It had seemed to cry for goats. He remembered saying at the time that every island ought to have goats on it, and forthwith he and Randy and the boys had rounded up a couple of dozen head and brought them over. What a wild time and a mad trip that had been! Aye, brother!

He couldn't imagine himself doing such a thing now. It seemed so lacking in purpose. For years all his actions had been with purpose; since the beginning of the war he had had to plan every move, to live with logic, to calculate every element from wind force and ocean current to the roll of the vessel and the trajectory of a shot. The smallest oversight meant the difference between defeat and victory, life and death. It was a little difficult to place himself in his old shoes—which no longer fitted!— and channel his mind to the boyhood romanticism of islands and goats.

But no, what he'd done was more than just a spurt of romanticism. Oh, there was that, too, what with being raised on *Robinson Crusoe,* and finding occasional coins and seeing the bones of old ships whitening on the beaches—but there was also purpose. Unconscious perhaps, but purpose just the same. Without quite realizing it, he'd been trying to preserve something when he bought the island. We go through life, he thought, buying things seemingly without purpose, things we don't really need or even want, all because they have special connotations and give us a grasp on desires that are often unknown to us.

When he acquired the island he'd been trying to preserve something in himself and of the past, something precious and intangible that even in those days he had felt to be slipping from him. Well, the war had taken what he had been, and changed him, but if any particle of his old self remained, he would find it over here.

His mind became occupied with Bella. He was still thinking of her when he fell into a fitful troubled sleep. When he awoke hours later, suddenly, he had an almost frightening awareness of her as if his mind, in sleep, had raced onward and dealt with equations that his consciousness had refused to tolerate.

He lay still, listening. The surf was quieter now and he could hear faint sounds all about him: the scurrying of a small creature over the pine needles, little rustlings, chirps and twitterings of warblers coming awake and testing the hour, and farther off the squawking of a gull and a single melodious measure from a mockingbird. There was a predawn chill to the air. The moon had vanished and a thin fog had washed away the outlines of the trees. The fog made a dim unreality of the man who stood watching him hardly a dozen feet beyond the dull embers of his campfire.

That it was a man did not come to him instantly. He saw the shape, and his eyes sought to interpret it as the trunk of a tree. Then it moved slightly, retreating, and with the shock of comprehension he lay staring a moment while a quick tightening went through his body. Abruptly he spun over on his elbows away from the fire and sat up in the shadow ready to spring. But the figure, an indefinite and amorphous shape, had merged quietly into the dark of the pines.

He crouched motionless for more than a minute, lis-

tening while he searched the dark, but any sound of re-
ceding footsteps was blanketed by the muttering of the
surf. Finally he got his pipe and filled it and lighted it
with a coal.

Here now, he thought. What the devil is this?

Had the fellow merely seen the fire or smelled the
smoke of it and come over here to investigate? But why
was he so curious? Why was he out poking around at
this hour?

Odd, but the man's stealth and his quietness made him
think of Branch. In the woods Branch was like an Indian. But of course it couldn't have been Branch. Ridiculous thought. There was Lassaphene over at the
reservation—but why would the keeper be prowling
about? Probably it was just a Negro, or some homeless
veteran who had come over here to live.

A sudden bird chorus told him that the dawn was near.
He kicked sand over the remains of his fire, got his bag
and went down onto the misty beach. He undressed,
took a quick plunge in the surf, slapped himself partially
dry and drew on his clothes, and drank from the trickle
of water running across the sand. The sky was lighten-
ing when he hoisted his bag and set out to cover the final
miles.

There was hardly any wind this morning and for a
long time the mist hung low over the dunes. It began to
lift as the sun rose, and burned away abruptly as he
neared his destination, so that the lighthouse was disclosed to him all at once, a gleaming white shaft rising
high above the dunes in the golden morning.

He stopped, dropped his bag and stood looking at it
with his lips drawn tight across his teeth. Presently he

went on until he was less than a hundred feet from it, and stopped again. His heart began to pound uncomfortably. His eyes darted with a curious intensity from the tower and the small service shed beside it to the two neat white cottages nestling close together behind the mounds of driven sand that had smothered the retaining wall. Wisps of breakfast smoke rose from both chimneys. He glanced briefly at the larger cottage on the right, traditionally the home of the keeper, and his attention centered on the other, a far older and more compact structure that showed the hand of the masons who had built the tower. Did something move at one of the front windows? The little veranda shadowed them and he could not be sure. He had the uncomfortable feeling that he was being observed from the windows of both cottages, but no one appeared.

A rooster crowed. It had the small shrill sound of a bantam cock. Bella, he remembered, had kept bantams. She had been very fond of them.

His hands began to clench and unclench at his sides. Suddenly he knew he had no business taking this job. He was an intruder. What a fool he was for even daring to come here! Bella had arranged her life—or rather had rearranged it. It would be better for them both if he never saw her again. What they'd had was gone. Maybe, after all, it had been only an illusion, a madness born of the times. It would be wiser to lock it with other illusions in the attic of his memory.

For nearly a minute he stood irresolute. Then he fought out of his aloneness and the lines in his face harshened. There had been no way to fit Bella into his plans, and in his mind he had always kept her apart. Now the matter had resolved itself. Perhaps it was better this

way. He must somehow accomplish what he had set out
to do, and if staying here awhile would be of any aid,
then he must stay.

His will clamped ruthlessly on his single purpose, and
he picked up his bag and strode forward.

As he climbed over the driven sand to the gate of the
keeper's cottage, the door opened and Captain Lassaphene, in baggy work trousers and pea jacket, came out
on the veranda. The keeper paused a moment, frowning
while he fingered his goatee. Then he came slowly down
the steps. In the center of the short boardwalk crossing
the small sunken yard he stopped, his long gray scholarly head tilted slightly, a question on his thin weathered
face. His restless lower lip seemed to accent the question,
but he said nothing. His act of stopping where he did
precluded any invitation to enter the yard and even made
being in the vicinity of the gate seem in the nature of
a trespass.

Max forced himself to a civility he did not feel. "Good
morning, sir. Clabo sent me over to help you. I'm—" he
started to give his real name, but checked himself—"I'm
Max Call."

"Hmm. I remember you. Clabo used the title captain
in connection with you. Is that correct?"

"Aye, sir."

"You are modest enough," Lassaphene said dryly,
"considering the preponderance of colonels these days.
However, we do not recognize military titles over here."
His voice, save for a faint asperity, was modulated and
rather matter-of-fact like that of an old calculus teacher
Max had known. But the modulation seemed to come
with an effort. It was as if the man had something ex-
plosive in him that he sought to control.

Max said, "The title is not military, and no one asked for recognition of it."

"So?" Lassaphene plucked at his goatee. "Clabo told me you'd been in the army."

"Does it make any difference these days?"

"If you can take orders and do as you are told, it makes no difference whatever."

"I'll endeavor to give satisfaction, Captain."

"Hmm. You are a seaman, I take it?"

"Aye, sir."

"Very well. I prefer a seaman. Who you are or what you were is of no concern to me. While you are over here you will remember that you are simply a hand in the employ of the lighthouse service, and living on government property. You will, er, conduct yourself accordingly. Mr. Haik, next door, is expecting you and will itemize your duties. You will be directly under his supervision, until he is able to carry on without help. So. You may report to him now."

With a curt nod, Lassaphene turned and went up the steps and entered his cottage without so much as a backward glance.

Max fumbled for his pipe and thrust it between his teeth. He stood biting it angrily a moment, then removed it and spat. Oh, the devil, he thought. Maybe the bastard values his privacy. At least he's being fair.

He peered grimly at the other cottage, suddenly dreading the next few minutes and wishing there had been some way to warn Bella of his coming. But she must know by now, he decided. She's been expecting someone to come, a man named Call. If she saw me walk up from the beach she must have recognized me. Surely she recognized my voice. If she's been watching, listening, she must have heard everything we said. The damned places are so close together. . . .

He crossed the drift of sand to the next yard and went slowly up to the little veranda. He hesitated, drew a deep breath and mounted the steps. All at once his heart was pounding furiously.

There was no need for him to knock upon the door. It was already unlatched, and slowly swinging open to admit him.

CHAPTER 8

I

HE SAW her as he reached the threshold, and something turned over in him and left him momentarily without the armor of his will. He stopped and almost tremblingly lowered his bag.

She stood just beyond him in the little hall, one hand on the door and the other at her throat. She was a tall and rather sturdy young woman in her middle twenties, with dark hair and Latin coloring, and full rounded modeling in her cheeks and chin. The modeling was medieval and almost like a mask—not because it was immobile but because of the eyes, which were odd. They were hazel, and too pale for the rest of her, so that they seemed to belong to another person. It was as if her Latin self had been superimposed on an entirely different sort of woman, who remained hidden and unsuspected until she looked at one directly.

This morning the eyes that stared at him were very wide and showed the whites.

He clamped his jaws and for a moment could not speak. At last, calmly and in a voice intended for other ears, he managed to say, "My name is Call, ma'am. Max Call."

"Yes, I—I know. I . . . we . . . we've been expecting you." She might have been repeating lines not yet committed to memory.

She was barefooted, he saw, and wore a gray polka-dot dress and a white apron. With a pang he remembered the dress. It still became her though it was faded. Her thick hair, which fell in a waterfall of ringlets over her shoulders, had been hastily pulled back and tied with a scrap of ribbon.

"Have you had breakfast?" she asked.

"No, ma'am."

"Ben—my husband—had a bad night with his leg. I'm not sure, but I think he's asleep now. If—if you'll come back to the kitchen . . ."

He followed her quietly down the hall, and out across a small latticed porch that connected the separate structure of the kitchen with the cottage. Here she turned and closed the door behind them and stood leaning against it with her eyes shut.

"Oh, Jesus!" she whispered. "Oh, Jesus God!"

She opened her eyes and stared at him intently so that for an instant they widened and again showed the whites. She reached forth and touched his arms and his jaws. Then her hands went to his chest, warm and hungrily alive on him. They crept around him, and suddenly she was pressed tightly against him, trembling, clinging to him, her face buried in his shoulder.

Her voice came muffled under his chin. "When I looked out and saw you, saw it was you . . ."

"I'm sorry. There wasn't any way to let you know."

"Oh, Max, why didn't you come back sooner?"

"I came back as soon as I could." His hands were uncertain on her, rough, almost angry. They fumbled as if they might push her away. "Why the devil didn't you wait?" he demanded.

"I waited as long as I could. I waited years—years."

"I've been gone only three years, or a little over."

"You've been gone a lifetime."

"They had me chained. Then I got sick. I thought I'd never break away. Did you get my letters?"

"I got one—just a little note during your trial." She looked up at him. "Just that. And months later I heard around town that they'd given you life. I thought I'd die. But I waited. I kept telling myself that you'd break away, or that when the war was over things would change and they'd maybe let you go. Peace came and I kept on waiting, and then Daddy died . . ."

She stopped and turned her head, listening. From somewhere in the house he heard a man's voice, querulous, thick, calling her name.

She drew away. "That's Ben. What'll I tell him?"

"That depends. I've got to be careful; they may be looking for me in town. What does he know about me?"

"Nothing. I mean, I reckon he's heard about you, but of course he'd never guess . . ."

She pressed her knuckles against her mouth. "Maybe

I ought to say I knew you before, but had forgotten your name. It'd make it easier. I mean, I could say you used to help Daddy during the war. Ben, he wouldn't know. He's from home. I grew up with 'im. He didn't come here till just before Daddy died. It might be smart if I told Ben you used to work with Daddy, and then went over on the east coast awhile—and that you came back here looking for work. That way he wouldn't be askin' too many questions about you."

He nodded. "Maybe you're right."

She opened the door and slipped out noiselessly, leaving the faint nostalgic aroma of herself clinging to him, awakening memory, bringing memory suddenly violently awake so that his thin nose dilated and he stood twisting the back of one of the kitchen chairs as if he would tear it apart. It made no difference that the years had changed her—for they had robbed her of something: her face was thinner and her mouth that had laughed so easily had acquired a sort of angry petulance. But the vital and responsive magnet of her had been untouched. She was still Bella.

The fact of it was suddenly upsetting. He had known he would have to face it and deal with it. But it had caught him like a cross sea in a storm and poured over him, leaving him momentarily helpless.

He took off his jacket and sat down at the table. His glance went restlessly about the small whitewashed kitchen with its pine table and cupboards, its little bricked-in stove and its cistern pump beside the sink. It was all as neat as a pin, and about as impersonal. There was a fire in the stove, but even the homey symbols of teakettle and coffeepot did not give a homey feeling to the place. This was merely a spot to prepare food. Almost the only personal touches were the sunbonnet and cap hanging by the door.

He peered with sudden curiosity at these evidences of the man and woman who had joined their lives and who lived together in this cottage and ate in this kitchen. Again came the thought that he was an intruder here. Whatever his feelings for Bella and his claim to her, they had been set aside by her marriage. It was beyond him to temporize with the fact. She belonged to another man. Who or what that man was made little difference; she was that man's wife and this was their home.

All at once he got up and began moving in a torment about the kitchen; in his confusion of mind and soul he felt caged, trapped, and suddenly wished he could feel free to walk out of here and go his way. But it was too late now. They needed him here at the light, and he had committed himself.

He was thinking of Garden Key when Bella returned.

"Ben would like to see you," she said. "Maybe it would be a good thing if you came in and talked to him a few minutes while I'm fixing his breakfast."

He followed her back through the hall and across a neat little parlor with grass matting on the floor. It was sparsely furnished with a cot between the windows, a marble-topped table holding a lamp and a large Bible, and a few walnut chairs that must have come from her former home in town, for the antimacassars and the green upholstery seemed familiar. At the doorway of the adjoining bedroom Bella paused and motioned him in ahead of her.

"Ben, this is Mr. Max Call, who used to work with Papa. Mr. Call, my husband." She turned to go, saying, "I won't be long. The coffee's all ready."

The room was small and dark, and smelled of stale tobacco smoke, urine and sweat. The mosquito bar had been drawn back from the plain wooden bed that sagged with the weight of the man who lay on it. He was a big man, a powerful man, thick-bodied and heavy-boned, a furious-featured Eric the Red with a great chest matted with a wiry pelt nearly as thick and bright as the hair on his head. Everything about him from his huge red-knuckled hands to his beetling brows and knotted sun-bitten jaws suggested animal force held in angry restraint. He lay with his bullish head and shoulders propped against a mound of pillows, wearing only a blue work shirt, unbuttoned, and with his lower body half covered by the rumpled sheet. Thrust stiffly in front of him was his injured right leg, tightly bound in splints. He was sweaty and unshaven, and evidently in great pain—which he made no attempt to conceal.

He groaned and extended a hot sticky hand. "Glad to know ye," he said hoarsely, but with a quick sharp probing of his little blue eyes that somehow belied his pain and his helplessness. "Sit down. Don't mind me. I ain't fitten to talk to nobody. Never closed my eyes all last night or the night before. But sit down. Make yourself to home."

"Thank you."

What a bull of a fellow! he thought, as he settled himself in the wooden rocker by the bedside table. What was such a man doing in a place like this? For surely Haik didn't fit into this sort of life. You can be as odd as you please—but without certain inner reserves you've no business as a lighthouse keeper. It disgusted him to know that this was Bella's husband.

Haik's eyes were little blue red-rimmed flames under

his beetling brows. "I wouldn't take ye for no ship-wright," he thrust out abruptly. "How'd ye happen to be workin' for ole man Tacon?"

Max explained casually that he was a naval architect by profession, and that his association with Nolly had been largely in the redesign of vessels for wartime use. "But there's no work now," he added. "I haven't had a thing hardly for months. Just odd jobs. I was helping Clabo when Lassaphene came around."

Haik grunted. "I'm glad ye ain't exactly no stranger. I reckon we'll git along. But ye'll have to watch it. By God, ye'll have to watch it close. We don't want no trouble."

"Eh? Why should there be any trouble?"

"Ye'll find out, mister. Lassaphene, he makes work. An' he lives by the rules. Ye're goin' to have to read up careful on them rules. Bella, she'll help ye, an' show ye about the light. An' after breakfast I'll tell ye about the other work. But mind now, everything's got to be done jest so, or we'll hear about. *I'll* hear about it first, 'cause he'll blame me. I been blamed for enough. By God——"

A fly settled on the exposed foot of his bandaged leg and began crawling ecstatically across the swollen toes. Haik jerked the sheet viciously and managed to cover the foot. The sudden movement jarred his leg and his face contorted with a wild caricature of pain. He groaned loudly and swore. His oaths rolled forth with a low vehement fury. Then he began to feel sorry for himself. "Hit don't give me no rest," he said piteously. "Day an' night, it jest throbs an' throbs. Like somebody was hittin' me with an ax, over an' over."

"It must be terrible," Max said gravely.

"Oh, God, ye jest can't imagine it!"

"How did it happen?"

Haik momentarily forgot his pain. "Didn't Lassaphene tell ye?"

"No. He wasn't in a very conversational mood."

"That bastard! The way he acts ye'd think I liked bein' laid up like this. As if I'd broke my leg a-purpose. An' 'twas all his fault, the son of a bitch! He wanted the tower painted. Blast 'is soul, it ain't been six months since I painted the tower. But like I say, he makes work. He's all spit an' polish. Everything has to be jest so. Anyhow, I started in to paint. I was bein' mighty careful. I don't like high places. They sort o' git me. You afraid o' high places, mister?"

"No, they've never bothered me."

"Then ye're lucky. Anyhow, I was swingin' from a bosun's chair, about halfway down the tower. I got me a cramp in the foot. I couldn't move. Hit tied me up somethin' terrible. I yelled for Bella, but before she got to the tower the damn line got away from me. Dunno how it happened. Jest one o' them crazy things. I fell forty feet an' hit the edge o' that li'l boardwalk out there. Broke my shinbone clean as a whistle. It was the afternoon Lassaphene was over at Clabo's. Soon's he got back he worked on me while his wife an' Bella held me. I reckon he done a fair enough job, but the bastard blames me for breakin' it."

"Accidents happen."

"Yeah, but tell *him* that. Anything for an excuse to git rid o' me. But he ain't goin' to do that. You hear me, mister? I worked damn hard to git this job, an' I'm hangin' onto it." Haik stopped. He closed his eyes and groaned, then gave Max a knowing nod. "Me, I got friends over in the city. Big people. Ye got to be well

connected to git anywhere these days. I'm a shipwright
by profession, but like you say, there ain't nothin' doin'
in that line now. Anyhow, I wanted somethin' steady.
Hit's a good life, keepin' a light. That is, if'n ye're head
keeper."

Max was trying to adjust this statement to his opinion of the man when Bella entered with a large tin tray.
She carried it around to the opposite side of the bed and
set it down on the sheet beside Haik. On the tray were
coffee, pie, scrambled eggs, sirup and a huge stack of
johnnycakes.

"There are more cakes if you want them," she said.
"How does your leg feel?"

"How d'you think it feels?" he growled. He closed
his eyes and groaned, then scowled at the food. "I can't
eat nothin'. I couldn't swallow a goddam bite."

"Well, try it anyhow, Ben. It'll maybe do you some
good."

She looked at Max. "Your breakfast is ready, too.
You'd better come back and eat it while it's hot."

Max followed her through the parlor. As he turned
into the hall he glanced covertly over his shoulder and
saw Haik forking a huge mouthful of eggs.

In the kitchen Bella closed the door softly behind
them.

"That *man!*" she said fiercely.

Max looked silently at the table. It was neatly set for
two. There was berry pie, a platter of scrambled eggs
and another piled with crisp brown johnycakes. He had
been very hungry, but now suddenly he had no appetite.
He watched Bella go over to the stove and turn four
cakes in the iron spider.

"Why don't you sit down and start?" she said. "You must be starved."

"All right." But he remained standing.

Bella hovered over the cakes, then scooped them up and brought them to the platter. His eyes followed the movements of her hands as she went back and slid the spider to the cold side of the stove, and brought the coffeepot over to the table and filled two cups. She had pretty hands. They were a bit too large perhaps, but the fingers were long and smoothly rounded like her arms. They looked strong and capable. The shape of them reminded him of old Nolly's hands. There had been good blood in her father. To the town, of course, he'd been only another shipbuilder. But Nolly was far more than that. He was a master craftsman, an artist. He could draw beautiful plans for vessels, and he had the ability to inspire those who worked under him and bring those vessels into being.

But except for the hands, and an almost flawless skin and coloring, Bella in no way resembled Nolly.

"What was your mother like?" he asked.

"My mother?" She laughed unpleasantly. "That's a funny question. I never knew her. She ran away with another man when I was a baby. We were living in Trieste then. Daddy brought me over to America soon afterward, and we settled in Mobile."

"And that's where you met Ben?"

"Yes."

She looked at him a moment with that odd widening of her eyes, so that for just an instant he had the feeling that he was under the speculative scrutiny of the other woman; it was as if the stranger of the eyes had adjusted the mask in order to view him more clinically. Then she came over and put her hands on his chest. Suddenly she was clinging to him again.

"Oh, Max," she wailed, "I hate this place! I hate every damn thing about it!"

"You didn't have to marry Ben."

"You don't know. You just don't know."

"I don't know what?"

"You don't understand how it was with me. It was awful. When Daddy died, there wasn't anything left. And I hadn't been well for a long time. You see, I—after you left I—I almost had a baby."

His hands tightened on her arms. "Tell me about it."

"There wasn't much to tell. When I heard you were captured I—it was an awful shock. I was getting pretty well along, though it wasn't showing yet. No one knew. Then I found out they were giving all privateersmen long sentences and that it might be years before I ever saw you again. So I got rid of it."

"You did *what?*" he said harshly.

"I went to an old colored woman and got rid of it."

He turned away from her suddenly and bunched his hands in his pockets. "That was a hell of a thing to do," he said.

She stared at him almost in fright. "Why do you say that? What was so wrong about it?"

"For one thing it might have killed you."

"It—it almost did."

"And anyhow it was wrong."

"You wouldn't have expected me to have a bastard, would you?"

"Oh, plague and the devil, that's not the idea! If we hadn't cared for each other it might have been different. But I cared a lot for you. Didn't it occur to you that I might have wanted our child?"

"You wouldn't have wanted a bastard."

"How d'you know I wouldn't have? I intended to marry you when I got back. Why didn't you wait?"

"I've been trying to tell you!" she cried. "Can't you listen? Can't you try to understand?"

"I'm listening."

"I—I wasn't well, like I said. And I didn't have any money."

"You might have tried going to my mother. If you'd told her all about it she'd have helped you."

She sniffed. "A lot you know about women. Your mother wouldn't have had anything to do with me."

"You wouldn't say that if you'd known my mother."

Her mouth curled. "I don't remember your ever offering to introduce me to her. After all, I was only a Tacon. And she was one of the mighty Ewings."

"You needn't talk that way. I intended for you to meet her at the right time. My mother never was high and mighty. She was a lady."

"And what's your idea of a lady?"

"Someone you can always depend on to do the right thing. Money and position have nothing to do with it."

She sniffed again. "You would say that."

"Well, it's true. It's what you are inside. And by that rule I'd call your father a gentleman, even though he was poor and a foreigner. He was a fine man. You ought to be proud of him."

She stared at him incredulously.

"Now," he demanded, "will you tell me why you felt called on to tie yourself to that favor-currying carpenter in there?"

"Oh, you——"

There was a small sound next door, a little clatter as if someone had stepped on a loose board. Bella's lips thinned; she turned from him suddenly and slipped to the rear window. She tipped the blinds carefully with her finger and peered out.

Her voice was an angry hiss. "There she is again! Always snooping around out there."

Max went over and glanced through the blinds. Outside stretched the kitchen yard with its plank walk crossing the sand to the outhouse and the barn. There was a single palm, and a straggling grape arbor hiding the enclosure for the chickens. To the right, beyond a low masonry wall, was a similar yard. Of the keeper's cottage little was visible save the cistern and a portion of the back porch. He glimpsed Lassaphene's niece going up the steps with a rusty watering can in her hand.

"That's Mrs. Maynard," he murmured.

"Oh, you know her, do you?"

"I saw her over at Clabo's Saturday."

"She thinks a lot of herself."

Bella turned from the window. She glanced at the breakfast table. Suddenly her chin began to quiver. "Oh, Max," she said unsteadily, and raised her apron to her eyes, "I—I never thought I'd see you again, ever, and I didn't have a penny and didn't know what to do, and I did the only thing I could—but you just *won't* understand. You're not even glad to see me." She began to cry softly.

He had never seen her cry. He had never associated her with the thought of tears. She had always taken life with a smile and a quiet chuckle as if she were sure of herself and her strength. In his mind she was vitality and remembered laughter.

"Oh, hell," he muttered. He went over and put his arms around her. "Oh, hell!"

II

Charlotte set the empty watering can on the edge of the porch and stood there a minute looking back over the yard. Her eyes traveled with a sort of wistful concern from the little fig tree she had planted during the winter to the spindly clump of gardenias, and the oleander switches along the dividing wall between the two cottages. The fig tree seemed to be coming out, but the gardenias looked sick and she was still in doubt about the oleanders. Her vegetable patch, far out back in a bit of low ground near the woods, was doing fairly well, but these things in the yard needed more attention. Maybe it was a mistake to expect anything to thrive here in the sand, so close to the sea. But still, other people managed it.

Once her glance went past the wall to the assistant keeper's house, but she did not see it. It was there before her eyes, but unconsciously she denied its existence. To have admitted its presence would have meant having an awareness of its occupants, and she did not want to be aware of them. They were strangers, alien, products of a country she did not wholly understand and had every reason to hate. By completely ignoring them, denying them, as one might ignore a flaw that would otherwise spoil one's appreciation of a gem, she could keep the island apart, a separate world untouched and unsullied by the world she had known.

Until coming here it would have been impossible for her to imagine such a spot as this. She had never seen the ocean before and had never been nearer salt water than Baltimore. But in the months since her arrival on the island she had become passionately attached to it. Everything was new and strange and absorbing—the tall pines and the green clumps of palmettos, the glittering white slash of sand against the hot blue of the Gulf, the almost magical groves of palms, the myriad sea birds and the great eagles and the fairy egrets, the wild goats and the occasional deer that watched her curiously from the dunes whenever she went shell hunting along the beach: all these had contributed to a measure of happiness she had never expected to find anywhere. Her happiness was but partial, for only the presence of David could have made it complete. Yet she knew very well that David would have been miserable here. He would have been appalled by the utter wildness and remoteness of this place, nor could he have stood for long the entire lack of the cultural and literary fare that had been his life. Poor gentle David! Sometimes, in her absorption with the island, she felt almost a traitor to his memory. Yet only the emptiness of not having David had made it possible for her to feel as she did.

Recently, for the first time in her life, she had become interested in gardening. Just what had started it she did not know, although in the beginning it had been forced upon her through a desire for foods that otherwise would have been impossible to obtain. In the city, where she'd bought all her vegetables from the huckster, she'd never questioned their source. Looking back she was a little amazed at the narrowness of her sheltered existence there; even the miracle of the seasons had almost escaped her. But out here she had come to have an awareness of innumerable miracles that had formerly gone unnoticed. To plant seeds and shrubs, to see them sprout and turn green with new growth, was to glimpse resurrection, to be given a promise and a proof that life, even though it may cease, is exempt from total death.

Religiously she tended the garden and the yard. Usually she started in after breakfast, for it had become her habit to rise early and walk some distance down the beach for a surreptitious dip before anyone else was stirring. But this morning her routine had been upset. Before reaching the beach she had seen a man approaching in the distance. She had guessed instantly who he was, and had fled back to the cottage. It would have been an ordeal to pass any stranger on the beach. Strangers, no matter where encountered, were always difficult for her. But something about the man Call had upset her, and she preferred to avoid him altogether.

As she stood now on the porch she raised her head and again her eyes encountered the cottage next door. This time she saw it. And abruptly she realized that she was listening. She could hear the voice of the man Call in the other kitchen. There was a sort of unsettling intensity in the man's low vibrant drawl, although the words were indistinguishable.

Suddenly furious with herself, Charlotte turned and quickly washed her hands and face in the basin by the door, and went in to where her Aunt Emily was setting out the breakfast dishes. Her Uncle Simon sat at the table with the Bible closed in his lap, his forefinger marking a page. He looked drained and a little feverish;

he hadn't shaved yet and she wondered uneasily if he had been out on another one of his excursions last night.

The new man was under discussion. Emily was saying, "You might have invited him in for breakfast, Simon."

"Mrs. Haik will take care of him," he answered patiently.

Emily sighed. "You and Charlotte! You're both so funny about people. Goodness alive, I should think you'd want to see a new face at the table once in a while."

Charlotte looked at her in horror. "Certainly not for *breakfast,* Aunt Emily. And anyhow, a person like that . . ."

"Oh, now, what was so wrong with him?"

"You saw him," Charlotte said acidly. "You don't miss very much."

Emily laughed. "Indeed I don't. God gave me eyes to see with, and I don't intend to go through life with them shut. But the man didn't look so bad to me. A little, er— what's the word, Simon?"

"Irreconcilable," he said mildly.

"Yes, of course. Irreconcilable. You have such a command of language, dear. Anyway, I had a good look at him through the window awhile ago, and I didn't see anything about him that a good solid meal wouldn't help."

"A solid meal wouldn't help his manners," Charlotte said.

"What's so wrong with his manners, dear?"

Charlotte got the blue willowware bowls and went over to dish the oatmeal. "I wasn't aware that he had any manners."

Emily peered at her mischievously. "If you're think-

ing of the way he stared at you over at Clabo's, maybe
he thought you were pretty—as Mr. Clabo does."

"Please. That's becoming rather sickening. I'm not
seventeen. I'm nearly twenty-seven, and I know only
too well what I look like. Anyway, that wasn't the way
he stared at me. The man was full of hate. To be perfectly honest, he sort of frightened me. Whatever made
you hire him, Uncle Simon?"

Lassaphene plucked at his protruding lower lip. "Oh,
availability, I suppose." But it was not entirely that, he
knew. It was because the man Call was a seaman. He
had known that from the first, in spite of what Clabo
had said. He remembered the man's walk, and that reserved "Good morning, sir" on the tavern veranda. A
landsman might have ignored him, or spoken in a different way. But in the greeting—and notwithstanding
Charlotte's opinion—there had been a sort of quarter-
deck politeness, a deferential acknowledgment from a
younger man to an older one who has followed the same
calling. It had rather amused him to pretend to believe
Clabo's story of the army background, for obviously Call
was not too happy about his past. But it did not matter.
Call was a seaman, which meant that he would approach
his job with the respect that no landsman could ever feel
for it.

Lassaphene had quitted the sea with some reluctance,
and only because his health was no longer equal to the
rigors of the Atlantic. But he had a strong feeling for
the service he was in, and he had come to have a regard
for his present post that was more abiding than anything
he had ever felt for a vessel. It was his opinion that no
man, who has not experienced the dread of a black night
and a lee shore, has any business around a lighthouse.

For that reason he deplored the politics that had thrust a person like Haik upon him in the capacity of assistant.

At the thought of Haik his lower lip moved soundlessly as if in punctuation of his unspoken epithets. What a bungling inept fool! Why, the man wasn't even a proper shipwright. Look at that plank he'd replaced in the sloop. What a mess! Cut shy, split at the ends and patched with putty . . .

"Simon," his wife interrupted, "for heaven's sake, forget about Mr. Haik and say the blessing so we can eat breakfast."

"Eh? Who said I was thinking of Haik?"

"You were thinking of something that made you angry, and he always makes you angry."

CHAPTER *9*

I

MAX drank the last of his coffee and took out his pipe and frowned at it. He did not look at Bella. He wanted suddenly to be busy, to be out of the house and away from her and doing something with his hands. He stirred and said, "I'd better go and see that husband of yours and find out what he wants done."

Her lips compressed at the harshness of his voice. "Please don't talk like that."

He said brutally, "He *is* your husband, isn't he?"

"Yes, but just in name. I—I don't live with him, really."

"Then you had no right to marry him."

145

"Oh, Max, please!" she said desperately. "I've been trying to explain——"

He thrust the empty pipe between his teeth and stood up.

She swallowed and begged quickly, "Don't go yet. We've hardly had a chance to talk about anything."

"We've talked enough for the present."

There was a deep anger in him. She wondered if he was still thinking about the baby. Oh, Lordy God, she thought, why was I such a ninny as ever to tell him anything like that?

"I haven't told you about the light," she said. "Please. Sit down and have some more coffee. You'll have to know about the watches."

He sat down. "The watches?"

She flew over to the stove and filled his cup. "Yes. We keep regular watches here. They won't affect you too much—except that you'll have to eat supper alone. You see, this is really our dinner we're having now. Being on the second watch, I go to bed in the afternoon, for I have to be up from midnight on. Captain Lassaphene has the first watch. He always lights the lamp, and stays up till midnight. Then it's Ben's turn—or rather mine. I always take care of the light anyway, and sign the log. You won't have to worry about any of that, except to watch the log for instructions."

"Where's the log kept?"

"Up in the watch room. That's the space in the tower just under the lantern. I have to be up in the lantern every morning at dawn, to put out the light and clean it, and let down the curtains so the sun won't hurt the lenses. I—I was working up there this morning before you came, and saw you 'way down the beach. I just saw you for about a half minute, and then the fog hid you. I guessed you were the man Clabo was sending, but of course I didn't dream it was you."

She stopped and looked at him intently a moment. "Max, when Ben's leg gets better and you leave here, what are you going to do?"

"I'm not sure yet. I've got plans."

"What are they?"

"I can't tell you about them now."

"Why not?"

"I just can't tell you." He took a long draught of the coffee and frowned. "Anyhow I can't do anything without money. I've got to raise money somehow."

"You mean for a pardon?"

"Pardon be damned!" he spat out. "You think I'd buy favors from my enemies? I'd rather be dead." He got up, mumbling, "I reckon I'd better get started."

"You haven't finished your coffee."

"I don't want it."

She stood up. "Max."

"What is it?"

"You—you make me feel awful," she said tremulously.

"Now what have I done?"

"It—it's what you haven't done. You haven't acted like you're really glad to see me. You—you haven't even kissed me."

"I don't think we'd better start that."

"But you—you came here, knowing I was here. Didn't you come here to see me?"

"Partly." His jaws knotted. "If it hadn't been for you, wanting to see you again, I'd be dead now. There were times when just thinking of you, wanting to be with

you again, was all that kept me alive." He was not looking at her as he spoke. His eyes were on a remoteness
and he was speaking to a vision in his mind, a woman he
had created from memory during the long black emptiness of the years of nights. His mind turned reluctantly
from the vision, knowing it was better than the original,
so much better that he wondered how he had ever contrived the perfection of it. "But everything's different
for us now," he went on harshly. "You've got to realize
that. You're married to Ben. I don't care who or what
he is, you're married to him. I can't come into another
man's home——"

"Oh, damn Ben!" she interrupted furiously. "He's no
husband to me! I hate the sight of him. I told you we
don't even live together." She bit her lip. Her eyes had
become very pale and greenish. "I can't help it how
things are. I want to get away from here. I can't stand
it much longer. I—I've been planning to leave. If you
hadn't come . . ." She stopped, and then said slowly,
"When the time comes for you to leave, Max, I'm going
with you."

He opened his mouth and closed it, and looked down
at the floor.

In sudden fright she said, "Don't you want me?"

"Of course I do," he answered quietly.

"You don't sound like it."

"But I can't take you. Not the way things are. I
haven't a thing, not a penny. We'd have no place to go."

"We—we could make out somehow."

"Without money?" He shook his head. "But it isn't
just that. I'm not free—I mean, I wouldn't be free to be
with you. I've something to do, something of the utmost

importance. It's going to take time and every dollar I can scrape together."

She looked at him strangely. "Can't you tell me about it?"

"Later, maybe. I'd rather not talk about it now."

"I wish you'd tell me. Maybe I can help."

"There's nothing you could do."

"I could help you get money, maybe."

"Where would you get money?"

"I didn't say I could get it. I said maybe I could help you get it. I'm not sure. It's just a chance."

From the set, implacable look on his face she couldn't tell whether he believed her or not, or what he was thinking. She had never been able to tell what was in his mind. Beyond him, through the west window, the dunes were glaring in the hot morning sun, reflecting such a brilliance that the patch of sky above them seemed almost black. The surf was a slow dry grinding, as if an idiot sat out there rocking a long box full of pebbles. Oh, the horrid sameness and loneliness of this place! For an instant she had the feeling of being trapped in a nightmare, and deep in the void of her soul a silent scream exploded in rebellion.

He turned toward the door, saying, "We can talk later. I'd really better get started."

Her hand rose, making a gesture toward him, then she clenched her lip and let her hand fall back at her side.

For nearly a minute after he was gone she remained standing in the middle of the kitchen with her eyes closed and her hands pressed tightly together. She felt stifled and weak, and her thighs ached. A tremor went over her, and she opened her eyes and saw the dirty dishes on the table and then remembered that this was Monday.

Suddenly as if she were possessed of a demon she tore into the routine of the day, driving herself all morning cleaning the house, looking after Ben, sorting out the weekly wash and planning dinner while the clothes were heating in the copper boiler on the stove. Once, as she carried rinse water from the pump to the tubs on the back porch, she saw Max coming from the barn with a paint bucket and a coil of line. She watched him a moment while he started across the drift of sand toward the lighthouse, her eyes following the movements of his long lean body. It was decisive in the sunlight, hard-etched lines and shadows, and she could feel it flowing with remembered power. Again a weakness came over her; then it passed and she went in and prodded the clothes in the boiler with a sort of fury, so that it sloshed over and a cloud of scalding steam shot up from the hot stove.

She had an impulse to cry out and seize the boiler and hurl it across the kitchen. She rushed through the rest of the work, hating it, hating herself, wanting to fly out of herself, dissolve, vanish into another and less mundane existence. Somehow she got through the dinner hour, managing to be occupied while Max ate and allowing herself little chance to talk with him. She felt incapable of speech. Her mind seethed without thought.

There was no truth in the story of the baby. It had been a fabrication of the moment, something born spontaneously with the sudden wish that the thing really had happened to her. It had come forth as a snare and a plea for sympathy; but far more than that she had seen it as an explanation, an excuse for her marriage. For surely, she had believed, if such a thing had actually happened he would sympathize; he would see her helpless in circumstance, ill and driven to accept the first honorable offer of security. It would never do for him to guess that her main desperation had been a physical need, and that in the beginning Ben, with his appearance of virility and a rare job in the offing, had seemed the answer to all her needs.

The story, conceived on the instant, had tumbled from her without a thought. His reaction had astounded her. She would never have dreamed that he would feel that way about a child. She was not maternal. And so it had been beyond her to imagine that a man like Ewing might not only be capable of loving such a child but could actually desire it and attach no stigma to its birth.

But the thing was told, and now it was impossible to retract it. Any denial of it, she knew, would only worsen her position and make it more difficult to re-establish their old relationship. At any cost she meant to have him back. It made no difference that his status had changed, for it had never mattered in the past; they might have been two strangers who had met in a wood and found in each other a rare completeness that had answered for everything. That there was another side of him she had never reached, a mental and emotional being made up of complexities, seemed of small importance.

Somehow she would get him back. But she would have to be careful. It would never do to throw herself upon him. Not the way he was now. So much had happened to him, and he was so bitter. . . .

"Oh, Lordy God," she breathed aloud. "Why didn't I wait?"

Still, how could she have waited? Things had been

awfully hard. There'd been no way to keep the house, what with taxes and a mortgage and no money coming in, and it had been almost impossible to earn anything. She had a few friends scattered around, of course, but most of them were over in Alabama. There'd been almost no one to turn to, except Ben.

At the thought of Ben she writhed inwardly, and again came the feeling of being trapped in a nightmare. It was so quiet. Just the ticking of the clock in the parlor and the low rasping of the surf, and the nothingness of the afternoon stretching on into nothingness . . . and she was lost here in the quiet with Ben yonder in the bedroom and Max somewhere outside at work and the people next door who were not people but only disembodied eyes. . . .

The sudden striking of the clock reminded her that it was time to get some rest. She tiptoed to the bedroom, saw that Ben was asleep. She went inside, slipped out of her clothes and drew on a nightgown and a cotton wrapper. She started out to the cot in the parlor, but stopped in the doorway and looked back at Ben. He was spread-eagled in sodden slumber, so that his great nude body had the semblance of death, like a hairy Norseman lying slain. Sleep robbed it of the suggestion of furious power. It had become neuter flesh. The mouth sagged open, the belly showed its fat, and even the genitals lost their symbolism, for they seemed curiously inadequate for so large a man.

A hundred times Bella had looked at her husband as she did at this moment: with her eyes widening a little and her lips bunched and ugly as if she wanted to spit upon him.

Oh, damn you! she thought. Damn you, damn you, damn you! You're not even half a man. You're nothing.

Abruptly she turned from him and crossed the parlor and sank down on the cot. She felt ill. For a long time she lay with her eyes closed, trying to sleep. But sleep would not come. Her thighs ached. Tears filled her eyes and began to flow down her cheeks.

II

For the present the only salvation lay in work. And there was enough of it waiting—so much, in fact, that Max wondered what Haik had been doing with himself during the past year. There was the tower to paint, the barn to repair, the walks and the retaining walls to fix, and there were innumerable small tasks from clearing the sand drifts from the gates to patching the pier on the other side of the island. But the tower came first. Every inch of it had to be gone over and painted and put in perfect repair.

Max began on the tower. Work, he told himself. Don't think; just work, use your hands. He worked methodically, trying not to think, trying to force all of himself outward through his hands. He hauled block and tackle aloft on a line, made it fast to the high iron gallery surrounding the lantern, then lashed himself in a bosun's chair and spent the rest of the morning dangling like a spider down the shady side of the tower. The sea and the sky and the island did not exist. There was just this spar of masonry on which he hung, lost in space. The hands worked, managed lines, toiled with brush and scraper. But the hands remained remote. The laborer was someone else. He was apart from the laborer; his thoughts tugged away into a maelstrom of anger and loneliness and frustration.

At noon he avoided Bella, unaware that he was being avoided; he ate quickly and left.

Again the hands toiled and he tried to put himself into them and be the laborer. But again his mind tugged away into the maelstrom. He raged at Bella without hating her. He raged, hating life. Life had betrayed him again. Life was always betraying him.

During the middle of the afternoon the wind freshened from the sea. Squalls darkened the horizon. The dangling lines slapped against the tower. He looked down at the swaying earth, thinking of Haik falling and wondering how it would be to fall. But there was a treachery even here. It wouldn't kill me, he thought. It wouldn't let me die if I wanted to.

He cursed the rising wind and the gusts which made it impossible to work. Finally he descended and went out to the barn to mix paint for the ironwork.

The barn was little more than a long open shed with one end enclosed to form a workshop and storeroom. There was a spring wagon under the shed, and back of it, just beyond the woodpile and the pump, was a rough corral of cypress poles where the reservation's mule dozed under a pine. He went into the shop and tried to draw himself out of the maelstrom while he sought the materials he needed and mixed powdered red lead with oil and turpentine in a pail. He had hardly finished when he heard the rain coming. Scattered drops struck the shed like a spray of bullets, and suddenly the rain was thundering on the roof. He went and stood by the wagon, half exhausted but furious that he should be trapped here by the rain, held here with his thoughts.

The squall passed and briefly the sun shone. He hurried to the tower with the pail of paint.

It thundered, and curtains of rain swept in from the sea and beat against the tower, making a low roaring inside, but he was scarcely aware of it as he went up the spiral stairway. He had been desolate with a sense of loss, now he burned with an overwhelming resentment. He raged. He wanted to strike back at life for everything it had denied him. He visioned the child that might have been, and the brightness of love and his home, and the faces that were dead, and the plans and the hopes that were nothing and the ships that would never sail; and all these injustices and might-have-beens were gall and acid in him, so that suddenly he hated even Cassius for the promise that held him here.

How foolish he'd been to promise! What folly to have tied himself here! Wait a month or more? Blast hell and heaven, what a waste! He was throwing away precious weeks when he ought to be out making arrangements, raising money and men. . . .

He stopped to get his breath, then drove himself on, cursing the endless steps and the fever that had sapped him. He gained the watch room with its table and log-book and tins of oil and boxes of supplies—wicks, lamp chimneys, polishing rouge, cloths and innumerable accessories for tending the high altar of the lamp in the great glassed structure of the lantern overhead. Again he stopped, leaning against the table while his breath rasped through his teeth, then he surged up the short ladder into the curtained lantern.

His resentment and fury had been mounting as he climbed. He had come to the top, but he was in the pit. He had been like this on the Bay of Cárdenas, and on · the night of Meriwether's death. He set the pail down, having momentarily forgotten what it was or why he had brought it up here. In his inner storm he was almost oblivious of the storm that raged around the tower. He leaned back against the iron framework and closed his eyes. He beat his fists together and cursed.

Someone spoke. The words did not carry above the wind and the gush of rain against the glass, but he heard the voice. The voice was small and remote, yet it was very clear. It had the clarity of a bell in the distance.

He opened his eyes. One of the heavy curtains that darkened the lantern through the day was partially raised. The light coming through it shone on the altar— the great gleaming, shining and sacred creation of prisms and lenses, the perfection of polished glass and metal to which every creature and thing on the reservation were subject. A belt of prisms had been opened, exposing the bright heart of it, the lamp. Standing beside it, a frightened vestal, seemingly ready to fly on the instant, was Lassaphene's niece.

"You!" he burst out, staring at her as if she were a ghost come to plague him, suddenly hating her for being here, hating her for everything she represented in his mind. She had no right to be here, no right whatever to be here at this moment of nakedness. It was incredible that she was here, hardly three paces from him. The fact that he had failed to notice her made him furious.

She stared back at him from beyond the belt of prisms. The shaft of light sharpened her thin sensitive face and made her wide-opened eyes seem liquid and enormous, like pools of amber. He saw her lips move, but no sound came from them. Then abruptly the gush of rain ceased and there was only a soft dripping on the glass. It was suddenly very quiet here in the lantern. Again her lips moved, as if she felt impelled to speech but resented the necessity of it.

"Why are you so full of hate?" she demanded in her small but extraordinarily clear voice.

"Because life is hateful," he snapped.

"People are," she corrected. "They make life what it is. But it's foolish to hate them."

His mouth became an ugly slash in his gaunt bronze face. "Give 'em the other cheek," he rasped. "You Puritans! Isn't that what you preach? That the meek inherit the earth? Bah! Six feet of it!" He snorted and glared at her a moment. "But I'll strike back. I'll keep on striking back as long as there's breath in me. But you don't know how it is to feel that way. You'll never know."

"I do know." She bit her lip and turned away. "That's the only reason I bothered to speak to you—in spite of your unpleasant attitude and your conduct the other day at Clabo's."

"Eh?" He rubbed his cheek as if she had slapped him.

What did she mean? What could she possibly understand of the way he felt? Then suddenly his anger evaporated, and he realized how rude he must seem; looking at her now he had only the impersonal dislike he felt for individuals of a class, people whose way of life had always been opposed to his own. But it was no excuse for rudeness. No woman had ever accused him of that in the past.

He said perfunctorily, "If I've been offensive, I'm very sorry. You have my apology. As for the other day at Clabo's, I had no intention of staring at you like a lout—if that's what you mean. But, well, you were a sort of curiosity. I mean, it just happened that you were the first white woman I'd seen in a long time."

"Oh." She bent over the lamp. Her hand moved hastily on the brass with a piece of chamois. "I didn't understand." She glanced back at him quickly with a line between her eyes, then bent over the lamp again.

He picked up the pail of red lead. He felt strangely calm. "I'm sorry to have—disturbed you. I had no idea you were up here. I'll go below and work."

"You may as well remain," she said, without looking around. "I'm nearly through."

He set the pail down. "Do you work up here every day?"

"Yes."

"I didn't know."

"No one knows—except my aunt. I'll appreciate it if you don't mention it to anyone."

He shrugged. "Very well. It's none of my business."

She peered up at him quickly. "I don't expect you to see how I feel about it, of course—the light hardly means anything to you. But so many things can happen if you're not careful. The wick has to be trimmed just so—if it isn't, it can't be adjusted properly, and it might even smoke. And then there's the oil and the polishing and the cleaning. . . ."

"I thought the Haiks were supposed to take care of all that."

She frowned and closed the belt of prisms and carefully wiped them with a cloth. "They're supposed to," she said quietly.

"Then why should you bother about it?"

"It's no bother. And it saves friction. Mrs. Haik is a little careless at times, and it always puts Uncle Simon in a temper when he finds something wrong. Even little things like fingerprints and spilled oil. So I always come up here in the afternoon when everyone's asleep. I enjoy it, really. I suppose even after the new people come . . ." She thrust cloth, chamois, scissors and a small box of tools into a basket, gave one searching look around the lantern, then moved over to the ladder with the basket. She was a slender high-breasted woman with a body that seemed to belong to a girl who has not quite reached maturity. Her movements were quick and deft without being nervous; as she turned and the light struck her pale reddish hair and her oddly sensitive face with its sharp nose and short upper lip, he realized that she was painfully shy and that it must have been an effort for her to speak to him at first. But under the shyness he sensed an immense calm.

She gathered her white skirts and started down the ladder, then stopped. "You must be very careful if you paint in here," she warned. "If it spatters, you must wipe it up immediately. And whatever you do, don't get anything on the lenses." She smiled faintly. "This is Uncle Simon's holy of holies; if he found a drop of paint where it didn't belong he'd fret for a week."

"I'll be careful. You mentioned new people coming. Are the Haiks leaving?"

"Why, I—I didn't mean to say anything about it. But I suppose it doesn't make much difference. They must realize it themselves. They're here only because of, well, political connections. Local ones. To remain here another year they've got to have the approval of both the head keeper and the inspector from the Lighthouse Board. The inspector is due almost any day now. So . . ."

She started down the ladder. When only her head and

shoulders were visible she suddenly hesitated and he saw she was looking at his feet. Then she lowered her head and vanished into the watch room.

He frowned down at his feet. Before starting to work on the tower he had partially rolled up his trousers. His bare ankles were still exposed, showing the rings of red left by the ankle irons.

A half hour before sundown Captain Lassaphene came out of his gate, crossed the sand drifts and walked slowly around the tower, noting the freshly painted areas below the gallery and the lines leading down and neatly belayed to stakes in the sand. Satisfied, he went inside and climbed to the lantern. He was wearing his cap, a light jacket and a pair of old serge trousers, and as usual at this evening ritual carried a spyglass under his left arm. He entered the lantern with the air of a master arriving on his quarter-deck.

He raised the curtains, opened the glass door to the gallery to clear the air of the reek of fresh paint and glanced around at the dabs of red lead covering the spots where rust had been chipped from the ironwork. He nodded. The fellow Call seemed to know what he was about. Haik, the fool, had always ignored the rust and painted directly over it.

He looked at his watch, then his eyes lifted to the west where the sun was dying in immense splendor beyond the pass. It lacked ten minutes of sundown. Patiently he circled his glass cage, studying the purpling sea, the red bay, the details of the island spreading away on three sides of the tower, strangely parklike and primeval. Absently he traced the reservation road that led from the barn and wound in broken threads through the pines. It skirted little cypress ponds and areas of marsh and tyty, and, nearing the bay, vanished beyond a log cabin on a hillock. He raised his glass to view the cabin. It had been built during the war and used by the soldiers stationed here as a sort of secondary observation post. He swung the glass to the right and was about to lower it when he saw movement.

Far over near the barren neck of sand connecting Little St. George with the main island were two figures—seemingly a man and a boy—made slow and minute by distance. They crept over an open area, together and now apart, halting and going on, buglike in erratic and meaningless progress. Through the glass the child became a bandy-legged troll in pantaloons. The man walked with a limp. In the marsh-bordered cove a quarter of a mile beyond them a catboat lay at anchor.

He tried to project himself through the suddenly wavering glass. In the halting movements he could see design.

They're measuring, he told himself. By heaven, they're measuring. They must have found the other cannon. Aye, they *must* have found it! They're trying to make a triangulation!

He almost forgot the lamp. When he turned to light it he was more than a minute late. He hurried now, impatient, trembling. He closed the gallery door, adjusted the lampwick, waited just long enough to check the height of the flame and started below. In the watch room he paused to make a brief entry in the log, then hastened down the stairway. But in the base of the tower he halted, and stood there twitching his hands in a sudden fever of anxiety and suspense and indecision.

What should he do? What would be the best thing to do in the circumstances?

At once he saw the answer. There was only one thing that could be done.

He went out, closed the tower door and hurried back to the cottage. In his bedroom he opened his sea chest and took out a Colt army revolver. He turned the cylinder, made sure that each chamber was capped and loaded, then thrust it in his belt and carefully buttoned his jacket over it.

He found Emily and Charlotte on the back porch playing with the gray cat's litter of kittens.

"I'm going for a walk," he said. "Charlotte, if I'm not back by nine, go up and check the lamp."

"Yes," she said. "Of course."

Emily said, "What's the matter, Simon?"

"I'm just nervous," he muttered. "I have to walk it off. When it comes on me like this, there's nothing to do but walk." He turned abruptly and went back through the cottage and out into the early twilight.

For a while afterward the two women were silent. The kittens crawled around them unnoticed. Finally Emily said, "He was all right at supper."

"Well, you know how he is," said Charlotte.

"But he's getting worse. He was out all last night, you know."

"I suspected it."

Again they were silent.

"Sometimes," Emily began presently, "I wish we hadn't come here. I think he would be better off in another place, one nearer people."

"But he can't stand people, Aunt Emily! No more

than I can. You know how it upsets him just to go over to the city."

"You two! I never saw a pair like you."

"Well, we've both had our troubles. And being of the same blood I suppose it's only natural that we should react in much the same way. He's terribly nervous, but at least I think he's happy over here."

"I don't know. Sometimes I think he's got Josephine on his mind."

"Oh, now," said Charlotte.

"But I do!" Emily said almost plaintively.

"You shouldn't feel that way."

"I can't help it. It's my being the second wife, I guess. And we were married so late in life. . . . What was Josephine like?"

"I hardly remember her—except that I always hated to go there. I have a vague impression of a sad-sweet little woman who lived on pills and prayer. I think that was her way of trying to hold Uncle Simon home, but all it did was drive him back to sea. Mother always said that she died on purpose just to make him feel sorry for her."

"Some women," Emily murmured darkly. She got up and caught one of the kittens that was about to tumble off the porch and put it in the box with the mother cat. "They're worse dead than alive, because you can't do anything about them. She unsettled him. And then he had such a hard time afterward, losing his vessel and all and drifting for days on the Banks, and it so cold. I don't know. I think he feels hounded. Or guilty and that he's being punished." She shook her head. "And now this other thing. I mean, he's so nervous anyhow, and it would take so little to unsettle him completely. Ever since he found those cannon he's been on fire."

"Well, any man would if he believed the story about them."

Emily sniffed. "I'm not a man, praise be, and I don't believe the story and I don't want to see the cannon. The only thing I'm willing to believe about the cannon is that Josephine's ghost had a finger in the finding of them. He's not acting as any other man would act. He won't talk about it, but that's all he thinks about, day and night. He's on fire inside. It's driving him to the brink. That's just what it's doing to him—driving him right to the brink. And it's no use talking to him. It just makes him worse. He's the captain. You can't tell the captain how to run his ship. That's why I wish we were nearer people. We're so remote here, so far from any help. If anything should happen . . ."

Charlotte said nothing. All Emily said only echoed what she herself felt. She had tried to hide it from herself, pass over it, pretend that it was nothing to be worried about. But it was time to worry. He was beginning to act just as her father had acted before he shot himself. There was that same feverish intentness, that singleness of purpose, that terrible inner tightness that was getting worse daily. Her father had only been trying to launch a new publication, a small literary weekly— but it had been just as much of a will-o'-the-wisp as this matter of old cannon and hidden wealth. The publication had failed, and her father had put a bullet in his head—but not because of financial failure. That was the least of it. He'd had such hopes for the weekly, such an absolute belief in it. He'd seen in it a literary revival, the dawning of a golden age. But he hadn't anticipated laughter. Who cared for aesthetics? He'd realized too late that all the country wanted was materialism and machines. Yes, and war.

Oh, the futility of it! The waste!

And now here was her father's brother, a man long hounded by devils, following another illusion to a precipice.

Certainly it was time to worry.

As she climbed the tower at nine, Charlotte was thinking of David. If only he were here, and she had him to confide in! And yet, suppose David were here? How could he help? This wasn't the sort of thing for a person like David. He would be lost in any kind of violence.

She entered the lantern, and abruptly came the memory of the new man, Call, as she had seen him here during the afternoon. He knew violence. He had lived with it and it seethed in him, and yet it wasn't the main part of him. She was amazed again at her temerity in speaking to him. Never in a thousand years would she have believed herself capable of reaching out as she did. In the past she would have fled. She'd been a little frightened of him at first, but that had passed quickly. She'd seen something under the surface—just what it was impossible to say—and there had come over her a ridiculous impulse to shake him and attempt to point out truths that he seemed to have lost sight of. Why?

Had she herself changed so much during the past year? Of course she had changed. All at once she realized that Call hadn't actually frightened her. He had merely startled her. Come to think of it, nothing frightened her any more. She had no real fear of anything, except people as a whole, en masse, crowds. She was afraid of the great crowd and hated it for what it had done to her. In the future she would avoid it. But she feared nothing else, not even death. She had seen death and knew it at its worst, and once she had craved it. She didn't fear the shark that had streaked for her one night in a burst of phosphorus while she bathed. She continued to go into the surf whenever she wished. Nor had she feared the wild hogs down the beach, or the great rattler she had seen over in the pines. She, the shy one who had always fled from people, had come to feel an affinity for these things of nature. Out here in this remoteness she had for the first time come to understand something of life and feel herself a part of it, and know a oneness with nature and the earth that had bred her. Fear life? Fear the lightning and the violent sea and the winds and the wild creatures of the earth? Not when she knew this closeness to them. Life could only startle her and bring a primeval prickling to her neck—as had happened to her this afternoon when the man Call had burst in here upon her. He, too, was a part of it.

Suddenly she wished she knew him better. Perhaps he could be of help.

CHAPTER 10

I

MAX parted the mosquito netting he had hung in a corner of the lattice porch and crawled in onto the pallet Bella had arranged for him. There was a spare room in the cottage but he had refused it. He would have felt trapped and stifled in there. This was better. Far better. He stretched out, sighed once in utter weariness and was instantly asleep. It was barely dark.

He awoke long afterward, his body still strapped and immobile in weariness but his mind clear and suddenly occupied with the thoughts that had filled it before he went to sleep. In the night's stillness the surf was a sullen undertone to the small sounds of crickets and distant whippoorwills and the occasional sleepy scolding of gulls. In the cottage he sensed movement and knew that Bella was up.

While part of him listened to Bella, aware of her and following her movements as a compass needle follows a magnet, he found himself considering her calmly and dispassionately. She was not as he had remembered her. What had he really seen in her in the first place? In the remembered Bella, under the richness and the laughter and the earthinesss of her, there had seemed to be deep wells of understanding; to clasp her had been to drown himself in her. Had that been only an illusion? Had the romantic—the man who had bought the island and put goats on it—merely endowed her with qualities that he had needed to find in those days, in the terrible urgency of the times? Perhaps that was it. Man must always seek comfort in woman. He comes from woman, his first comfort is the cave of her, and it is to the cave always that he turns for comfort when in need. It is a law as old as life. Bella had been Woman.

Suddenly he heard her nearer. He became more sharply aware of her. There was the soft pressure of her bare feet on the hall flooring. She was approaching; she had reached the door; now she was on the porch. All at once he saw her, vague beyond the mosquito netting.

She came over and stood silently by the pallet, and he could feel her looking down at him. Then she stooped, and he closed his eyes and pretended sleep, though his blood was suddenly pounding with the vital scent of her.

"Max?" she whispered.

He tried to open his eyes, to turn toward her, to answer. He was bound. He wanted her, but the wanting was a remembered wanting. It had nothing to do with the present. His wanting was almost an agony, but his body was chained. It was as if toil and fever and long hardship and contaminating death had robbed him and left him impotent with only the memory of desire.

"Max?" she whispered again, almost plaintively.

But something lay dead between them. It was dead with the thought of the child, dead with the knowledge of Ben over in the corner room, dead because illusion had fled from it.

He heard her sigh, rise slowly and move away through the hall and go outside. Then there were only the small sounds of the night and the undertone of the surf and a faint snoring from the corner room. She could have reached in and touched him, but she had not tried that. It seemed almost that she had been afraid to do that, afraid of a rebuff. He thought of her loneliness and how her life was here, and the note of plaintiveness in her voice. Suddenly he felt sorry for her.

Unaware of the trap of pity, he felt sorry for her.

Bella pulled on a pair of sandals and went down on the beach and walked. It was too early to relieve Lassaphene. At midnight she would enter the tower, take a small brass lantern he always left burning just within the entrance and climb to the light. She would check the height of the flame with a rule, make any slight adjustment necessary and stop in the watch room on the way down to sign the logbook. It was her duty to repeat the ritual every two hours thereafter, although it was seldom that she did so. It seemed a ridiculous precaution. Usually after the midnight check she would go back to the kitchen, fix coffee and a few sandwiches, then return to her cot to doze or read till dawn. Occasionally she would glance out of the window to see that the light was burning. Only when it seemed dim would she bother to check it. Later, after turning it out at sunrise, she would make triple entries in the logbook. It saved a great deal of what she considered entirely unnecessary climbing.

Tonight in a fit of depression she walked far down the beach, removed her wrapper and sandals, then waded out in the shallows and sat down, letting the spent surf foam about her. She sat there a long time idly washing herself while she stared off into the pale dark, hating her lot and feeling sorry for herself and wondering what it would be like to swim out and drown—yet knowing she would never attempt it. If Max had been awake she would have found some excuse to stay and talk with him, but she had not dared to awaken him. The time was not right for that. But if he had been awake . . .

Sullenly she eyed the waning moon; her mood darkened. She thought of Ben. "Pig!" she muttered. "Pig! Pig! Pig!" The dirty sloppy fat-bellied useless hunk of nothing! Why did he have to break his leg? Why couldn't he have fallen on his thick head? Why did life have to be so—so awfully the way it was?

"I've never had anything I wanted," she said angrily.

She had never considered exactly what she wanted, but to her mind came visions of luxury and ease. She felt pinched by poverty and she wondered what it would be like to spend a month in New Orleans at the best hotel. But not alone. It would have to be with Max. She closed her eyes and imagined nights of love.

A sudden explosion of small fish about her interrupted her sensual reverie; she saw the phosphorescent streak of something large darting through the surf and she sprang up with a cry of fright and ran to the beach. She picked up her wrapper and sandals and carried them until her body had dried before putting them on.

As she neared the tower she saw the Lassaphenes' cat foraging near the water's edge. She had always hated the cat, suspecting it of having killed some of her bantam chicks. At the sight of it she was possessed by a sudden murderous rage. She stopped, looked carefully around until she had located a short heavy piece of driftwood, then stealthily got it and approached her victim.

But the cat, suspicious from past experience, darted away. She hurled the heavy stick at it and missed.

Seething, she went on to the tower.

Bella did not realize she was late until she entered the tower door and saw Charlotte Maynard coming down the stairway with the lantern.

In all the months the two women had lived here, in cottages only a few yards apart, they had exchanged hardly a dozen words. Charlotte, in fact, had seldom seen the other except from a short distance, although more than once she had been aware of Bella's secret observation from behind the shutters next door. That Bella disliked her she knew instinctively. Her own dislike, founded on a glance that had shown only a distant and unpromising shore, she had put aside with her denial of Bella's existence; for months Bella had been as impersonal in her mind as some next-door stranger in a crowded city.

But now as she reached the bottom of the stairway and raised the lantern, she saw the other woman close for the first time. The lantern light reduced Bella's face to the basic of black and white; and Charlotte thought: How odd—it's like a Florentine mask, or a drawing by Dürer. Then she saw the eyes, the very pale eyes that did not go with the mask. The eyes were staring at her viciously.

She held out the lantern, thinking, *The woman's a devil, and she's dangerous.* But she said quietly, "I checked the flame, Mrs. Haik, and it's all right. I left the logbook for you."

Bella did not snatch the lantern. She merely reached forth and took it firmly, but it was as if she had snatched it. Without a word she turned and started up the stairway.

II

Beyond the bedroom window the morning sun touched the hillocks and the rolling waves of sand, gilding the crests and leaving the valleys filled with deep blue shadow. The shadows of the tower and the cottages and the outbuildings were long cool blue avenues across the dunes. There was no wind this morning, and no surf. The sea made a restless rippling along the beach that had the sound of tearing silk. The splash of a porpoise was audible here in the room.

Bella set the breakfast tray on the bed and stood looking down at her husband. Her face was a stealthy pool in which something had recently drowned.

"Did you sleep well?" she asked sweetly.

"Sleep!" he snarled. "I ain't slept none since——"

"You were snoring like a pig when I got up. You ought to wash and shave. Then maybe you wouldn't look so much like a pig."

He stared at her. "Bella, I don't think ye like me sometimes."

"I'd like you better if you were cleaner."

"There you go pickin' on me again. If'n I warn't flat on my back . . . Where's that feller Call?"

"Out on the back porch—shaving."

He glowered at her. "Oh, ye figger I oughta shave 'cause he does, eh?"

"I just think you'd feel better."

"Ain't nothin' gonna make me feel better till I kin git up an' walk." He scowled at the breakfast tray. "I swear to God, I think that bastard next door musta done somethin' to them lines, jest so I'd fall."

"Why would he do that?"

"Ye know damn well why he'd do it. He do anything to git rid o' me."

"Pshaw! There're better ways than that of getting rid of you."

"How d'ye mean?"

"I've told you before, but you won't listen to me. Just wait'll the inspector comes."

"He won't have no say-so."

"Oh, yes, he will! It's up to him and Cap'n Lassaphene. Those people in town, they maybe got you the job—but they sure can't keep you here if the others don't want you."

He looked at her furiously while she turned with a little shrug and moved to the door. She stopped in the doorway and turned slightly and said almost as if in afterthought: "Ben, when I went up to put out the light a little while ago I saw Cap'n Lassaphene coming home around the marsh. He'd been out there all night."

He stiffened and his mouth came open; then, oblivious of his leg, he lurched upright in bed with his big hands knotting on the sheet.

"Ye sure o' that?" he demanded hoarsely. "Ye sure he was out there by the marsh, all last night?"

"Of course I'm sure. He wasn't on duty last night. That Maynard woman took his place. I met her when I first went to the tower. And he was out all night before last, too."

She watched him a moment with only a faint widening of her eyes while his neck and jowls swelled and his face darkened as if it would burst with blood. Then she added, "I think he must have found something. I mean, he was acting sort of funny."

"How was he actin'?" Ben asked quickly, his eyes like little blue marbles popping out at her.

"Why, he kept stopping and looking at something. I couldn't tell exactly, he was so far off. But he stopped four or five times, and seemed to be looking at something in his hand."

Ben swore. He sank back against the pillows. He looked sick.

She said, "Well, what are you going to do about it?"

"What kin I do?" he cried. He beat his fists upon the mattress like a frustrated child. "How kin a man do anything when he's strapped down here like this?"

She looked at him silently. Finally she came over and sat down in the chair.

"Maybe what he found didn't amount to much," she said. "You know how he is—always picking up shells and one thing and another on the beach. But on the other hand, if it's really true about those cannon——"

"Ye know damn well hit's true," he interrupted. "Ye wouldn't catch Lassaphene spendin' his nights out there 'less'n there's somethin' to it."

"Well, Ben, if it's true I think it's time you got some

help. I think you ought to tell Max—Mr. Call—about it and get him——"

"No! Nothin' doin'! I ain't takin' *nobody* in on this."

"Do you want Cap'n Lassaphene to get it all?" She sniffed. "You make me tired! Here you are laid up with a broken leg and it'll be weeks before you can get about——"

"By God, I'm goin' to be up in another week! All I need is a peg leg to strap on, an' a crutch. I kin whittle them out right here. If'n you think I can't git about with a peg an' a crutch——"

She stood up. "Suit yourself. A week from now and it may be too late. And anyhow, we won't be here long after the inspector comes. You mark my words. But it's your business. I was just trying to be dutiful and help you. I don't know how much you expected to find, but I'd rather have part of it than none at all. And you certainly won't get anything unless you tell Max what you know and get him to help."

He glowered at her. For nearly a minute he said nothing. Suddenly his little blue eyes seemed to flame. "So hit's Max, eh? Ye're gittin' mighty goddam friendly, an' him only here a day."

She turned away from him to hide her own sudden anger. He was so stupid about so many things—but trust him to notice a little detail like that! She sniffed, then forced herself to turn around and pretend surprise.

"What's the matter with you? Papa and I always called him Max. You make me tired! Here I am trying to help you, and you won't listen to me. Don't you see he's the only chance you've got? You've got to get somebody. Who's it going to be if you don't get him?"

He lay back with his head against the pillows, slowly

twisting the sheet between his big hairy hands. Finally
he closed his eyes and expelled a long breath that was a
groan of defeat. "All right," he muttered. "I reckon I
might as well tell 'im. I don't see no other way out."

"Well, go ahead and eat," she said. "I'll send him in
when you've finished."

She started through the cottage toward the kitchen,
but at the end of the hallway she stopped and leaned
back against the wall, smiling. She wanted to laugh,
shout, dance. She could feel her blood racing.

An hour ago, well, an hour ago it had been just another
day. Then there had come a sudden comprehension of
the thing she had seen, and a quick knowledge of what
she must do. It had been like the abrupt opening of a
door in a blank space where she'd only hoped a door
might be.

All these months she hadn't believed it. She'd watched
it going on, the sly maneuvering of Lassaphene and Ben,
both suspicious, wary, one trying to avoid the other and
each trying to slip away unseen and gain that narrow
neck of the island without the other knowing. And
Clabo, yes, even Clabo had been out there often. From
the tower lantern she had watched each of them on oc-
casion, searching, probing with a long iron rod, absorbed
in the kind of hunt that a woman couldn't take seriously.
How could a woman take any stock in such things when
all her life she'd seen the boys and men at home going
off on just such excursions? It was just a sort of game
with them, a pastime like hunting or fishing. They'd
sneak off and make a holiday of it and have fun and
come back drunk, and once in a long while somebody
would find a few little things, though nothing of much
value. She supposed there actually was a lot of wealth

scattered about. After all there'd been so many piracies along the coast, and Lord knows how many wrecks. Every mile you traveled you'd hear a different tale about something. That business of the cannon had been only another one. But, Lordy God, who'd have thought——?

It was seeing the look on Lassaphene's face. Just that look. If it had been on any other face—Ben's, say, or Branch Clabo's—it wouldn't have meant so much. But to see a man like Lassaphene who had never shaken the reefs out of his dignity and let himself go . . .

If it had happened yesterday she'd have missed it. Yesterday it had been foggy when she went up to put out the light, and she hadn't bothered to get the little spyglass kept in the watch room and take it up for a look around. But this morning had dawned clear and she'd taken the glass up with her—and with the first sweep of it she'd picked up Lassaphene running. Captain Simon Lassaphene with his cap and his dignity gone and his gray hair a mess, out there running, carrying his long iron probe in one hand and hugging something tightly to him with the other. Not running *from* anything, or even running exactly. But hurrying with his thin body bent forward and his face wildly alive like, well—like a small boy who'd just caught his first fish. That was it; that was just how he looked—the probe trailing like a fish pole and his other hand hugging his prize, afraid it would wriggle away from him before he got it home. And every once in a while he'd stop, and give quick jerky little glances around, and then look at the thing he carried. Twice she saw him rub his sleeve over it as if trying to polish it. He was too far away for her to make out what it was, but it was obviously metal, and heavy.

She'd been shocked for a moment, for it was like look-

ing on an indecency to see a man like Lassaphene in such
a state.

In beholding the drama of the effect, she was tempo-
rarily blind to the causal drama. Then it hit her, the
thing she hadn't believed all these months. Ben and
Clabo and Lassaphene were right. *There was something
out there in the sand.*

What it was she did not even try to guess. She was not
interested in the nature of it. That part of it was unim-
portant. All that mattered was the fact of it, the un-
questioned value of it. Instantly it opened a door where
no door had been.

When she took in Ben's breakfast tray she had nothing
in her mind save a consciousness of the open door, and a
feeling of how she would have to maneuver in order to
reach it. Instinctively she knew she had better remain
indifferent and rather impersonal in front of Ben, as if
what she'd seen hadn't really set her off. It never took
more than a word on that subject to set *him* off. He'd
been frothing ever since he'd hurt himself, and it would
be yeast enough just to give him the bare facts about
Lassaphene. She mustn't let him get suspicious about
her own side of it. That little piggy brain of his . . .

But now she'd managed it. It was all arranged.

The next thing was to tell Max.

Bella took a deep tingling breath and hurried on to
the kitchen.

Max had finished cleaning and was waiting for her at
the breakfast table. He glanced up briefly as she entered,
then looked at her again, more sharply. Her pose was gone
and excitement had wiped out a heaviness that the years
had thrust upon her. He saw the brightness of her eyes,
the alive tightening of her face. At this moment she

looked just as he had always remembered her. The thought struck him with a little pang.

She closed the kitchen door quickly. "Max!" she whispered. "I've something to tell you!"

Then a little veil seemed to come over her face; the aliveness was still there but she was suppressing something, holding it back. Her lips parted and closed, then she came over to the table and sat down. She looked at him intently.

"Max, do you remember what I said yesterday, about helping you, I mean? You know, we were talking about money."

He nodded slowly.

"Max, if you had a lot of money, what would you do with it? I mean, where would you go, and all?"

"I'd probably start immediately for Mexico," he said quietly.

"Mexico," she said, and looked at the wall seeing strange distance. "Mexico. Is it nice there—pretty? Could people live well there and have nice things and be happy—like they were here before the war?"

"I suppose so," he said without enthusiasm. "But of course. A person can find anything he wants there. And it's beautiful."

She was silent a moment. Then her eyes turned from distance and she looked at him intently again.

"Max, if—if I help you to get some money, a lot of it, all you want, will you take me to Mexico with you?"

He was toying with his fork. He set it down carefully and his lips thinned. "But I wouldn't be going to Mexico to live. I'd be there only a short while—a few weeks, a month or two. You wouldn't want me to go away and leave you there, would you?"

"Leave me there? But why? Why couldn't you just take me with you wherever you went?"

"That would be impossible."

She stared at him. "Max! What is it you're planning? Is it so important?"

"I'd rather not talk about it."

"You're funny. I don't understand you sometimes." She got up and went over to the stove. She was suddenly upset. All at once she faced him again. "But, Max, after you've done this thing you're planning—I mean, you'd be coming back, wouldn't you?"

"I suppose so."

"Well, what about then?"

"I don't know. I haven't thought that far ahead."

He frowned at this sudden discovery. It was true, he hadn't thought that far ahead. His mind had never traveled beyond the accomplishment of his mission. Why was this? Was it because he had never allowed himself to think beyond a certain point—or was the mission itself the ultimate, the end?

He said, "But this isn't getting us anywhere. It's all hypothetical."

"No, it's not!" she cried instantly. She came over to him slowly and said in an intense half whisper, "It's true—we *can* get the money! I *know* it now!"

He hitched his chair around to stare at her, and she said, "I mean it, Max—it's true! Listen—if I can help you to get what you want and do what you want to do, will—will you take me to Mexico with you?"

It shocked him suddenly to be faced with the issue. He might desire her, but he didn't love her. And she was another man's wife. What was more important: his own personal code, or his mission? But what was any code if he could save the lives of other men?

"Yes," he said, smiling thinly, temporizing. "Even if you were the witch of Endor——"

"You'll take me with you, truly?"

"I'll see that you get to Mexico."

Suddenly she slipped down into his lap and ran her fingers through his hair, tilting his head so that he was forced to look into her eyes. Abruptly she pressed her lips down on his, happily and then hungrily and prolonged as if she would devour him or merge herself into him. When she drew back she was gasping. "Oh, God, it's been so long. . . ."

It was hard to tear his hands from her. His abrupt and terrible wanting of her stifled thought and blinded him. He looked away and shook his head, then took a deep breath and placed his unsteady hands under her armpits and forced her gently to her feet. "Now wait a bit," he ground out. "We're getting ahead of ourselves. We aren't in Mexico—and I don't even know what it's all about."

"Just listen to what I have to tell you!"

"No, not here," he muttered. "You're too close. Get around on the other side of the table. I can't think when you're so close."

She giggled and went around the table. "You do love me, don't you?"

"You're a bargaining witch. Plague and the devil, pour my coffee—and tell me what this is about."

She poured coffee and brought the things over from the stove and sat down. He thought: What's the difference? I owe it to her, I suppose. She's miserable here and I ought to take her away anyhow, no matter what happens. It isn't her fault that she's tied to that fool, or that she's the way she is. We're victims of damned circumstance, both of us. What has she to look forward to, or I?

But as she sat down and he looked across into her pale intense eyes, he suddenly remembered the Maynard woman's eyes yesterday in the tower. Bella's eyes were wrong. She should have had those of the other woman. What color were they—a sort of brown? No, amber, a kind of deep melted amber. Some hurt had smothered in them, but they were at peace now. What was it she had said up there yesterday? . . .

Then he stiffened, abruptly attentive, for Bella was saying: ". . . three cannon, but only two of them have ever been seen. The story is that you've got to find all three of them and line them up a certain way before you can—but you've heard of the story, haven't you?"

"Yes," he said quietly. "There are several versions."

"Well, I thought it was just another one of those— you know—tales. Until this morning. I thought Ben and the others—Mr. Clabo and Cap'n Lassaphene— were wasting their time. But a little while ago when I went up to put out the light, I saw Cap'n Lassaphene 'way out there by the marsh, running."

He sat motionless, silent, visioning the way Lassa- phene had run while she described it. That's the way a man acts when he first finds something, he thought. It gets in his blood and he goes a little crazy. He wants to shout and tell all the world, and then he wants to run and hide what he's found so no one will know. I was the same way.

He thrust his hand deep into his pocket and felt the

smoothness of the single coin there, but he did not take it out. He sat with his fingers touching the coin as if it were a sort of talisman, remembering the day he had found it and how it had gleamed there in the sun, not a hundred yards from one of the cannon. There'd been a high wind the day befdre and it had shifted a lot of sand. If he'd come along any later the drifting sand would have covered the coin again and he would never have had the experience of seeing and picking it up—the very personal experience of doing something thrilling and extraordinary the first time. If he were to find ten thousand coins they would never give him quite that winged feeling of wild elation that amounted almost to drunkenness. He'd shouted and scrabbled in the sand, and then he'd run furtively as if all the island had eyes. He'd been only a boy then, but from then on the island had mystery. Perhaps that was why, years later, he had bought the place, so he could retain that intangible something that men lose when they cease being boys. What was it Cassius had called it? Fey? Whatever it was, something had happened to his responses; he felt only a little numb about what was going on, and faintly angry. But he could understand how Lassaphene felt.

Bella said, "What's the matter with you? You don't act a bit excited!"

"I'm not," he said. "I'm just thinking."

"Well if you aren't the—but eat your breakfast. We've got to see Ben."

"Eh? What has he to do with it?"

"I've been telling you! He knows. He knows all about it. That's why he's nearly crazy, because he can't do anything. So I talked him into taking you in on it. We wouldn't get very far without him. If we tried it by ourselves he'd soon smell a rat and cause trouble. This way we've got 'im with us, helping. Don't you see?"

"Yes, of course," he said absently. Lassaphene and Branch Clabo and Ben—all three of them, he thought. All three of them, wary flies after the honeypot. And now Lassaphene had found something.

Was it just a stray find like the coin—or had Lassaphene finally stumbled on the honeypot?

The morning was cool but sweat was running down from his armpits. He could feel it trickling along his skin so that his faded shirt clung to him when he moved. He drank part of his coffee. Suddenly he thrust his chair back.

"Let's go in and see Ben," he said abruptly.

CHAPTER *11*

I

BRANCH CLABO lay motionless in bed. Lily Bright hovered beside him, nervously lacing her long yellow fingers.

"Please," she said. "Can't I do somethin' to ease you?"

"Go on," he mumbled. "Leave me be."

"I jes' wants to help you," she pleaded.

"I don't need no help."

"But you been here three days, an' you ain't hardly moved! You's painin', an' you's mad too. Sho, I kin tell. Did you an' Cap'n Max have trouble when you took 'im to the island?"

185

"Aw, hell an' dingbats, why don't you mind your own damn business!"

She turned away from him, then came back. "Please, how kin I help you 'less'n I knows what ails you?"

"I tole you I strained myself," he growled impatiently. "You can't do nothin' about that."

She sighed. "If'n you jes' knowed how I worries 'bout you."

"Then stop worryin'. I'll be all right."

"Can't I bring you some coffee?"

"I don't want nothin'. Leave me alone."

"Mebbe a li'l whisky'd fix you up."

"All right. Bring me a glass."

She hurried down to the taproom and returned quickly with a glass of whisky. He was sitting up in bed now, leaning back against the wooden headboard with his lips thin and bloodless and his eyes small and hard. He took the glass and drained it in long gulps and gave it back to her.

"Now leave me be," he ordered.

She moved reluctantly to the door, then turned and looked at him across the bare ugly room with its sagging floor and water-stained walls where the paint was peeling from the wood. Worry shadowed her eyes and yet made her beautiful. She knew he saw her only as a fixture to be used and enjoyed when needed, but the pattern had been set long ago and she did not mind it. She was sure of the pattern, for in it she was indispensable. Her only fear was that something might change it.

He's really a good man, she thought, but wished he did not have his terrible and insatiable longing for wealth. She hoped he never found his father's money.

If he did she knew she would lose him, for then he would no longer be shy with white women.

She smiled suddenly and said, "Don't it help a little to know what you got downstairs in t'safe?"

He thought of the handful of Federal notes Ramsey Dau had given him. At another time the knowledge of the security they brought would have given him pleasure, but at the moment his only feeling about them was an uneasy one of guilt.

"Forgit it," he muttered, then ordered angrily, "Go leave me alone!"

She stared at him in quick fear, unable to understand his reaction. Finally she turned and went downstairs. She did not share his guilty feeling. More than a week ago she had urged him to do what Dau wanted, and to her way of thinking it had been a wise move, the only smart thing to do in the circumstances. Now everything was safe, and they had Dau for a friend instead of an enemy.

When she was gone, Branch unbuttoned his shirt and looked at the great bruise on his side. The bullet must have struck the rod he'd been carrying and slammed it against his ribs. It was like being hit by an ax. It had knocked him flat, knocked all the air out of him.

He closed his eyes and again felt the impact of the big bullet; there was the sound of the shot and the earth flying up to meet him and the sting of sand in his face, and then there was the effort of trying to rise and the numbness and sudden sound of another shot and still another, and ahead of him in the twilight that was nearly night the glimpse of Hermes falling, kicking.

That in a way was the worst of it, seeing little Hermes

fall like that and thinking him dead. But it had pulled him to his feet and he'd run and caught up Hermes and carried him down to the skiff. Hermes had only tripped over something, and was all right, but it had been an awful feeling for a minute. Together they'd managed to get out to the boat. He'd left his rifle on the boat, and if he'd only been able to handle a rifle with one hand he'd have gone back ashore and settled the thing that night.

How many shots? Four? Five? Quick ones, too, and heavy lead. Sounded like an army revolver. Max didn't have one and he didn't know about Lassaphene, but he was sure there was no stranger living over on that part of the island, so it must have been Lassaphene.

"I'll fix you, mister," he said in a low monotone.

Then he thought of the cannon.

For three days the thought of the cannon had been bursting upon him blindingly day and night, driving away all other thoughts. Suddenly his hands shook with the vision of it and again he saw it there in the late afternoon with the palmettos growing over the breech and the rest of it nearly buried in the sand so that it looked more like a drift log than what it was. A bronze cannon, mottled black and gray and green and so much like a log that he'd stepped right over it. He'd have gone right on walking if Hermes hadn't taken a poke at it, and turned him around fast with the sound of metal on metal.

The third cannon.

"Oh, Christ, help me," he said. "I got to git back there. I can't wait no longer."

Carefully he swung his feet out of bed and slowly, painfully, drew on his trousers and his sandals. His whole left side felt as if it were caved in, but maybe it was just a broken rib. Getting out ought to make him feel better.

"I got to know what's goin' on," he mumbled. "I better git over there fast."

He went down and found Lily Bright in the taproom. "Where's Hermes?"

"Workin' on Cap'n Max's boat. Wh-what you aimin' to do?"

"I'm goin' to the island. Help me git ready."

It was when he limped out to the dock and saw Max Ewing's battered old sloop that his feeling of guilt returned. The sloop was back in the water now and Hermes was pumping it out. He wished suddenly that the craft were somewhere else, so that he would not have to see it and be reminded of Max and all the things Max stood for. Just looking at it made him question his deal with Dau, made him feel the wrongness of something he did not want to feel was wrong.

Then all at once the angles of his flat face sharpened and he began snapping the fingers of one hand across his thumb. Everyone knew the catboat, so why announce himself on the island by sailing over there in it? Why not sail over in the sloop and leave it at the lighthouse pier? Then everyone would think he'd just brought it over for Max, and gone on back home with Hermes in the other boat. Sure, that was the way to work it. And Hermes could sail over for him later.

He reached the island late that night and made the sloop fast to the pier. He was very tired and the least movement had become an agony. For a few hours he stretched out on one of the bunks and tried to sleep, but long before dawn he was up and transferring his equipment to the skiff he had towed astern. When the skiff was loaded he cast off in it and tried to row along the shore. The agony was too much, and he crawled aft and began sculling with one of the oars. After a long while he came to the marsh. He turned into the first channel and poled the skiff as far up into the saw grass as it would go. He was nearly exhausted by now, and it was almost daylight. The cannon was close, but if it had been miles away he would have gone on, impelled by a necessity that took no accounting of his ills.

A quarter of an hour later he crawled through a fringe of palmettos near the edge of the timber and saw the vague loglike shape of the cannon twenty yards ahead. His mouth was open and he was panting like a winded dog.

There had been a light fog during the night and the surface of the sand was still damp. Far plainer than the cannon were the fresh footprints all around it.

He sank down panting with his fists clenched in the sand, staring at the footprints while he silently raged.

II

Bethsheba stood by the side gate, her body turned so that the new moon would not shine over her shoulder. Uneasily out of the corner of her eye she watched the approach of the four soldiers on the street, but she pretended not to notice them until the dog Teal, crouching at her feet, gave a low growl.

The soldiers halted by the gate and grounded their arms. The corporal in charge frowned at the chain and padlock under Bethsheba's hand.

"All right, auntie—open up!" he demanded.

"Whuffo?" she asked. They were hardly more than boys, she saw. Just raw recruits of the occupation force. "What y'all wants hyar, white folkses?"

"Never mind what we want! Open the gate before we break it down!"

Bethsheba swelled. She thrust her great black ugly head over the top of the gate and bellowed, "Who you thinks you talkin' to? You lay hands on dis gate or try comin' in dis yard, an' de Lawd help you 'cause you'll *sho* be needin' help!"

The quartet stared at her. "Now look," said the corporal patiently. "We don't want trouble, but we have our orders. We have to search this place. Isn't this Cassius Drew's house?"

"Naw, suh! Hit's my house!"

"Doesn't Mr. Drew live here?"

"Sho, I rents de po' harmless ole gent'man a few rooms—but hit's *my* house an' *my* yard! Jes' go down to de co'thouse an' see whose name hit's in an' ask who pays de taxes! I don't care *who* give you orders! My name's Bethsheba Washington an' I's a freedman in good standin', an' I *knows* my rights! Whuffo de army hyar if'n it ain't to uphold de Freedmen's rights? Jes' you try bustin' in on my rights an' see what de Bureau does to you!"

The soldiers wanted no skirmish with the all-powerful Bureau that dictated to the army. They held a low consultation. Presently they departed.

Bethsheba waited until she could no longer hear them in the distance, then she hastened to the barn door.

"All clear," she whispered, and hurried back to watch the street again.

From the blackness of the barn came more than a dozen men. Most of them were elderly and had long been active in local government. The acids of time and trial had marked them all in the same way, so that they looked a little like brothers in the moonlight. They moved quickly across the dappled shadow of the yard, slipped through a hole in the garden fence and vanished among the trees next door.

Cassius went over and touched Bethsheba on the shoulder. "Bless you," he murmured. "If I can keep out of jail a few weeks longer . . ." Then he added, "Have you managed to find out anything of our Maximilian?"

"Ain't found out nothin', Marse Cass'us."

"I'm getting worried. I expected him to slip back and see us more than a week ago. Now it's absolutely necessary that I get in touch with him."

"Is hit about de pardon?" she asked hopefully.

"No such luck. But we need him. He's the only person who can help us now."

"How kin he help with him a-havin' to stay hid all de time?"

"He can handle everything over at Clabo's."

She shook her head slowly. "Marse Cass'us, I don't think he's over at Clabo's no more."

"Why do you say that?"

"If'n he was dat close, he'd a-been in to see us by now. An' I knows Marse Branch ain't over thar 'cause I was talkin' to dat ornery Pinchy down at de Bureau an' he happened to say he'd been lookin' fo' Branch Clabo an' couldn't find 'im home."

"Hmm."

They were silent a moment. Then Bethsheba said,

"If'n there's trouble round hyar, you gonna find dat Pinchy sittin' right on top o' hit. Dat's an' ornery bad nigger."

"Yes, I'm very well aware of it. That's one reason I've got to locate Maximilian. Has Janus come back from fishing yet?"

"I looks fer 'im in de mornin'."

"Then send him in to see me. I think it's time we told him about Maximilian."

Cassius went into the house. He lighted a candle in his study and sat down at the table to write a note, then shook his head and blew out the candle. Better not commit anything to writing. He wished he knew the date the army was leaving town. But that, however, was one important secret the forces of evil were guarding carefully. The army would just leave suddenly, and overnight a handful of renegades would take over the town.

He considered appealing to the district military governor to leave the troops. Then he snorted. Appeal to the hangman to spare the noose! "Hell's mischief," he muttered. "They're too busy cutting down fruit trees. Of course *that's* important."

What could he do? What could any of them do? The day of darkness was almost upon them. That couldn't be stopped. You couldn't stop it unless you had civil rights and could govern yourself. But when you had no rights, no arms, not even the right of free speech or the right of self-protection . . .

No, you couldn't stop what was coming, but with luck you could mitigate some of the evil. If you could make a show of force, and keep the mob from being armed, and then close the saloons and be ready for trouble when the army left . . .

Across the hall he heard his mother talking in her sleep. "Celeste!" she said sharply to a servant long dead. "Celeste! How many times must I tell you to keep that pipe out of your mouth while you're cooking your master's bouillabaisse!"

Cassius smiled, then a little tremor of dread went through him. If he died first, who would take care of her? What would happen to her in the days ahead?

Then he thought of the more immediate future. He wished fervently that he could see Maximilian this very night.

III

This was the Lassaphenes' Saturday to go to the mainland. Usually Lassaphene had the mule hitched up before daylight, ready to drive to the other side of the island and get an early start across the bay. But by two in the afternoon there had been no preparations for leaving. The wagon stood untouched in the shed and the mule still dozed in the corral.

Bella peered through the kitchen shutters, listening. It was cool here in the cottage, but outside the sun was a sword. From the pines out back she could hear the locusts shrilling in the heat. The surf was a hateful grating that lay under all other sounds. How much longer? she thought. I can't stand it much longer. Something's got to happen.

She left the kitchen and moved soundlessly across the lattice porch and along the hall to the front door. It was siesta hour, but she had no thought of sleep. Behind her in the living room she heard Ben say, "Can't ye see nobody?"

She turned and entered the living room where Ben sat in a rocking chair with his injured leg resting on a stool. He was using his jackknife to trim down and cut designs in a rustic crutch Max had made. On the floor beside him was a heavy walking stick with the drying bark peeled in crude patterns like the crutch. A child might have cut the patterns, but even a child would not have kept on like this, endlessly elaborating until the design was obliterated.

He just sits there and does that all the time, she thought. I'll go crazy if he keeps on. And it's been three weeks since I was away from here. Jesus God. If Max would only . . .

"There's nobody next door but Mrs. Lassaphene," she said. She ranged the room, a restless panther, barefooted and wearing only a long yellow cotton wrapper. She said irritably, "Why don't you do your whittling on the porch? It won't hurt you to sit out there."

He overruled her with an obscenity. "I'm tryin' to think," he growled. "I don't like the look o' what's goin' on. Where's Call?"

"Working out in the barn."

"An' that Mrs. Maynard, ye sure she ain't come back?"

"I'd have seen 'er if she had," she said sulkily.

"I wish to hell I knowed where she went this mornin'. Why didn't ye send Call to follow her?"

"You make me tired! How could I send him after her when I was up in the tower trying to watch where she was going?"

"All right, all right. Ye needn't git riled."

"Anyhow," she said, "I told you where she went. The last I saw of her she was heading for that big palm grove. I'm sure she went in there. And I bet you anything that's where Cap'n Lassaphene's digging. She's gone there to help him. Isn't that where you found the second cannon?"

"Yeah." He scowled furiously at the crutch and with a stroke obliterated three inches of carving. Suddenly he said, "Go git Call. Hit's time I had a talk with 'im."

She started for the hall, but he looked up abruptly and said, "Wait a minnit. I been wantin' to ask you somethin'. How d'ye feel about that feller?"

"How do you mean how I feel?"

"Hit was your idea, gittin' 'im in on this. But I ask ye now, what's he done, heh? Jest tell me, what's he done?"

"He's done all he could, Ben. Up to now it's been the dark of the moon. You can't expect anybody to do much out there on a black night."

"Well, by God, Lassaphene seems to be doin' somethin'! I don't put no trust in that feller Call! He's like all the rest o' them educated fellers. He's runnin' deep. He's been runnin' deep ever since Clabo brung 'is boat over here an' left it. How do we know he ain't a-goin' to grab everything when the time comes, an' take off some night in that boat o' his'n?"

She shook her head angrily. "He wouldn't do that."

His little bright porcine eyes were suddenly full of suspicion. "Ye like 'im a heap, don't ye?"

"I know what kind of a man he is," she snapped. "There's no reason for you to talk that way."

His face reddened and purpled. "Always standin' up for 'im! Ye can't fool me! Sure ye like 'im!"

She stamped her foot and blazed, "Do you want me to get him for you, or don't you?"

"All right, by God, go git 'im—but put on some more clothes! Ye ain't got no goddam business showin' yourself around like that—to him or nobody else!"

"I'm not putting anything more on! It's hot and I'm decently covered up and comfortable—and don't you curse and talk like that to me!"

She left in a fury. She had been spending much more time with her toilet lately, and the yellow wrapper was especially for Max. It was subtly revealing and she knew she looked her best in it. There was furthermore the nagging consciousness of the Maynard woman next door and the knowledge that Max had twice been over there to work on her shrubs. Not, of course, that he could ever see anything in such a person, but at the same time . . .

On the back porch she stepped tremblingly into a pair of slippers and went slowly out to the barn, trying to compose herself before she got there.

She found Max in the shop, fitting a new handle to the ax. He looked at her sharply and put the ax aside.

"What's the matter, Bella?"

She clenched her fists. "Oh—that—that——" She went over and pressed her body close against his. "Hold me!" she whispered. "Hold me tight!"

He put his arms dutifully around her, and unconsciously fled from her by seeking escape in another image. For no reason it seemed there came to him a vision of the Maynard woman's eyes. Those eyes had known hurt, but there was something strangely calming in their quiet depths.

"Ben acting up again?" he asked.

"Oh, God! That man! I can't stand it much longer— I just can't! What's happening, Max? How much longer have we got to wait?"

"I don't know. Right now it's Lassaphene. I can't do anything while he's out there by the palm grove."

"But *what's* going on out there? Ben wants to know! He wants to see you! He's in a fit! What're you going to tell 'im?"

He shrugged and thrust her gently aside. "Leave it to me," he said, and started slowly for the house.

"Be careful," she whispered behind him. "He's beginning to think things about us."

It suddenly infuriated Max that he should have to be answerable to such a man. But he'd been expecting trouble. He'd seen it coming for days. Ben had done nothing but sit in there and fume; and now with Lassaphene digging out yonder on the neck of sand where the island narrowed, Ben was like a boiling kettle on a hot fire of suspicion and anxiety.

In the parlor Max looked down wearily at the big seething redheaded man. "There's something you want to know?" he said quietly.

"Ye're damn right there is!" the other burst out hoarsely. "Why ain't ye keepin' an eye on things? What's goin' on out yonder? What's Lassaphene doin'?"

"He's out there digging."

"But *where?* By God, that's what I want to know—*where? Where?*"

"I told you yesterday. He's still in the same spot. Just east of the big palm grove. He made a triangulation on the three cannon and he's digging around there in circles."

"Then why ain't you out there on the neck watchin'? Tell me that! Ye want that bastard to git away with everything?" Ben Haik was sitting up, his leg forgotten while he pounded the floor with his crutch. He was almost shouting. "I don't like the look o' this! Ye're holding somethin' back! By God, when I took ye in on this ye swore to play fair with me an' tell me everything——"

Bella, standing in the doorway, suddenly stamped her foot. "Ben, for heaven's sake! Quiet down! Do you want Mrs. Lassaphene to hear everything you're saying?"

"Shut up! Keep out o' this!" He swung back at Max, waving his crutch. "How do I know ye ain't a-holdin' out on me? By God, hit's mighty damn queer——"

"Luff up!" Max suddenly ordered. "You're acting like a damned fool."

"Ye can't talk to me that way! I ain't havin' it! I'm runnin' this show! Ye hear me?"

Max turned away in disgust. He started for the hall.

"Hey!" Ben cried. "Jest a minnit there! Where d'ye think ye're goin?"

"I'm through," Max told him shortly. "The deal's off."

"Like hell it is!"

Bella gave a little gasp, and Max turned.

Ben had jerked a derringer from his open shirt. "Don't move or I'll blast ye!" he bellowed. "Ye're tryin' to take advantage o' me! Sure, I know how ye figger! Ye're runnin' deep on me! Instead o' bein' grateful ye're tryin' to take advantage o' me 'cause I'm laid up an' nigh helpless! Yeah! But ye ain't gittin' by with hit! No, by God! I'll kill ye first!"

CHAPTER *12*

I

MAX ignored the weapon. He sighed and said a little wearily, as if to a child, "Listen, Haik: I've known all about the cannon for years—long before you ever heard of them. That's why I came over here. So you're the one who should be grateful—for you'll get nowhere without me. I know this island as you'll never know it. And I know exactly what Lassaphene's trying to do out there. And I know he's wrong."

"Heh? How d'ye know he's wrong?"

"Remember the story of the cannon?"

"Sure I remember it!"

"How does it go?"

200

"How come I should tell it all to ye if ye've heard it?"

"I want to hear your version of it."

Ben scowled furiously. "Well——" He lowered the weapon. "All right. Hit's to do with that there fort them English built over here in the old days. Ye know about the fort?"

"Yes."

"Well, seems like they had a heap o' pay money an' stuff on hand, an' the French—some say hit was that La Fitte bunch—anyways they come an' tried to take it away from 'em. But the English had hauled the money out in the night an' buried it in a big triangle marked by three cannon. The way it goes, ye got to find all three cannon an' line 'em up jest right. Ye got to triangle 'em, I mean, an' then square it, an' dig where the fourth cannon u'd be if'n there was one."

"And then the storm?"

"Yeah. There come up a big breeze o' wind that blowed sand over the cannon, an' nobody could find 'em afterward."

"It makes a good story," said Max. "But if you were awaiting attack, would you take three cannon you might be needing badly and drag them all over the sand at night just to mark where you'd hidden your valuables?"

"Well, now, I dunno. But that don't matter. Them cannon are out there! I seen two of 'em! So've you!"

"Did you take a good look at them?"

"Sure, but hell, they're jest cannon. Jest old cannon."

"Haik, I've studied all three of them. They're not English cannon—they're Spanish. And they're strung out over a half mile of sand. Furthermore the fort the English had over here was miles away from them." He spread his hands. "But that's just one story, Haik. I've heard half a dozen tales about those cannon, and they're all different."

Haik said nothing. He looked out of the window. He cowled and puffed out his lips. The derringer sagged in his hand, forgotten. Finally, absently, he uncocked the weapon and thrust it back into his sweaty shirt. Suddenly he looked up.

"But Lassaphene found something! Ye know he did!"

Max shrugged. "So have other people found things. Just stray objects. But finding whatever he did and locating the third cannon have got Lassaphene excited. He's staying out there on the neck all the time. And so long as he's out there I can't do anything myself—unless you're anxious to make a deal with him."

"I don't want no truck with Lassaphene!"

"Neither do I. Very well, then. You see how matters stand. Even if you were able to try it alone, you'd get nowhere without me. So if we continue our partnership, it'll have to be entirely on my own terms. Financial and otherwise. No—none of that! Plague and the devil, you'll keep a hitch on yourself—or you can go whistling!"

He stood watching Haik a moment, then went on quietly, "But I'll not take advantage of you. I never make promises I don't intend to keep. But from now on I'll manage this, and there'll be no questions out of you. Is that clear?"

Max returned to the barn. He felt better now that he'd had it out with Haik, though he hardly expected anyone so inflamed not to be troublesome later. But it had galled him to be driven by circumstance into such a dubious partnership, particularly when the man had not the slightest claim to what might be hidden on the island. If one reduced it to a matter of rights, he supposed that he himself possessed all personal rights, even if power-less to enforce them. After all, he owned the island.

Even so, it was impossible for him to look upon the object of his search in any sense of personal ownership. To *that* he had no right—except the right of a trustee. He had come to have an almost fanatical view of this trusteeship. It was as if the wealth in the sand had been placed there long ago by a farseeing fate, to be held in escrow until he, finally, could use it for the purpose for which it had been intended. Clearly in his mind he saw it as belonging to a cause. It was the power that would tear open the casemates on Garden Key. It could be used to destroy the vultures that had come to pick the bones of his homeland. It was the solution to everything.

All this would have seemed nebulous and even fan-tastic if he had had the least doubt of what the sand would yield. But he no longer had any doubt. He was certain of what he would find. And by now he knew definitely where it lay. All his hates and his hopes, his furies and his future were channeled into a singleness based upon this certainty of what he would find. He did not consider failure.

As he stood a moment looking out beyond the corral and the garden toward the curving belt of pines his lips thinned against his teeth and his body tightened with a quick surge of excitement. It was impossible not to feel it. But with the excitement came an instant worry that Lassaphene might suddenly see the truth. He himself had guessed it months ago in prison, and now that he was sure of it he was a little amazed that no one else had thought of a thing so simple.

He went into the shop and finished fitting the handle
to the ax. Then he wandered restlessly about the shed,
wondering what to do. Today he had expected Lassaphene to be away. He had counted on it. He wanted
badly to be out near the marsh bordering the neck, using
the daylight hours to study the task that lay ahead. It
was hard, in fact, to restrain himself and not go rushing
over there.

"Damn Lassaphene!" he muttered in a wrath of im-
patience. "Confound him, damn him and blast him!"

He considered hiking across the island to see about his
sloop. It had been very decent of Branch to bring it over
and leave it at the pier, but the hull was still in need of
attention, for Hermes had done little more than give it a
coat of bottom paint. He knew he ought to go over and
work on it while he had the chance.

He started irresolutely down the road, but after a few
paces he turned and went instead to the tower.

It was not until he had climbed all the way to the
lantern that he began to wonder what had ever possessed
him to come here.

He opened the gallery door to let in the fresh air, then
parted one of the curtains and studied the distant palm
grove where Lassaphene had gone. The grove shim-
mered in the heat and beyond it the dunes stretched
away in a glittering haze. His eyes hurt to look at it.
He turned away, seeing in his mind all that was going
on at the grove and annoyed only by the knowledge of
Lassaphene's presence.

At the gallery door he paused and looked idly across
the width of the island in the direction of the pier. The
pier and the boats moored there were hidden in the distance beyond the pine tops, but portions of the island

road were clearly visible. The man approaching along
the road was a white mark a half mile away, a white
moving dot in the green parklike area of the pines.

Suddenly troubled, uneasy, he studied the moving dot.
It was not Clabo, for there was no suggestion of a limp.
Nor was it Lassaphene, for the keeper seldom wore white.

Who would be coming over here? And why?

He turned and slowly circled the light, frowning, and
got out his pipe and filled it. With some logic he tried
to convince himself that neither the man nor his mission
were of the least importance to him, but he could not
shake the feeling that a finger had touched him and
gently swung him from one channel to another, so that
momentarily he had lost his objectivity.

On the seaward side of the lantern he paused and
absently moved the curtain, thinking of Cassius while he
peered down at the beach. Instantly he forgot Cassius.

Below him Charlotte Maynard was struggling over the
drift of sand from the beach, heading toward the tower
entrance.

What the devil did she want? Or had she merely come
early to clean the lamp?

He took out his tinderbox and methodically went
through the ritual of striking a spark on the tinder, shaking it to a flame and lighting his pipe. Then he stood
smoking, waiting.

Presently he heard her coming up the ladder from the
watch room. Her head appeared in the opening. Seeing
him, she hesitated a moment then came slowly on into
the lantern. Under her bonnet her face looked pale and
drawn, showing a faint spattering of freckles across her
cheeks.

She leaned wearily against the iron framework until

she got her breath. "Thank heaven," she managed to say finally. "I hoped you would be in the tower. I—I prayed you would be."

He got the work stool and carried it over to her.

"You'd better sit down," he said.

She sank gratefully upon the stool and drew off her bonnet. She closed her eyes and pressed her hands over them. Abruptly she looked up at him.

"Tell me something: Why are you here this afternoon?"

"I don't know. I just came. I'd been wondering."

"I think you're here because for the past hour I've been hoping I'd find you here. Or do you believe in such things?"

"I always have," he told her gravely.

She sighed. "Most people draw a circle around life and say it's just so. I'm glad you're not like that, because I need your help. I—I've been wanting to talk to you for a long time. Now things are coming to a head."

"Tell me what's wrong."

"Do you know where I've been all day?"

"Aye."

"Then you—you know all about what's going on?"

He nodded.

She started to speak again but looked away, biting her lip. He saw that her long thin deft fingers were clenching the bonnet ties, twisting them as if she would tear them.

"Ease up," he said gently. "You're as taut as a weather brace in a breeze." He moved over to the opposite side of the door and sat down on his heels, facing her. He had seen her only a few times since their first meeting here in the tower and usually it had been in passing, for he had long finished his work about the lantern. Except for the brief occasions when he had helped her with her shrubs, they had exchanged hardly a dozen words. Yet she had been often on his mind, increasingly so after discovering her eager interest in all growing things, and he no longer had the least feeling that they were strangers.

"I'll be glad to help you in any way I can," he told her. "What seems to be the trouble?"

"It's Uncle Simon. He—I think he's losing his mind. This is the third day he's been out by the palm grove, and he won't come home. I've tried to reason with him— but he ran me away. I—I don't know what to do! If I were only a man . . ."

"If you were a man you'd leave him alone. I know what's got into him. He'll work it off. They always do."

"Oh, no!" she cried, shaking her head quickly. "You don't understand. This is much more serious than you realize. I've seen it coming on for weeks, and tried to ignore it—but it can't be ignored any longer. And Uncle Simon means so much to me. He helped me when I needed help, and he's the only blood relative I have left. He——"

"Now wait," he interrupted. "I tell you there's nothing to worry about. Haven't you ever seen anyone with gold fever before?"

"Gold fever!" She sprang up, suddenly agitated, and began moving about the lantern. "If it were only that! You don't realize how we feel about this place, how much it means to us. All the money in the world wouldn't give us the peace that we've found here. But this thing is destroying him, destroying everything. If you could realize how desperate——"

He stood up, looking at her curiously, frowning. "I

guess I don't quite understand. Why do you say desperate?"

"Because——" She moved to the light. Her hand trembled on the belt of lenses. Suddenly she turned and faced him.

"No one knows this," she began, her voice almost a whisper. "Not even Aunt Emily—although she suspects. She's his second wife, and doesn't know all that happened. He had a lot of trouble once, and went insane. This excitement over the cannon is bringing it on again. I know the signs. He's been getting a little worse each day. So drawn up inside. So tight. Oh, it's awful to see that tightening in him! Unless we can do something, and do it soon, it's suddenly going to snap. Then he'll be violent. He may kill himself—or one of us. He—he carries a loaded pistol all the time."

She stopped. She closed her eyes a moment and took a deep breath. When she looked at him again she seemed quite calm. "I'm sorry," she said in her small clear voice. "I didn't mean to get excited. I hardly ever do any more. But I've been upset all day. It's a—a terrible problem. I hate to bring it to you when you have problems of your own. But we're going to have to do something."

His pipe had gone out. He scowled at it and, turning, tapped the ashes from it against the gallery door. While he thought of Lassaphene his eyes followed the tracery of the island road. It was with a little start that he again saw the approaching figure in white. The man was much closer now.

Charlotte Maynard said, "If only he hadn't heard of those cannon . . . But they're all he's thought about for weeks. Do—do you believe the story about them?"

"Which story?"

"There's more than one?"

"Aye, I know a dozen."

"Is—is that one of the reasons you came over here—so you could do some searching too? Please—I don't mean to pry. But if you're going to help me I think I ought to tell you the truth. I've seen you go out in that stretch of sand in the evening where Uncle Simon goes. And I know more about you than you may think."

"Some things are evident," he said a little harshly, and glanced down at his ankles.

She bit her lip. Her eyes were suddenly amber pools of compassion. "I wasn't thinking of that—and it isn't very evident now. Aunt Emily hasn't noticed, and she seldom misses anything."

"Go on," he said.

She shook her head, and for an instant the light played across her hair and her thin sensitive face so that he caught a dynamic and multidimensional impression that he had hitherto missed. The thought crossed his mind that she was a woman you had to look at twice to see, for the first look was a lie; she wasn't plain. There was a beauty in her that was too elusive for a casual glance.

She said, "I've no right to go on. I just wanted you to know that I understand how you feel, and why. Or at least part of it."

The hollows in his face deepened. "Maybe we'd better think about your Uncle Simon."

"Well," she said uncertainly, "that's why I asked about the cannon. Because of the effect of what he might find."

"He won't find anything," he said.

"But he's already found something! That's what

made him worse. He—he found a crucifix. A beautiful thing of wrought gold. He carries it with him all the time. He won't let it out of his sight."

Max took the coin from his pocket. "I found this nearly twenty years ago. But it doesn't mean much— except to establish the fact of something."

She looked curiously at the coin but did not touch it.

"So much must have happened here," she murmured. "I felt it when I first came. Mystery. It's all right to delve into it if it doesn't become an obsession. I don't know which would be worse for him—to stumble suddenly on a great treasure, or to go on following the will-o'-the-wisp. I—I've been praying he won't find anything more, hoping maybe he'd just wear himself out and in time get over it. But he's been in a frenzy all day. If he stays out there much longer . . . Do you think it would help if we went to the grove and you talked to him?"

"I doubt it. I think he'd resent me. To make him angry would only make him worse."

"But we've *got* to do something!"

"Aye. Let me think."

He moved around the light, chewing on his empty pipe.

She turned to the gallery door and looked out. Suddenly she said, "There's someone down there near the barn. It's a colored man."

He looked down toward the barn and saw the figure in white standing beside the woodpile. The man had taken off his wide straw hat and was wiping his face with a bandana while he peered uncertainly from one cottage to the other. The shadow of the trees lay upon him so that he seemed to have no individuality of race; he was just another black man in cotton shirt and pantaloons.

Charlotte said, "I can't imagine what he wants here. Were you expecting anyone?"

"No, hardly. No one knows where I am except Clabo."

She drew on her bonnet. "I'll go down and find out what he wants."

"Wouldn't you rather have me go?"

"I don't think you'd better. I'm only guessing about you now—but unless I'm very wrong you shouldn't be seen by anyone from the city who might possibly remember you."

"Thank you. I'll wait for you below. There's no use in your climbing all the way up here again."

He closed the gallery door, then followed her to the base of the tower. He waited within the shadow of the entrance while she crossed the drift of sand at the side of the Haik cottage and vanished around the back.

While he was still adjusting all she had said into a new conception of her, and wondering what possible course could be taken with Lassaphene, he saw her returning. She had a swift effortless way of walking as if her body weighed nothing.

She entered and said, "It's *you* he wants to see! He said to tell you his name is Janus."

"*Janus!*"

"You'll see him?"

"Of course. He's my old servant."

She studied him gravely a moment. "Before you go, let's decide something about Uncle Simon."

"Hmm. I can hardly make a suggestion until I've had a look at him and possibly talked to him. And that's going to be a little difficult. We haven't spoken since the morning I came here. He made it clear that I'm just a foc's'le hand while I'm working on the reservation."

She stood silent, lacing her long thin fingers together. Finally she asked, "Is there a moon tonight?"

"Yes."

"Well, if he doesn't return this evening in time to light the lamp, I'm going out to the grove again."

"Do you want me to come with you?"

"I wish you would. Maybe we can think of some way to get him to come home."

"All right. Where shall I meet you?"

"Down the beach where the big log came ashore. I'll light the lamp at sundown, and then start down there."

"I'll be there."

He stepped down from the entrance and began moving swiftly toward the barn, but after a few paces he slowed. His elongated shadow, stretching beside him in parody over the sand, seemed to strain away from him like a troubled jester.

II

Charlotte watched him thoughtfully until he was out of sight around the cottage, then she sat down on the tower steps, took off her slippers and shook the sand from them, and drew them on again. Forking away in front of her were two narrow boardwalks, one going to each of the cottages. As she stood up and moved to the fork her attention went unconsciously to the Haik cottage, whose front windows looked almost directly into the tower entrance. Her glance was merely for assurance; she had the feeling of being observed—which was just her state of mind, she thought, for surely the Haiks had long been asleep at this hour.

But with a little start she discovered that Bella was

awake, and watching her. She could see the dark shape of Bella's head in one of the parlor windows.

Charlotte bit her lip in annoyance and moved quickly along the right-hand walk to her gate. But every step of the distance she could feel the silent malevolence of the other woman's stare. That devil! she thought. What's the matter with her? Why does she hate me?

She stopped abruptly at the gate. Good Lord, she thought, she's jealous—of *me!* Of course—she saw us both go into the tower. She thinks I'm after him, that we planned to meet there.

With an inexplicable flash of temper she thrust the gate open and hurried into the house.

Emily was in the parlor, sitting in the rocker by the corner window. She was rocking slowly, monotonously, while she knitted. The bone needles were making a furious little clicking, but her face seemed composed.

"About time," she said as Charlotte entered. "About time. Landsakes, you've been gone all day."

"I—I was helping him," said Charlotte.

"You—helping him!"

"Why, yes," Charlotte said innocently. "It's getting rather exciting. I mean, there's certainly something out in that stretch of sand—you can almost feel it. I don't blame him for wanting to stay out there."

"I want to know when he's coming home."

"Tomorrow, probably. He's still probing around the grove. You can't expect him to stop until he finishes that part of it. It would upset everything. Please don't worry about him. Really, I think he's having the time of his life."

She wasn't sure anyone as sharp as Emily would swallow the lie, but at least Emily wanted to believe it. The clicking of the knitting needles had stopped.

"I'm going to take a nap," she told Emily. "I'm dead tired."

She went into her room, undressed and crawled wearily between the cool sheets.

Emily came down the hall and paused at her door. "Charlotte," she said, puzzled, "what were you and Mr. Call doing running back and forth at the tower?"

"Oh, it wasn't anything. I mean, some colored man came while I was looking at the lamp, and I went out to see what he wanted. But he'd just heard Mr. Call was over here at the reservation and had come to see him."

"I didn't know. I was just curious. I was there in the front room and saw you two coming and going, and I thought you looked angry about something when you came in. It seemed so funny to see you angry."

Charlotte thought, You never miss anything, do you?

"I was rather put out," she told Emily. "That Mrs. Haik was up and she kept staring at me all the way down the walk. She saw us at the tower."

"She's in love with that man," Emily said slowly. "And I wouldn't put anything past her. I've a very strong suspicion she knew him long before he came here."

Charlotte was silent.

Suddenly Emily said, "Simon isn't right. He—he's reached the brink. I know it." Her voice broke slightly. "I wish you wouldn't try to hide it from me. I've kept away because you've so much more influence with him than I—but please don't pretend any more. It—it doesn't save me anything. Tell me—did you ask Mr. Call to help you?"

"Yes," Charlotte said faintly. "We're going to the grove tonight to see if we can get him to come home."

CHAPTER 13

I

Max turned past the chicken yard and the grape arbor and saw Janus waiting under the shed. He broke stride and nearly stopped at the sight of the sturdy brown man in the ragged pantaloons and wide palmetto hat. In his memory Janus was a neat figure in a fitted jacket; he wore polished shoes and gave answer in diction that was better than that of most whites. But now only the patient face of Janus was familiar.

The brown man stared at him, and came forward slowly. And suddenly the palmetto hat was tossed aside and Janus ran up to him, blinking, and silently caught

215

his arms. They hugged like brothers. There were tears on the brown man's cheeks.

"Look at you! Oh, Glory, look at you!"

"Look at *you!*"

They shook each other.

"You been here all this time, all this time—an' I didn't know!"

"There was no way of telling you, Janus. How did you find me?"

"Mr. Cassius told me to find you. He wants to see you. Said you'd been at Clabo's, but didn't know what'd come of you. So I started out yesterday. Had to get rid o' that boy o' mine first. He's a Bureau boy—you know about the Bureau?"

"Aye, too well."

"Rather do without 'im—but it takes two to fish. Paid 'im off an' got 'im drunk—then I went to Clabo's. Mr. Branch, he wasn't there. But I talked to Lily Bright. She told me that 'Mr. Call—' " Janus smiled—" '*Mr. Call*' was working here at the lighthouse. So here I came. Lord, Lord, my boat never sailed so slow!"

They moved to the shed, talking, and sat down in the shade beside the wagon. They filled their pipes and lighted them, and studied each other.

Janus said, "What they've done to us! I think old Cap'n saw this coming. I think that's why he sent me to school."

"Then why are you fishing? Why aren't you over in the city taking advantage of your education? You could be on top."

"You think so?" The brown man looked down at his bare toes and wiggled them in the sand. "Mebbe I could—if I'd play ignorant an' do as the Bureau an' that man Dau—you know about him?"

Max nodded. "I know."

"Well, he's not the only one. If I'd do as they'd want me to do, swallow their lies and sign papers I wasn't supposed to know how to read, I'd get along fine. And if I could turn against the people that were good to me, that brought me up to be as good as any man, why, I'd get along better. But I'd be wasting the education that old Cap'n gave me. An' I wouldn't have any self-respect. You see? So I go fishing. I like it out on the bay. I stay out there all I can because I sure don't like it ashore." Janus looked sad. "It's bad there. Mighty bad. Did Mr. Cassius tell you how bad it is?"

"He told me enough. Do you know what he wants with me?"

"He didn't say. There were some people coming, and he didn't take time to explain. He just said to find you an' bring you to 'im fast. Can you leave now?"

"Not very well." Max stood up, frowning. He went out of the shed and studied the sun and came back, thinking of his promise to Charlotte. "I can't possibly leave this evening. We're having a little trouble here. Er, both keepers are sick. It may be several days before I can get away. I wish I knew why he wants to see me, how important it is."

"I think it's very important, Cap'n."

"Could it be about my pardon, do you think?"

Janus shook his head. "Can't be that. I'm always askin' about the pardon. He'd have told me. This is something else. I got a sort of feeling he wants your help."

"But, good Lord, how could I be of any help to him?"

"I don't know. I'm away too much to mix in things—and I don't have anything to do with the Bureau. But that boy that works for me, he's signed up with 'em. He's no-account, but at least he tells me a thing or two. So I know there's something goin' on over in the city. That's why I put up with that boy, so I'll maybe hear things I'm not supposed to hear."

"What do you think is going on now?"

Janus got up and wiped the palms of his hands on his pantaloons. He was obviously troubled. "Cap'n Max, you remember that man Pinchy that used to belong to Mr. Branch?"

"I certainly do."

"Cap'n, that's a bad black man. I don't think people realize just how bad he is, or just how much power he's got. He thinks he's got royal blood in 'im—says his papa was a king of the Matabele. A lot of those ignorant colored people believe that, and he's got such a hold over 'em that the Bureau favors 'im every way it can. Cap'n, I look for trouble. I look for bad trouble soon."

Again Max felt the echo of what Cassius had told him. Yet it was nebulous except for a half-remembered black runaway, a spindly light-fingered rascal with an easy tongue and a head full of schemes. But there was hardly enough to Pinchy to give it form. After all, what was Pinchy in the shadow of Dau? And what more could Dau want when he had practically everything? Why should there be trouble?

Across his mind passed the names of Dessalines and Toussaint L'Ouverture; then he shook his head at the thought. They were giants, and Pinchy was but a pigmy. Why all these murmurings of trouble, these fears? But perhaps, after all that had happened, they were to be expected. This was a time of uncertainty. No man could rest easy. With things as they were one could always expect trouble of sorts—not anything of great violence as Janus implied, but certainly many kinds of trouble— and years of privation and bitterness and sudden flaring hatred and the slow anguish of inevitable death under the hand of oppression. Later, no doubt, he would be in a position to do something about it, pardon or no pardon. Damn the pardon anyway! The one thing he could do was to take Garden Key and liberate the prisoners there.

Everything in its place. He could do nothing here now. He was powerless. But in another week or two his promised period of waiting would be up. Then he would see Cassius—and have something to show him. From then on matters should proceed very swiftly.

Janus was looking at him curiously.

"What are you thinking about, Cap'n?"

"The future," he answered shortly.

"You scare me," said Janus. "You're not like you used to be. There's something in you."

The brown man came closer and touched him on the arm and peered up at him with his sad, patient and intelligent eyes. "Cap'n, I feel for you. Every day you've been gone I've felt for you. They've wronged you. It's something a man can't get over easy, if ever. But I hate to see it all coiled up in you like a rattlesnake. It scares me. Remember what old Cap'n said to us once—after we'd gone hunting an' you'd got in some trouble with a man an' were brooding about it the next day?"

"What was that, Janus?"

"He said: 'We have only today. Tomorrow rests with God, and yesterday with Caesar.' I've thought of that a lot since the day he said it. He was mighty wise, old Cap'n was."

"Aye. There was never anyone like him."

Janus said, "He gave me to you when you were a boy. You always were my Cap'n, an' you always will be. Everything I have is yours. If there's anything I can do for you that you want done, I'll do it. If you need money, I got it. I got more'n two hundred dollars hid away; it's yours any time you want it."

Max swallowed. "Thank you, Janus. I didn't realize that I still have a brother."

"Cap'n, I don't know what Mr. Cassius wants to see you about, except that it's mighty important. What shall I tell him?"

"Tell him I'll sail over the first evening it's possible for me to get away. Surely it'll keep a few days. You might explain to him the situation here: one of the keepers is just recovering from a broken leg. The other seems to be losing his mind."

II

He was waiting by the drift log at sundown, and watched her coming swiftly along the beach, moving with that effortless walk that in the distance made her seem more like a girl than a woman. She was bareheaded and carried a basket in the crook of one arm. A few slim-winged terns circled her and occasionally she would reach into the basket and toss them crumbs which they caught in the air. Once one of the birds lighted on her arm; she fed it with apparent unconcern and without changing pace. As he watched her it seemed to him that she was spirit to the terns and as much a creature of the island as they.

But he saw that her face was grave when she reached the log.

She gave him a half-smile, and said quickly, "I brought a little lunch for him, and something to drink. I think he's got enough to eat, but this is just an excuse. I don't want to appear obvious to him."

"I'm still in doubt about my part of it," he said. "I don't think I'd better be seen at first—unless it's absolutely necessary. You know very well that just seeing me will antagonize him, especially in these circumstances."

"I've thought of that. I believe the best thing will be to approach him quietly—if we can get close to him without being noticed—and see how he is. If he seems rational I'll go up to him and try to talk to him alone. After that we'll just have to do whatever seems best. I'm praying he'll be so tired that he'll be willing to come straight home with me."

"If we can get him home, have you got something in the medicine chest that'll keep him quiet for a while?"

"Aunt Emily is taking care of that," she said grimly. "She'll give him a cup of tea that'll hold him in bed for the next two days."

She had hardly paused at the log. They were moving swiftly along the beach.

"Don't hurry," he told her, realizing how tense she was. "It'll be black dark long before we can get out there. Then we'll have to wait for the moon."

"But it was bright last night," she insisted.

"Aye, but it's thickening. We won't see a star unless the wind hauls."

She slowed for a while, but presently she was walking as fast as ever. The terns followed, circling, then flew away as the twilight deepened. He swung along silently beside her.

At last she said, "Was this the first time you've seen Janus since you—since you returned home?"

"Yes."

"Were you glad to see him?"

"It was like finding a lost brother," he said quietly.

"And he was your slave?"

"If you want to put it that way. Father gave him to me when I was a kid. We've never thought of our Negroes as slaves."

"But of course he *was* a slave. How does he feel now—about being free, I mean?"

"He's not very happy over it. But you couldn't expect him to be. He's no fool, and Father gave him a good education. He knows what's going on over in the city. He doesn't want any part of it."

"Any part of what? What are you talking about?"

He stopped. "You mean to say that you don't know what's going on over there—and in fact all over the South?"

"I—I wasn't aware that anything unusual was happening. But then I never go to the city. I came down here on a ship from Baltimore. I've never seen the South, and know very little about it. I spent most of my life in Philadelphia. I—I think I should tell you that it would be difficult for me to have much sympathy for a—for either the South or its issues."

"Then what the devil are you doing down here?" he demanded.

"This isn't the South, or even a part of it," she said, moving on down the beach. "This is an island. It's almost out of sight of the mainland. It's entirely different and remote from anything I've ever known. I came here because I—because I was very unhappy where I was. I wanted to go someplace where I'd never see people or have to come in contact with them again. It was as much for my sake as his own that Uncle Simon asked for duty here. He'd visited here and knew what it was like. I love this place. I wish I owned it so I'd never have to leave it."

He scowled at her, and paced her in silence. The twilight deepened.

"You're angry," she said presently. "I'm sorry. I was only trying to explain to you a little of how I felt and why I'm here. If I were partisan I wouldn't be here. And if I have any hate left in me it's for the war itself and what it did to people. We're both victims of it."

"Aye, but I don't intend to take what it did to me without doing something about it!"

At the harshness of his voice she glanced up at him quickly, but said nothing.

They walked on silently for a while. It was almost night.

Finally she said in her quiet voice, "I remember what you told me the first time I talked to you. That's a terrible way to feel. Don't you realize the waste of it— that you'd just be throwing yourself away for no purpose? Can't you see that it's all one country now—and that you ought to work for unity and harmony?"

"Unity!" he spat out abruptly. "Harmony! Those are fine words to use when the prisons are jammed with men who did no more than fight for their homes—and when all the country is overrun with buzzards who've flocked down to steal everything they can get their hands on! Bah! You'd better go to the mainland and see what's happening. The country's defenseless." His hands reached and clenched upon the night as if it were an enemy he would rend. His voice harshened to a rasp.

"Let me tell you about the Freedmen's Bureau and people like Dau, and what they're doing—and what it's like to come back and find the last of your family dead and your home gone and everything confiscated. But maybe I should tell you first about prison. Aye, you know I've been there—and you've guessed that I must have escaped. Then I ought to tell you how I got there, and what it's like to be dealt with as a criminal instead of as a prisoner of war. And maybe, when you've heard it, you'll see why there are many thousands of us who can never feel anything but hatred and contempt for a government that has neither honor nor any regard for human rights.

"I'll tell you first about Randy . . ."

It was black dark when he finished and the night was so still that it seemed even the sea had been listening. The woman seated near him on the low hillock above the beach was all but invisible. For a long time she said nothing, and so quiet and remote was she that he almost had the feeling of being alone.

Then suddenly he felt the quick hesitant pressure of her fingers upon his arm. Still she did not speak, but the shy touch of her hand was like that other involuntary reaching the first day in the tower. She had spoken then from within herself; now there was no need for words. And now instantly any antagonism he felt toward her vanished forever. She became close, personal, intimate in his awareness of her.

He had almost forgotten Lassaphene. The palm grove

was nearly a half mile away; it was impossible to go on until the moon rose or the night cleared.

After a while her voice came to him, very low and disembodied in the dark. "There was a time when I felt almost as you do. I wanted to get a rifle and go out and kill. You don't believe me, do you? You don't think I'm like that. But women have that in them. I wanted to do violence, only I wasn't able, so I went all to pieces. I'm sure David would have been horrified if he had known I could be that way. He didn't have any violence in him. He——"

"Who's David?"

She must have turned her head, for when she answered he could barely hear her. "He—he was my husband. He was a journalist, like my father. He didn't believe in war—especially this one. He said it was madness. He denounced it, wrote against it and lost his friends because of it. For a long time he managed to stay out of it. Then he was drafted. He was in uniform only a few days. They snatched him out of private life, put a rifle in his hand and threw him into a marching column.

"I took what money we had and tried to follow. It was June, just four years ago. Late in June. A great many women were on the roads that week, riding from town to town any way we could, following the army across Pennsylvania. I'd never been in the country before, or that part of the state, and I don't remember the names of any of the places except one. I suppose the country was beautiful, but I hardly saw it. I can remember only the heat and the stillness and the dust along the roads, and of riding that last day with an old Quaker and his wife who had a son in one of the companies somewhere ahead of us. They were trying to catch up with him just as I was trying to catch up with David. There was something dreadful in the air. We knew what was coming, and it drove us on. We wanted to see our men again, if only for a few minutes.

"That morning—it was the first day of July—I remember we came to a crossroads store and tavern, and we stopped to water the horses. That was when I first heard the guns.

She stopped a moment. Then she said, "Did you ever go to a place right after a big battle had been fought?"

"No. All the fighting I saw was at sea."

She said, "The sea is clean. That's why I like it. It wipes out ugliness. There aren't the smells, and the flies, and the ground all torn up as far as you can see and every sort of thing imaginable scattered over it. Clothing and equipment and fragments of things . . . Oh, the litter! And everywhere there are pieces of paper. Letters. It's seeing those scattered letters that's the worst, almost. It makes it all doubly awful. Those pages and pages of handwriting where women have poured out their hearts to men, and men their last thoughts to women. All trampled there in the torn earth, among the stains and the flies. It's that death of something beyond the flesh that makes it so unutterable.

"But it was days before I saw all that. The guns kept up for three days, and during that time there was nothing I could do but wait there with the crowd at the tavern. Just wait and wait. Afterward I located some of David's company . . . and it was then that I learned I'd have to go out on the field to find him. I went with the Quaker couple. The—the dead had been laid out in long rows, and everywhere I went there were people trying to identify relatives." She stopped a moment. "It took me two days to find David. I don't think that poor couple ever found their son."

Beyond her he saw the moon rising from the sea, a dim melon slice that brightened as it rose. She took form against it and her face sharpened in silhouette.

"Gettysburg?" he said finally.

"Yes. You're the first person I've told it to, except Uncle Simon. I don't know what would have happened if he hadn't taken me in and looked after me. So you can understand how I feel about him."

She turned and peered at the moon. "Don't you think we can go on now?"

"Aye, I believe we can see all right."

He stood up quickly and gave her his hand. She took it and got to her feet, and for a moment afterward she stood there motionless looking at him, her eyes deep with shadow, and he felt the warm pressure of her fingers in his. Then she turned and began moving swiftly across the long waves of sand in the direction of the palm grove.

CHAPTER *14*

1

A LITTLE breeze began to brush the night, sweeping the
blackness from the horizon and piling it back into the
sky. The night brightened as stars showed in the east.
Now ahead, dimly across the rolling gray-white waves
of sand, they could see the palm grove, a dark oasis
stretching along the island's narrow neck. Vaguely beyond it lay a smaller grove, and around it like watchful
sentinels were scattered palms and small clumps of palmettos. There was no reality here under the moon, only
something secretive and strange.

Charlotte slowed. "He's around on the other side,

near the marsh." Unconsciously she spoke in a whisper.

"Aye, I know. We'd better bear to the right. When we reach the trees, you go on around to where he is. Don't pay any attention to me. I'll keep out of sight, but I won't be twenty paces behind you."

She began to hurry again, but after a few steps she slowed. Then she stopped. She stood very still as if she were listening.

"What is it?" he asked.

"I don't know. It's something I always feel when I come out here. Mystery, maybe. A sort of awareness of the past."

"Aye, I know what you mean. I've always felt it, even as a kid."

"Did you come here often?"

"Many times."

"To hunt treasure?"

"Not primarily—though it served as an excuse."

"Do you believe there's treasure here?"

He nodded. "I'm sure of it."

They were standing close, speaking in low tones while they studied the small sand hills, the clumps of palms and the distant fringe of the grove. It occurred to him that he ought to let her go on alone from here, and so avoid any chance that Lassaphene might see them together.

She said, "From what you told me this afternoon, I thought you didn't believe the story of the cannon."

"I don't."

"Then you're sure he won't find anything where he's working."

"Reasonably sure." He shrugged. "But one never knows. In a place like this, where so much has happened . . . where man and nature have always been violent . . . I think you'd better go ahead while I circle— he may be watching."

"Wait!" she whispered. "What's that moving yonder?"

To their left and halfway to the grove something appeared on one of the sand ridges. Then he made out a small herd of goats led by a shaggy old billy with great curving horns.

He chuckled. "Why, that's old Noah! He's the first goat I brought over. The time we had with him!"

"You—you brought these goats over here?" she said slowly, staring at him. "Why?"

"I was younger then. And I'd just got the place. I'd always wanted to see goats on it."

"You—this is *your* island?"

"It is unless it's been taken away from me recently. But I doubt that anyone would want it—at least the sort who're grabbing things these days. It would be about the only thing of mine that hasn't been touched— and that simply because it's worthless."

"I'd say it was worth a great deal," she murmured, "depending on how you look at it." She turned, saying, "I expect I'd better go along."

He waited until she had a good start, then he circled, keeping to the low areas and moving up in the cover of the scattered clumps of palmettos. The goats worried him. It was not like them to move about much at night. Generally they herded together at one spot and stayed there unless disturbed.

At the edge of the grove he flattened against a palm while he studied the black silhouettes of the close-growing trunks, then he went warily on, following Charlotte. He could catch occasional glimpses of her as she hurried around to the lee side of the grove. Finally he was near the spot where he had seen Lassaphene digging. He crouched and waited for the expected sound of voices, but they did not come.

After a while he heard Charlotte call, "Uncle Simon? Where are you?"

Still he waited, uneasy. He heard her call again and yet again, more urgently. There was no answer.

At last he stepped cautiously from his cover and approached the wide shallow pit where she was standing.

"He's gone!" she whispered.

"Maybe he went home."

"No, I'm sure he didn't! I'd have seen him. I was watching—he always goes home by the beach."

"Maybe he got around us in the dark."

"Oh, no—I'm sure he couldn't have. For one thing his eyes aren't too good. He'd have waited for the moon, just as we did. Something's happened."

She sank down on a fallen palm near the pit and sat there holding the basket with one hand while she beat her other hand on the trunk. "We got here too late," she said miserably. "We should have come straight out here after I talked to you in the tower."

"If he's in the condition you think he's in, our coming earlier wouldn't have helped. Anyway, he would have seen us coming in daylight. You can't approach this place without being seen."

He stepped down into the pit. "He hasn't worked in here for hours," he said. "The sand's bone-dry."

He got out and walked slowly around the area, looking at three small holes that had been abandoned. "I don't see any tools. What did he have with him?"

"A spade and a probe and—let's see: a knapsack and a canteen and a blanket—and his pistol."

She sprang up suddenly and went over to a slight depression at the edge of the grove. "He had his blanket spread out here when I talked to him, and his knapsack and canteen were on it. They're gone. Everything's gone."

"Well, he's certainly given up working here. And he hasn't been here for hours. What did you say when you talked to him?"

"Oh, I don't remember exactly—just anything to try to take his mind off of this. When I couldn't get him to come home, I pretended to be interested in what he was doing and to want to help. But at the same time I tried to question things. I mean, I said anything I could think of to make him doubt what he was doing. I even questioned his triangulation. I've seen two of the cannon— one's 'way up yonder near the beach and the other's over on the other side of the grove."

"Yes, I know."

"Well, I got him to tell me where the third one was, and I said wasn't it strange that they were so much in line, as if they'd fallen off of something; and then I said it seemed odd that anyone in a hurry to hide the fort's money would go to so much trouble and make such a difficult triangulation. In fact, you can hardly get a triangle out of it. I just mentioned the first things that popped into my head—but none of it did any good. He got angry. And finally he ordered me home."

"I see." He stared at her. "No wonder he's gone!"

"What have I done?" she asked plaintively.

"Don't you see what you've done? Plague and the devil, you of all people had to come out here and instantly put your finger on the truth! The triangulation must have worried him. He's no fool. Look—he tried four times to make his measurements come out right. The last time he just kept enlarging the hole. Then you came along and upset everything. Of course he got mad. But after you left he sat down to think it out. Now I'll bet anything he knows what actually happened!"

He strode around the pit and then back, suddenly worried and upset; he ran his hands through his hair, and took out his pipe and clamped his teeth upon it, but then thrust it back into his pocket. "Imagine—of all the people who've puzzled over this, it takes a woman to point out the obvious!" He took out his pipe again. "Sure, he knows what happened now."

She stood watching him curiously. "But what *did* happen?" she asked almost in a whisper.

He glowered at her. Abruptly he stooped and picked up a broken whitened conch shell. "How do you think this got so far over from the beach?" he demanded. "Look at it! Look around you! What d'you think happened?"

She did not move. He saw her eyes widen a trifle, then she gave a small "Oh!" of comprehension.

She was silent a moment. Then she said, "You're angry with me. Why are you so angry?"

"Oh . . ." He turned away.

"Does this upset things for you?"

"It's going to make it difficult for both of us. Now he'll keep on till he finds it."

"You're sure there—there's some sort of treasure?"

"There's no question of it!"

"But you . . . It wasn't why you bought the island, was it?"

"No, certainly not. Do you think I could have valued money above a spot like this?"

"Then why do you want money so badly now?"

He turned away without answering.

She said, "You needn't tell me. It isn't hard to guess."

Still he said nothing, and she said, "There's something in you that's frightening. I don't blame you for hating, and for wanting to do something about it—but there are so many ways to fight. I'd want to fight too if I were in your place. In fact, I would. But not the way you want to do it. Fighting for something you believe in is one thing—but revenge is something else. It's a terrible thing because it's so utterly selfish. It's an obsession. It's being possessed and driven by an evil spirit. If we were living back a few centuries ago they'd say that both you and Uncle Simon were possessed—although in his case he's destroying no one but himself."

She came over and touched his arm. "Please, if you have any idea where we can find him, tell me! Maybe he hasn't actually figured out anything yet. Maybe he doesn't quite know. It's possible that he's given up hope here and is just out there wandering. There's that chance. Maybe if we could get him home now and keep him there . . ."

"Come on," he said abruptly. "I think we can find him. Those goats—remember? I think somebody startled them."

They walked swiftly around the lee of the grove.

Once she looked up at him and said, "You're not really angry with me, are you?"

"Forgive me. Things just threw me off my course for a minute. I was angry only at circumstances. It seems

I've been running into circumstances ever since I got back."

They went on toward the ridge where they had seen the goats. They kept closer together now and were watchful, speaking little. Their feet made a steady rasping in the dry sand. As they started up the ridge she stumbled and fell to her knees; he helped her up and insisted on taking the basket. On the ridge they stopped, their shadows blending as they studied the dim moonlit sweep of sand ahead. The pale moon gave the night a smoky look and laid on everything a veil of illusion and deception. Ahead a jagged arm of marsh cutting in from the bay was like a raw cicatrice exposing a subcutaneous darkness. Patches of palmettos and tufts of sea oats covering little hillocks assumed fantastic forms, and they seemed to move unless closely watched. The sea was a faint muttering in the air, a deep living breath that gave life to everything.

The sudden crunch of footsteps brought them instantly around, but they did not see the man until they heard his voice.

"Charlotte!"

Then the thin intense form of Lassaphene detached itself from the shadow of a hillock and swung quickly up to the ridge. The man stopped a few paces from them and stood swaying a little, stiffly like a dry reed in a wind. He was wearing his cap and jacket, and except for a stubble of beard graying his cheeks to his goatee he seemed about as usual. But as he moved his head the moonlight suddenly pitted his face with deep hollows. His protruding lower lip was jerking soundlessly.

Suddenly his voice snapped and crackled at them, cut

at them with a fierce biting edge. "What are you two doing out here?"

"Uncle Simon," Charlotte began, "I came out to see you—and——"

"I told you to stay home!"

"Uncle Simon, please——"

"You've no business out here with this man! Go home!"

"Uncle Simon——"

"Go home this instant!"

Max could feel Charlotte's fingers tightening on his arm, but when she spoke it was in her quiet even way as if this were nothing unusual, as if Lassaphene were entirely rational and not dangerously on the point of an explosion. The man's voice had a tautness as if something in him were stretched to the utmost; he was tired, his body swayed with weariness, yet the body was as taut as the voice. Max did not take his eyes from him for an instant. Lassaphene was carrying no equipment save his pistol, which was thrust into his belt, but his hands were curved stiffly at his sides with the spread fingers slowly twitching.

Charlotte said, "Of course, Uncle Simon, I'm going right away—but Aunt Emily needs you. She isn't well. She needs you badly. Won't you please come with me?"

"Eh—Emily? She needs me?" The biting voice faltered for a moment. "Yes, of course—I'll go with you. I—I was going anyway. But go on—wait for me on the beach! By heaven, I'm not leaving till I've settled with this fellow!"

"Uncle Simon——"

"*Go on!*" he cried.

It was better to obey him. Max thrust the basket upon

her, urging her away. She started toward the beach, moving slowly.

Once she was on her way Lassaphene did not look at her. The biting voice suddenly chilled. "You've overstepped yourself. You've pried into matters that don't concern you. Now you've presumed. I'll not have my niece compromised by any prying recalcitrant. As soon as I return I'll give Mrs. Haik your wages. You are to be gone by sunup tomorrow. If I catch you on the island after that, I'll shoot you on sight."

Max opened his mouth, and closed it.

Lassaphene snapped, "No arguments!" His hand darted to his belt. He drew the pistol, and there was a little click as he set the hammer. "Get out of my sight—and don't ever let me see you again!"

II

Max took his time returning and it was after eleven when he got back to the cottage. There was a light in the kitchen, and he found Bella waiting for him.

"Well!" she said accusingly. "You've gone and done it! You've certainly gone and done it!"

He shrugged. "The captain's been here, has he?"

"You bet he's been here! There's your pay." She pointed to the table. "He told me that you would have to be out of here by morning. Now will you please tell me what's happened?"

He sat down wearily. "He's just got himself in a state that's all. How did he act when he came over?"

"I didn't see anything wrong with him! Just sort of tired—and mad at you. What's happened?"

He sighed. "I had a talk with Mrs. Maynard this

afternoon, and she wanted me to go out with her and help bring the captain home."

"Oh, she did, did she?"

At her tone he stiffened a little. "Yes, she did. He's been out there several days, you know. He hasn't been acting very rational."

She sniffed. "So *she* says! Well, I know better! He was certainly all right awhile ago!"

"He wasn't all right out in the dunes," he managed to say patiently. "He came up on us suddenly when we were trying to find him, and—well, he was most irrational. I don't mean out of his head, but just tired and strung up and excitable, so that any situation would look distorted to him. Anyway, he was in such a state that it infuriated him to see me with her. He threatened to kill me if he ever saw me again. He——"

"So *that's* it! And what were you an' that sneaky woman *doing* when he saw you?"

He stiffened. "Bella! I won't have that!"

"Oh, you like her, do you? Humph! I've seen you with her. I saw you meet her in the tower this afternoon. I know what she's up to! Anything to get her hooks into you!"

"Bella!"

"I know what I'm talking about! Now look what she's done to us! She's just a sneaky——"

He got up suddenly and shook her. "If you don't get off this crazy tack you're on, I'll pack up and leave right now. Damned if I won't—and the devil take you! Now calm down."

Her pale eyes widened upon him suddenly and showed the whites. Then her chin quivered. "Oh, Max . . . "

"Pour me some coffee," he ordered. "Then sit down and let's get this straightened out. It's bad enough to have Lassaphene suddenly drop his rudder without you putting your lee rail under at the same time. Mrs. Maynard's a lady, and it's time you realized it. As for Captain Lassaphene——" He frowned. "I wish I'd been here when he came, just to have heard how he acted."

She poured his coffee but did not sit down. Her face had a set blank look.

She said, "I told you how he acted."

"Is Ben awake?"

"No."

"It's just as well. You can explain things to him in the morning." He frowned again. "I'm sure Lassaphene must know I've been watching him, or at least suspect it. And it didn't help him any to find out he'd been wasting his time there in the palm grove. That's probably why he was in such a fury."

"Are you trying to excuse yourself?" she asked shortly.

"I'm not trying to excuse anything," he snapped. "The man's physically exhausted and emotionally overwrought. I'm just trying to figure how he'll be when he's had some rest. I've got to plan accordingly."

She sat down. They were silent for a minute.

Finally she asked, "What in the world are you going to do, Max?"

"I haven't decided yet."

"Did—did he really threaten to kill you?"

"Yes—and he meant it when he said it."

"Are you afraid of him?"

"If he's irrational—yes. But no matter what, I've got to take him into account. And of course I'll have to leave the reservation. There's no question of that."

"But—but where'll you go?"

He shrugged. "Not too far away, that's certain."

"Max, what about that cabin the soldiers put up during the war?"

"I've thought about it. I'll have a look at it tomorrow. If I stay there I'll have to go to Clabo's and get some things. What about you and Ben? Can you manage all right?"

She sniffed. "He can get around if he wants to. And if he isn't able to take me over to the city next week, I'll sail over alone. It won't be the first time I've done it."

She stopped a moment, then looked at him intently. "Max, what do you really think of that Mrs. Maynard?"

"Oh, for God's sake! he said irritably. "Can't you get her out of your mind? I've had enough for one day. I'm tired." He passed his hand over his eyes and stood up. "I've got to get a little rest before I go. But plague take it, don't let me sleep too long."

He went out on the porch and undressed and crawled through the mosquito netting to his pallet. Bone-tired, he collapsed and pulled the light cotton blanket over him. A weight of weariness closed his eyes.

But little thoughts like noisy children raced around in him and drove sleep away.

What did he think of Mrs. Maynard? He remembered the terns circling her as she came along the beach, and he remembered the things she had said, and her quiet way with trouble. Perhaps he could never bring himself to agree with her—but he could never pigeonhole such a woman and dismiss her.

III

He was up and on his way soon after dawn. To be forced to leave now, particularly today of all times, was the last thing he wanted. He hated to leave the island even for a day. Too much was coming to a head. He could feel it as he left the cottage, and it suddenly touched him like the cold point of a knife when he glanced back at the gate and saw Bella watching him from the kitchen window. Ben was still asleep, so she could have told him nothing yet. He wondered what she was thinking, for at that instant it seemed that the Bella at the window was the stranger he had glimpsed only at rare intervals.

When he gained the road he could not help looking back once more, but now the kitchen was hidden by the grape arbor. He could see, instead, a corner of the other cottage framed between the outbuildings. On the veranda there, a motionless silhouetted sentinel, was Lassaphene. The man seemed as taut and intense as he had been last evening.

Again there was the point of the knife, colder and sharper.

Max swung quickly down the road. On reaching the pines he shifted his bag to his shoulder and began to hurry. The main thing now was to sail to Clabo's, get his supplies and make it back here as soon as possible. He regretted the necessity of having to go to Clabo's, but there was no help for it. He had to have supplies. Furthermore, it might be important to be seen sailing away. He had no doubt that Lassaphene would climb the tower and watch for his sail, to make sure he didn't merely leave the area and hole up in one of the coves.

Presently he saw the log cabin over in the pines to his right, but he did not take time to go over and examine it. The spot was convenient, and Bella had insisted on meeting him there. It would have to serve.

But what of Charlotte? How could he get in touch with her? Somehow he must manage that.

He reached the sloop finally and got under way, and now his anxiety increased. He groped for it in his mind and tried to identify it, but it was no one thing. It was not Bella and the certainty that she was going to be a problem. Nor was it Lassaphene and the worry that the man would either lose his reason or suddenly see the answer to the matter of the cannon. Aye, Lassaphene was a worry—but off the reservation and away from Charlotte, even an irrational Lassaphene could be handled.

Perhaps his anxiety was the sum of everything, including his own uncertainties. There was Cassius—but that would have to wait. He couldn't afford to be worrying about Cassius now.

The wind had gone off somewhere to hide, and he tacked and drifted while the day dragged interminably. It was infuriating to be caught out here on this empty bay, lost in time and space with the thought of Lassaphene probing near the third cannon. . . .

Late in the afternoon, when he was more than a mile from Clabo's landing, the wind came out of hiding—and almost immediately he saw Branch Clabo's catboat sliding past the point on a course for the island.

He changed course to intercept it.

CHAPTER *15*

HE HAD expected to find Branch aboard, but as he came closer he was surprised to see no one but Hermes. He swung in near to the other craft and called, "Where's Branch?"

The little man stared at him owlishly a moment, then extended a tiny hand, pointing toward the island.

Max glanced at the distant ragged line of the island and saw, at the nearer point across the sound, a faint smudge of smoke. That was a signal Branch had often used when he was out after ducks somewhere and wanted Hermes to come and get him. But this time, of course, it hadn't been ducks. It had been Lassaphene. To be sure. Branch must have been over there for some time, keeping an eye on the palm grove to see what developed.

"Is Lily Bright at the tavern?" he asked.

Hermes nodded.

"Is she alone there?"

Hermes nodded again, vigorously, indicating that the coast was clear.

"All right, go on and pick up Branch. I just want to get some supplies. Lily can take care of me."

He came about and sailed for the landing, impatient to finish his business and get under way again. Already he could feel a weather change, which added to his worries. There would be wind tonight, probably more of it than he wanted. It might even turn into a sou'easter and hang on for days. That would be bad.

He had forgotten this was a Sunday, and realized it only after he saw the locked door of the trading post. But he found Lily Bright around in the kitchen and she let him into the post through the taproom entrance. She seemed glad to see him, but she was obviously in a mood. She had been drinking.

"Ain't been nobody round here for days," she mumbled. "Not for days."

"What's the matter, Lily?"

"Lot's o' things."

Silently she went about helping him gather his stores. At last she said, "Mebbe I done wrong."

"About what?"

"Things. Jes' things. Cap'n Max, d'you believe in God?"

"Yes."

"D'you believe God'll punish you if'n you do wrong?"

"I'm not sure about that, Lily." He hurriedly checked

off his list and began packing the articles into a box. "I've found the God I believe in only at sea. And I know if you break the laws of the sea, you'll suffer for it."

She said, "All I ever done was for Branch." Suddenly she looked up at him and asked, "Cap'n Max, did you an' him have any trouble when he taken you to the lighthouse?"

"No. Why?"

" 'Cause he stayed over at the island to fool around like he does sometimes, an' when he come back he'd been hurt. Says he jes' fell, but I think he'd been in a fight. Mebbe got shot. I dunno. He stayed in bed for days an' couldn't hardly move. An' Hermes, he acted mighty funny. Then Branch he crawled out o' bed, sick as he was, an' headed fo' the island again. He left mad. Mighty mad." She stopped, and then added earnestly, "Cap'n Max, don't you never let on I done tole you all this."

"No, of course not, Lily."

"Cap'n Max, all I cares about is makin' him happy. But all he cares about is gittin' his hands on a heap o' money. He oughta be happy with a roof over his head what nobody kin take away from 'im, an' plenty to eat—that's a heap more'n lots o' folks got these days. But he can't see hit. He keeps stayin' away, lookin' fo' somethin' he ain't never gonna find."

"He's on the way back now," he told her. "I saw Hermes going after him."

"Sho," she muttered. "I seen his smoke. I sent Hermes to fetch 'im." She did not seem happy about it. She was almost afraid, he thought.

He had little interest in Branch at the moment and he wanted only to get away, but he said, "Stop worrying about him. He'll be all right. I think he had a little trouble with Lassaphene—probably something to do with those cannon. But that's all over. Everything's going to be all right."

"No hit ain't," she said.

"Oh, come now. You've just been drinking too much."

" 'Tain't the likker," she said darkly. "Hit's what I done. I feels it hangin' over me. Hit's somethin' black. You—you got everything you wants?"

He frowned at his list. Something about her made him uneasy. Maybe, he thought, it was just a combination of the whisky and the weather. The weather change seemed to be upsetting everyone, including himself.

"Let's see," he said. "I ought to have a rifle."

She looked at him blankly, and he said, "I forgot to tell you, but I'm through at the lighthouse." He decided not to elaborate on that statement, and added quickly, "I'll probably live on the boat, and I'll need a rifle if I want fresh meat."

She said, "But we ain't got no rifles."

"Oh, I mean one of those Enfields," he explained. "You know. Those ones I brought in during the war, that last time. Branch said he still had them."

Her eyes widened a trifle and for just an instant he thought he saw stark fear in them. But that may have been only because of the way she was feeling. She looked away and said, "Us ain't got 'em. Branch, he had to git rid of 'em."

"Eh? How d'you mean?"

"Hit—hit was bein' talked around that he had them rifles, an' he got sort o' scared. I don't blame 'im. Them things was a live danger. So he taken 'em all out one night an' dumped 'em in the bay."

"Oh."

He was disappointed and a little irritated that Branch should have done that. He'd had plans for those rifles, although he had not mentioned it to Branch. But the thing was done and there was no help for it now. When the time came for rifles he'd have to get them in Vera Cruz.

He totaled up his bill and found he owed seven dollars more than he had. Well, he'd had to buy everything on earth from blankets to beans. "I'll pay you the rest the next time I come over," he said, sure that Cassius would have a little money from the sale of the jewelry.

She helped carry his load down to the boat, then stood looking moodily across the sound for some indication of a sail—though it was far too early for Hermes to be on the way back.

"Come out of it," he said. "You're worrying about nothing."

"I ain't worryin'," she mumbled. "What's comin' is comin'. I feels hit settlin' over me like somethin' black. When you does wrong, you got to pay."

"What have you done that's so wrong, Lily?"

"I can't tell you," she said, and turned quickly and started back up the path to the tavern.

He double-reefed the mainsail before he left, but he was scarcely three miles out into the bay when he realized he would never make it to the island tonight. It was getting dark quickly and the wind was coming in a steadily increasing rush out of the southeast, driving heavy seas ahead of it. In a larger craft, one as well equipped as Branch Clabo's catboat, it would have been a different matter; but the sloop was small and old, and her cordage bad. The only thing to do was to turn in

toward the city, and try to anchor as near Cassius Drew's
pier as possible.

Well, there it was. He'd been fighting a battle with his
conscience, trying to convince himself he ought to do one
thing when he'd known all the time that he ought to do
the other. Now nature had taken a hand.

In the dark he missed the Drew pier. By the time he
had made everything secure and waded ashore, naked,
and got back into his clothes, the blackness was so intense that he had difficulty determining where he was
and locating the Drew house. At least there was no need
for stealth. A cat wouldn't know her own kittens on a
night like this.

He fumbled at the gate, found it locked and boldly
climbed the fence. Teal announced him on the back
porch with a wind-muffled bark, but he had to pound the
back door for nearly a minute before Cassius heard him
and let him in.

So, at last, he sat once more in the dusty little study
and looked at the grim eagle face of Cassius in the candlelight, and again he was startled by the bite of age.

Cassius did not sit down at once. "Hell's mischief,
I've been walking holes in my shoes waiting for you! I
thought you'd never get here, Maximilian."

"I'm sorry, sir. I came as quickly as possible."

"Oh, I'm not blaming you! You came quickly enough
after Janus found you. I only wish I'd sent for you a
week ago. But I didn't realize then. It's all my fault!
If I'd only guessed in time——"

"What's wrong?"

"They're taking the troops away, Maximilian."

"Eh? Is that going to be so bad?"

"My God, man, if you sit on a barrel of gunpowder and light a match to it, is that bad?"

Cassius circled the room, his thumbs hooked at his back. "Don't mind me, Maximilian. I'm overwrought tonight."

"Everybody I've talked to lately seems overwrought. I think it's the weather."

"Oh, if it only were the weather! The situation was bad enough when you were here before—but it's become incredibly worse. I'm praying you can help. If we work fast, maybe we can manage something before the troops leave."

"When are they leaving?"

"If I only knew!" Cassius cried, suddenly beating his fists together. "If I only knew! That's the agonizing thing about it—there's a troopship down at the docks now; it's been there three days, and they may leave on it any day now."

"They won't leave with this southeaster blowing up— you can count on that. No vessel will be able to get over the West Pass bar by morning."

"Hmm." Cassius stopped his pacing. "I don't know why I didn't think of that. It gives us a little time. If you can manage to sail over to Clabo's first thing to-morrow and make the arrangements——"

"Eh? What the devil has Branch Clabo got to do with this?"

"He has everything to do with it! Everything! I sent for you because you're the only person on our side who could make any sort of a deal with him. He doesn't dare be seen talking with any of the rest of us—and he doesn't like us anyway. But you can handle him."

"But what——"

"Rifles!" cried Cassius. "Rifles! We've got to have them! They've disarmed us. That's one of the first things they did over a year ago—searched every house in town and took every weapon they could lay their hands on. Now they're pulling out and leaving us to a damned bunch of black renegades who are all set to take over everything. And I mean everything—police, courts, business, even our homes and our women. We're organized too—we're ready to set up a police force and other law agencies—but we'll have to do it legally, and we'll have to make a show of force before they'll let us do it!"

"But, Cassius, there aren't any rifles. I just came from Clabo's. He hasn't any."

Cassius stared at him. "You're sure? You're absolutely sure?"

"Of course. Why?"

"Because if we can't get rifles, at least they can't get them either. They're no better armed than we are, but it doesn't help us much. They completely outnumber us. God, I don't know what to say now! I was hoping——" He shook his head. "Somehow I had the notion Clabo still had some Enfields you'd brought in during the war."

"He did have. A lot of them. He had them when I first got back, over a month ago." Max stopped. He tapped the arms of his chair. Suddenly he stood up, flexing his hands, and walked around the table. Outside he could hear the dry rattling of the palms in the steady rush of wind; the house creaked and seemed to be floating in the vast current of that sound of rushing. He wondered suddenly how Charlotte liked the wind. Bella hated it.

"I'm through working at the light," he said. "Had a

scrap with the keeper—he's been in a difficult state of
mind. Anyway, I'm planning to stay on the island, so
today I went to Clabo's for supplies. I wanted a rifle,
and asked for one of those Enfields. Lily Bright told me
that Branch had got worried about having the things
around—seems there's been some whispering about
them—and that he took them all out into the bay and
dumped them."

"Do you believe that?"

"No. Not now."

"Did—did you talk to Clabo?"

"He wasn't there."

Cassius went over to his chair and sat down heavily.
"God!" he said hoarsely. "God!"

Anger coiled through the sickness in Max, but the sickness had come first. In spite of all that Branch had done,
it was hard to accept this final mark against him. Yet it
must be true. "I think I can see what happened," he
said. "They must have found out he had those guns, and
put pressure on him. The Bureau, I mean. And I'm sure
Lily had a finger in it, from the way she acted. Probably
urged him along. Wanted him to play safe with the
powers that be. I don't think Branch could have
realized——"

"That swine!" snarled Cassius. "Don't try to mitigate
the deed! There's no worse form of treason than to be-
tray your kind. And he did it! As sure as I'm sitting
here, he did it! If Branch Clabo had rifles a month ago
and hasn't got them now, he's sold 'em! That man never
threw a thing away in his life but his ethics!" He rose,
trembling, his fierce old eyes glittering in the candlelight.
"But enough of him! The thing's done and we——"

"I'll kill him," said Max. "If this thing breaks, and

there's trouble, I'll kill him. But maybe there won't be trouble. The troops haven't left yet. Maybe we can keep them here. Maybe——"

"We can't do a thing. I've written the district military governor. I've begged Tallahassee, and everyone in power. I've only been ignored or laughed at."

"Where'll these soldiers go when they leave here?"

"To St. Marks, I expect, to disembark for Tallahassee. They came from the garrison at Pensacola."

"Then why don't you telegraph the commanding officer at Pensacola, explain the situation and request that he send more troops—if these are being taken out of his jurisdiction. He probably has charge of all the troop placements in this part of the state. You'll get nowhere with politicians."

"I'll try it. I'll try it first thing in the morning—if I'm allowed to use the telegraph. I'll have to manage to get the message sent on the sly, or they'll certainly stop it. But I'll try it."

Cassius closed his eyes and sighed wearily. "Well, there's no use worrying any more about it now. We can't do a thing tonight."

They were silent for a minute while they listened to the wind. Max paced the room with the feeling of again being in chains at a time of need.

"Every damned thing happens at once," he muttered. "I'd give ten thousand dollars to be back on the island now. But my boat would never make it in this blow."

"You'll be safe here for a while. I can hide you."

"It's not that."

Cassius looked at him sharply. "What's the matter?"

"Oh, it's no one thing—except that the keeper knows

about that business of the cannon . . . and I've practically
got my hands on something."

"Don't tell me you've found the third cannon!"

"Aye. And you'll be surprised at the truth—the real
truth. I guessed it in prison. It's pretty simple."

"All real truths are basically simple—though we're
very good at complicating them." Then Cassius added
quietly, "Did you find the rest of it—the ship?"

"How did you know there was a ship?"

"By just thinking about it—as you did. I may as well
admit now that I found the third cannon years ago. It
was obvious that they must have fallen from a vessel
that was being driven across the island in a hurricane.
Of course, so few people realize what a big hurricane can
do. The Spanish were always losing vessels from the
Plata Flota along this coast. In fact, they've lost entire
fleets. As nearly as I could estimate it, that vessel was
driven diagonally for more than a mile across that sandy
low area."

Max said slowly, "Did you—locate the remains of the
vessel?"

"Yes. It's in that pocket beyond the third cannon,
near where the woods begin. Naturally it had to be
there—it couldn't have been driven any farther in that
direction. I only probed for it. I didn't attempt to dig."

"Why not?"

Cassius shrugged. "Remember what I said on your
first visit?"

"You said if you'd found it that would have been the
end of it. But you *did* find it!"

"Oh, no! We were speaking of gold. I found no gold.
I didn't want to find it. Money is only relative, and I

had more than enough of it in those days. Suppose I'd found it? What then? Why, I couldn't use it to buy back what I'd lost by finding it. For then it would all be over. That would be the end of it. But this way, in a sense, I still have it—like eternal youth."

"But you won't have it if Lassaphene or I get to working out there."

"Oh, yes, I will! When you've learned more of certain truths——"

"What are you talking about? Isn't the gold really there?"

"I'm sure it must be. But now I'm speaking of the verities. They are hard to impart. A man has to discover them for himself." He scowled and snapped his fingers. "Hell's mischief, what's the good of gold or philosophy at a time like this?"

"Everything happens at once. If it wasn't for that damned wind——"

"Thank God for it!" Cassius said fervently. "It gives us a little more time."

II

The wind came steadily out of the southeast, a clammy, sticky rainless wind that built up gradually through the night and the morning following. Far out on the exposed face of the island the two cottages felt the full intensity of it, and to the sound of its rushing was added the roar of surf and the hiss of sand against the windows. It seemed to Charlotte that the frame cottage was submerged in a great river of wind that poured around it and over and under it, and held it in a state of constant trembling while it fingered every opening. Once she made the mistake of unlatching the front door, and instantly the wind hurled her back and covered the floor with fine sand that had collected in drifts on the veranda. It was with difficulty that she managed to close the door and lock it. After that she used the rear entrance when she went outside.

Twice that first morning she climbed the tower, unsettled and nervous and not knowing why she came up here until finally, looking across the island through the spyglass, she saw the small log cabin near the road.

The sight of the cabin suddenly steadied her. He'll stay there, she thought. He'll want shelter and water, and it has a pump. Of course, he'll go straight there when he gets back. There's no other place.

She had no doubt that Max would return as soon as possible. It had upset her after he was ordered away that she had found no chance to speak to him. But she could manage that later. She studied the bay, knowing that he must have gone to Clabo's for supplies. Could he get back in this wind? She had never seen the bay so ugly, except last September when it had been lashed by the tail end of a hurricane.

At last, realizing that no small craft would be venturing out for some time, she went below and started back to the cottage, her skirts whipping and tendrils of hair flying from under the kerchief she had tied over her head. She moved with head down and her elbow over her face to shield it from the stinging sand. Suddenly, for the first time since coming here, she hated the wind. A hurricane was one thing, but at least it was soon over. A southeaster might hang on for days.

She entered the kitchen in time to see the conclusion of a little drama that had been going on all morning.

Her Uncle Simon was sitting at the table with a cup of tea in his hand.

Charlotte hardly dared look at him, or at Emily who was pretending to be busy at the stove beyond him.

"It has a foul taste," he muttered. "Perfectly foul."

"That just proves how badly you need it," Emily said.

"But it shouldn't be foul. It tastes like that tea you made the other night. It was foul too. I couldn't drink it."

"If you'd just taken it you'd feel better now," she insisted. "You need freshening. You need freshening bad."

"I'm not a cow," he said with some acerbity. "And it's *badly*—not bad."

"Yes, dear." She wisely refrained from the retort that at his age he was hardly a bull either. "Do drink it—I know you'll feel better."

Charlotte held her breath. She could see the cup shaking in his hand. He looked terrible. The tightness was still in him, almost worse it seemed, and he had hardly slept since ordering Max away. He had spent yesterday in the dunes, and most of last night pacing the cottage after the wind had driven him home. She and Emily had been biting their tongues to avoid crossing him by so much as a word.

Suddenly he raised the cup to his lips again, and drained it. For a while afterward he sat there, his face twitching while he stared out the window at the flying sand. Then he got slowly to his feet and went to the door.

"I'm going to take a nap," he said. "Don't let me sleep too long."

When he was gone Emily collapsed in her chair.

"God preserve me!" she whispered. "I thought he'd never, *never* . . ."

CHAPTER *16*

I

ALL morning Bella paced the cottage like a caged cat.
Sand came in under the doors and around the windows
and it was everywhere under her bare feet. It had been
in the eggs at breakfast and it still gritted in her mouth.
She could hear it rasping against the windows, striking
the windowpanes as if it would cut through the glass.
The wind was bad enough—the steady deadly monotony
of it tortured her soul. But the rasping of the sand
against the windows seemed to tear the skin from her
body and whip every nerve end raw. She wanted to
scream.

257

"Goddam ye!" Ben snarled at her. "Can't ye stop that fool walkin' around?"

"Oh, shut up!" she flared.

"Don't tell me to shut up!"

He glared at her, white around the mouth, and for an instant she thought he was going to hurl something at her. He was sitting on a stool, trying to fit the bended knee of his broken leg into the padded crotch of a peg leg he had fashioned yesterday after Max had left. The peg leg had a piece of heavy sole leather fastened to the bottom for walking in sand. He seemed insensible to the wind, but he had been in a fury ever since hearing about Max.

He strapped the peg leg to his thigh, then got his cane and stood up carefully, testing his weight on the bended knee. He took a step. He pivoted and took another step, and grunted.

"There, by God! Now I kin git out yonder an' see for myself what's been goin' on. If'n I been told any lies——" He stopped and his head jerked upward. He listened. "What the hell's that upstairs?"

She'd heard it too Something was up there.

She darted into the hall and glanced quickly up the stairway. She froze. Suddenly she was trembling.

Ben growled, "What's the matter with ye?"

"It's a bird!" she whispered. "A *bird!*"

"Aw, hell!"

"Someone's going to die," she whispered, backing into the room. "*Oh, God, maybe it's Max. . . .*"

"That damned bastard!"

She hardly heard Ben. Her eyes were on the bird. It had swooped down the stairway; now it darted toward the hall window. It struck the window, and its wings beat frantically against the glass.

She whirled into the hall and seized the broom in the corner. "Get out of here!" she screamed, wildly swinging the broom. "Get out of here! Ben, open the door!"

Ben stood cursing in the middle of the room. She screamed again as the bird flew over her head; then grimly, silently, she went after it, intent on killing it. She chased it around the hall and into the parlor, and back into the hall. Suddenly it flew upstairs, and she tore after it.

When she reached the top of the stairs it had vanished. She went through both rooms, searching carefully, looking in and under everything. She could not find it. Maybe it was a swallow, just an ordinary swallow. Maybe it had managed to get out through the chimney or a hole in the attic. Maybe—but it didn't matter what kind of a bird it was, or where it had gone, so long as it was out of the house. What mattered was that it had been here. She could still see it at the moment of discovery, when she had peered up the stairway and saw it looking down at her with its little round bright knowing eye.

Sand kept sifting into her cot that afternoon when she tried to sleep. That, and the memory of the bird's little eye, kept her awake until after nightfall. She slept at last, fitfully, and awoke suddenly with the clock striking midnight.

Hurriedly she lighted a lantern and drew on her robe. She hated the prospect of the dark night and the wind, but the tower bothered her more. All at once she was terrified at the thought of climbing up alone through the empty blackness of the tower. She could see the bird's eye again, and now she could imagine it in the tower, grown huge and looking down at her from every turn of the winding stairs.

"I won't go," she muttered to herself. "I won't go."

Then she trembled, thinking: *I'm* the one who saw it. It was looking at *me*.

She peered out the window at the light. It seemed bright enough. Surely it would burn steadily until dawn.

She took off her robe and sank down on the cot again.

At the first gray light of day she was up and on her way to the tower. The wind was so strong she still had to lean against it, but it didn't seem quite so bad as yesterday. Up in the lantern the lamp seemed perfectly all right; in fact the flame was higher than she had expected it to be, considering it had been left untended, but she assumed this was the result of the wind.

Impatiently she waited until sunrise, then put out the flame and hurriedly cleaned the lamp and lenses, and drew the curtains. Now she got the spyglass and parted one of the lee curtains to study first the bay and then the cabin.

There was no sign of the cabin being occupied. But of course Max would wait for better weather.

Or would he? He'd been gone two days now. Why hadn't he come back the first night before the wind got bad? Surely he could have managed it.

But maybe he was back. Maybe she ought to go over to the cabin and make sure.

She went down to the cottage and hurried to fix breakfast. She was suddenly excited over the thought of getting away from Ben and the cottage and at the possibility of seeing Max again, this time with no one around.

She said to Ben, "I think I ought to go over to that

cabin and see if Max is back, so we can sort of make plans."

"Make plans for what?" Ben growled, glowering at her. His mood was no better this morning. His eyes were bloodshot and he had a rank smell that was a mixture of tobacco and sweat and soiled clothes.

"We've got to keep in touch with him!" she said irritably. "After all, he's in on this thing with us!"

"Yeah," he muttered darkly. "Yeah." He clenched his big hairy hands and scowled at his leg, which was stretched out on the stool in front of him. He was not wearing the peg leg in the house, for it meant keeping his knee bent, which made it almost impossible to sit down. "How d'ye know," he said, glaring at her, "that he ain't run out on us?"

"He wouldn't do that!"

"Like hell he wouldn't! I know 'is kind. He'd skip an' leave if'n he'd found something. I bet we never see 'im again."

She got up, white with sudden anger and apprehension. "Don't tell me he's not coming back! I know better. He's probably at the cabin now. I'm going over and see."

She dressed and went out, leaving her breakfast untouched.

It was more than a mile and a half to the cabin, and long before she came within sight of it she wished she had taken the mule and wagon. Still, it was better to walk, for if she had taken the wagon someone in the other cottage would have noticed and been curious. Anyway, the wind wasn't bad here in the woods.

When she saw the weeds growing in front of the sagging door of the cabin she had a hollow feeling in her stomach. But she hurried and looked hopefully inside.

The leaves and the litter over the dirt floor showed that no one had crossed the threshold for months.

She stood a moment gripping her hands; then, because the bay was not much farther, she went on to the pier. There was no sign of Max's sloop anywhere along the lee of the island or on the bay.

Slowly she started back to the reservation. Now little doubts and uncertainties began to gnaw at her. She nursed them with her suspicion of Max, with her jealousy of Charlotte, and they grew large and hateful. She raged. Then she pitied herself for the little life had given her, and walked for a half mile in deep sullen dejection, and raged again. As she neared the dunes and heard the roaring of the surf and felt the pressure of the wind and the sting of flying sand, there came over her such a hatred for her lot and such a loathing for the place that all at once she wished she had left with Max. Oh, what a fool she'd been to let him go away without her! They could have managed somehow. There was some money in the house—it was as much hers as Ben's—and it would have seen them through.

For of course Max hadn't found anything yet. Wouldn't he have told her if he had? Or would he?

Actually he hadn't told her a thing about his plans. Not a thing. He's been acting strange for days. . . .

But there was a reason for that. Oh, yes, there was a reason. . . .

Bella had been moving with her head down, leaning against the wind. She did not realize she was nearly home until she found herself crossing the sand drift at the side of the barn. Now suddenly she looked up and stopped abruptly, for Charlotte had just come out of the farther gate.

In an instant everything in her was concentrating on Charlotte. Every sand-flayed nerve and sense in all her wind-tortured being gathered and whipped tau͏t ͏at the hated sight of Charlotte, and all her inner raging whirled to a furious focus.

Oh, yes, damn you, she thought, staring at Charlotte. *You're the reason!* And in the next moment she had lost all capacity for rational action, and was moving swiftly over the sand toward Charlotte.

Charlotte had been waiting half the morning for a chance to tell Bella about the light, but Bella had gone off down the road before she could catch her. Last night, after midnight, the lamp had smoked. Just by accident she had looked out of the window and seen it growing dim, and she had rushed to get to it before it blacked out. Bella had not appeared.

In her loathing of any kind of scene Charlotte would have preferred writing her grievance, but this was too flagrant a breach of duty to put in a note. Letting the lamp go unattended was a serious matter. Had her Uncle Simon been well she would have left it in his hands. That being out of the question, she had resolved to see Bella herself.

But now, suddenly, she forgot the lamp. This had nothing to do with the lamp. This was a personal matter between two women.

At the sight of Bella's face she stopped at the edge of the sand drift, and all at once in a heightening of perception she saw Bella in slow motion, saw the widening of Bella's eyes and the thinning of the mouth, and the hooking of Bella's strong hands. And she thought, *She's coming at me. She wants to kill me. I'm going to have to fight her.*

In the space of moments while she stood watching Bella coming toward her, a little chain of things raced through her mind and she thought: She blames me for what happened. She's been out looking for Max and he hasn't come back, and after the other night she's afraid she's lost him. Aunt Emily's right—she knew him before they ever came here and there was something between them, but she didn't wait for him when he went to prison. That's what it is. That must be what it is . . . and now she wants him back and she can't have him. She hasn't any right to him. She's not good enough to wash his feet.

Then in the second before Bella struck her, she thought: Why am I standing here? I'm not the kind of woman who fights like this. It isn't even civilized. Oh, Lord, what would David think?

Then there was the jarring sting of Bella's hand against the side of her head, so hard that she staggered and nearly fell. And there was a jerk and a quick angry ripping of cloth—for an instant sickening before she responded in fury at being half disrobed. It suddenly did not matter what David would have thought. David and everything behind her belonged to another world and a different life.

She struck back at Bella, trying to use her fists as she'd seen men do. Bella clawed her and caught at her sleeve and tore it from her, but she kicked and got her hands in Bella's dress and ripped it from throat to hem. Her kerchief came loose and the wind whipped her hair about her face so that she could hardly see, and she felt the sting of sand on her naked back. There was a taste of blood in her mouth. But she got her hands on Bella and they fell together and began rolling over and over in the sand, each struggling to choke, to pound, to claw, to bite, to do anything possible to gain an advantage. They were in too much of a fury to waste breath screaming their hate, and so they fought silently. They were soon nearly exhausted.

Charlotte tore herself away and rose half blinded to her feet. Her dress was gone and her underthings were in shreds. Dimly she saw Bella rise and lurch wildly toward her like a drunken apparition, and in a final little burst of rage she caught the heavier woman's arm and jerked with all her strength and sent her tumbling headlong a dozen feet into the sand drift. Then she turned and stumbled away.

Bella struggled to her knees. She managed to rise. She moved unsteadily to her gate and clung there gasping for breath, sobbing with little dry, thick, bitter sobs of fury and frustration. She had not been beaten—but neither was she the victor. She had never expected this thin quiet woman with her infuriating calm to possess such wiry strength, or to turn on her and fight so savagely.

Her hair was loose and streaming in the wind, and she was half naked and her body burned with innumerable scratches. She had a horrible crawling sensation in her stomach, and her hate became a tearing thing as if all her organs were in the grip of a band of iron. Little spasms of frustrated fury shook her so that suddenly she was trembling violently. She held tightly to the gate with her broken fingernails digging into the wood, and hot needles shot through and through her brain.

She wished she'd had a knife, a hatchet, any sort of weapon. Dimly with her reddened eyes she saw the ax sticking in the chopping block at the woodpile, and she thought: I walked right by it. I could have picked it up and killed her.

Aloud, in a voice that was tight and hoarse, she cursed Charlotte.

Finally she began to think of getting into the house.

She could see no one about. Apparently no one had seen the fight. She crept through the arbor, hesitated, then ran on to her back porch and tiptoed up the steps. The sound of the wind covered any noise she might have made as she slipped into the kitchen and closed the door.

She unbuttoned her shoes—almost the only things that had been undamaged—and pulled off what remained of her clothing. Her hands were still trembling in reaction as she tried to comb her hair and wash. In the clothes-basket in the corner she found a soiled wrapper and drew it on. At last she looked at herself in the mirror over the sink. One eye was swelling and there was a cut along her upper lip, which was getting puffy. She decided she could not face Ben.

She hid her torn clothing, then slipped into the hall and started up the narrow stairs.

From the parlor Ben called, "Hey, what kept ye so damn long? Come here!"

"I—I'm sick," she said. "I'm going upstairs to bed."

"What the devil's wrong with ye? Did ye see that feller Call?"

"No, he's not back yet."

"What'd I tell ye, huh? The bastard's run out on us!"

She did not answer. She could not. Speech, suddenly, was impossible for her.

She fled up the stairs, thankful that Ben was unable to follow.

It was not until she had thrown herself trembling down on the bed that she remembered the bird.

II

In the kitchen of the other cottage Emily said, "Except for those scratches on your face, you don't look too bad now. Not too bad. It's as though you'd been clawed by a cat."

"I was. She's all cat."

"After a glimpse of what you did to her, I'd say the same of you. I got just a quick look at her before she reached the house. You made a mess of her."

"That's good. I intended to."

Emily stared at her. "I don't understand you, Charlotte. Indeed I don't. I should think you'd be a wreck. Why, it's the most unthinkable——" She stopped, then said almost plaintively, "I wish I'd seen it!"

"I'm glad you didn't," Charlotte said quietly. "How's Uncle Simon?"

"I gave him some more tea. He got it down before he realized what it was. He wasn't quite awake. Now he's safe till tomorrow."

"Aren't you afraid of the effect of so much of that stuff on him?"

"Oh, no." Emily shook her head. "I've seen it used before. Right now I'm a lot more concerned about you. How do *you* feel?"

Charlotte supposed that after the reaction set in she'd

be a wreck, but at the moment she felt almost exultant. But of course she couldn't tell Emily that. It was a little difficult to understand it herself, for actually her body ached; there were deep scratches down her back and across both shoulders and they burned with the stuff Emily had put on them. There was a bad bite on her arm that was beginning to throb. But none of it seemed to matter. In her old life, worlds and years away, she would have felt degraded by any such exhibition of physical violence. But it hadn't affected her that way. She felt strong and sure of herself, for the first time in her life. Actually she hadn't done anything except protect herself . . . well, it was a little more than that. It hadn't been entirely self-protection. . . .

"I feel all right now," she told Emily. "Please, don't ever say anything to Uncle Simon about it."

"I won't." Emily looked at her curiously. "But what *started* it, Charlotte? What ever came over her suddenly to——"

"*You* know what started it."

"Oh—him."

Emily looked away, thoughtful. She went over to the stove and poured more hot water into the teapot.

"You'd better have another cup," she said absently.

"No, I've had enough, thanks."

Suddenly Emily said, "I think you'd better be very careful, Charlotte. There's no telling what she's liable to do now."

"I'm not afraid of her. She's learned I can handle her."

"That isn't it. You simply can't trust a woman like that. If she'd whipped you, it'd be all over. But she didn't. She caught more than she bargained for. She's dangerous now, and where there's a man concerned, I wouldn't put it past her to try to kill you. I'd be very careful climbing the tower at night. It would be just like her to hide up there and push you down the stairs."

Charlotte listened with part of her mind, but she was suddenly thinking of Max. She found herself wanting to see him again, badly.

III

Bella paced her room. She had refused to come down at midday, and Ben had fixed his own lunch. Now she could hear him hobbling about the house, muttering to himself. Once he called to her angrily but she paid no attention to him. She moved jerkily across the bare floor, sometimes stopping in front of the wardrobe to stare at nothing with widening eyes, or going to the bed and sitting down a moment—only to rise instantly as if her body were made of a steel spring. She could not sit still. She could not think. She was oblivious of any physical feeling except the iron tightening that had gone all through her.

The wind, the island, the cottage, Ben—everything that made up her life or touched on it was intolerable to her. She wanted to destroy. Had there been anything breakable in the room she would have smashed it, but there was nothing here but the wooden bed, the empty wardrobe, a table and a chair. All of her things and Ben's were downstairs.

There was no outlet for her mental storm, and it filled her with a blackness that pressed down on her mind and drove her, finally, back to bed. With twilight she fell into a tormented sleep, from which she awoke suddenly as on the previous night with the clock striking twelve.

She groped downstairs in the dark. But now, as before, she refused to go out. Rebelliously she waited until daylight before climbing the tower.

She made only a pretense of cleaning the lamp. In the middle of it, while she was polishing the chimney, a little spasm of awakening fury shot through her and she hurled the chimney upon the iron floor where it smashed into a thousand pieces.

She turned and looked angrily out over the island, seeing nothing at first but the hated dunes and the pines. Then suddenly her attention focused on the distant cabin. Even without a glass she could make out the faint dark streamer of wind-driven smoke slanting from the chimney. She caught her breath and stared.

Then in a flash, trembling, she was hurrying down from the light and back to the cottage. In her mind the cabin had all at once become an oasis in an intolerable desert. She longed to fly there, to see Max, to be reassured. If she could have that reassurance . . .

In the kitchen she collected herself and tried to think. Ben was outside—through the window she saw him leaving the outhouse and moving toward the barn. He was wearing the peg leg he had made and walking with it—with the aid of a cane—without too much difficulty. She whirled to the stove, got breakfast going, then ran through the house to the bedroom and dressed, combed her hair and tied it back, and tried unsuccessfully to hide the bruises on her face with powder.

In the kitchen again she gulped a cup of day-old coffee warming on the edge of the stove, ate a leftover johnnycake and a piece of half-done bacon and hurried outside.

She ran into Ben as she went around the side of the barn.

"Where ye goin'?" he demanded, staring at her.

"To see Max—he's back!"

"I don't believe it!"

"I don't care what you believe—he's back, and I'm going to see him!"

"Ye ain't a-goin' no place till ye've fixed my breakfast!"

"Go fix your own damned breakfast!" she snapped. "It's on the stove. And don't tell me where I can go or where I can't—I'll go where I please!"

She started away, but he caught her arm and jerked her around.

"Git back in the house!" he ordered hoarsely. "Ye're actin' mighty damn funny. All ye kin think about is that bastard Call. I don't like it. By God, I'm beginning to think there's somethin' goin' on between you two!"

Her eyes widened on him. She was suddenly trembling with pent-up fury. Her nostrils caught his sweaty smell; she wanted to spit on him. "Get your dirty hand off me," she said through her clenched teeth.

His big fingers tightened on her and he pulled her toward him with such force that he almost lost balance.

"Sure," he snarled, "there's been somethin' goin' on! I know it now! Goddam ye!" He struck her hard with the cane, and instantly she lashed out at him with her free hand, twisting and kicking, so that he was forced to turn her loose to avoid falling.

But he had gone too far. The storm that had been raging in her since her fight with Charlotte suddenly burst. She had hated him for months, and now she turned on him with all her accumulated furies. She spat on him. "Yes, you dirty pig!" she shrilled. "Yes! Yes! Yes! I had a lot to do with him once—and that's more than I can say for you! You're not a man! You're just a big dirty stupid fool!"

She backed into the woodpile to escape his cane, and groped wildly for something to hit him with.

With a little gasp that had the sound of joy she saw the ax. She caught it up fiercely with both hands and swung it at him with all her strength, and she continued to swing it until his body had ceased its spasmodic jerking on the sand.

CHAPTER *17*

I

WHILE he waited for the coffeepot to come to a boil in the fireplace, Max cut a limb from a young pine and used it to sweep out the litter of leaves on the cabin floor. He worked quickly, cleaning the place with a seaman's thoroughness and dislike of dirt, although his mind was on other matters. Occasionally he glanced out of one of the long narrow windows slotting the sides. The windows, covered by hinged planks that he had propped open with sticks, had been planned to give a clear view of every approach. The height of the cabin on the knoll made it possible to see a long stretch of the curving road, the landing and the pier, and most of the bay. A good glass would have disclosed details of the city nine miles away on the mainland.

A trace of smoke in the approximate area of the river mouth interested him for a minute. Was it the troopship? He knew it was still at the dock. It had to be, for he would have seen it if it had come out into the bay. Until dawn this morning it would have been impossible for it to leave. Last night the wind had moderated, but no skipper in his right mind would have attempted the pass in the black dark, even if the tide had been right.

The tide was high now—and it wouldn't be high again till tomorrow morning, the tides being what they were on this coast. He turned from the window, knowing he did not have to worry about the vessel for another twenty-four hours, when there would be enough water for it to get over the bar.

Bethsheba had picked up a story that the troopship had actually come in for repairs and would probably lie at the dock for a fortnight or more. It was a comforting thought, but he did not intend to be lulled by it. The vessel might leave any day. When it happened he wanted to know it.

One extra man with only a pair of old pistols might not have much effect against a mob well-armed with modern rifles, but when the time came the least he could do would be to head for the city and be with Cassius.

The coffee was boiling. He set it aside, greased the skillet with a piece of bacon and mixed up a stiff batter for a hoecake. The hoecake filled the skillet and he waited impatiently for it to brown, for he had not touched hot food since leaving Cassius Drew's house Monday morning.

What day was this? Wednesday? He frowned, thinking of the time he had been away from the island, and of the two days he'd been forced to spend on the boat. Monday morning he had looked out to see the boat dragging anchor—it was a poor homemade affair, that anchor—and there'd been nothing to do but to get aboard fast and break out the jib and run for it until he was far down by St. Vincent and had a little protection. Then had come the slow job of beating his way back up the lower bay yesterday and finally crossing to the tip of St. George.

Wednesday! Oh, hell, and he'd planned on getting back here Monday.

He fished the brown hoecake into a tin plate, smothered it with cane sirup and poured coffee. He sat down on the bench by the door to eat, but with a thoughtful glance out at the road he got up suddenly and heaped chips and bark in the fireplace until smoke was pouring up the crudely built brick chimney.

That would tell them he was back. Bella would see it first, being the first one up in the tower every morning, but maybe Charlotte would remember the cabin and climb up sometime during the morning for a look. Lassaphene never entered the tower until evening—if he were entering it at all now—although he did not care whether the keeper saw the smoke or not. Better to have it out with Lassaphene as soon as possible. The man would have to learn that he had no jurisdiction beyond the limits of the reservation.

As he considered the task ahead, Max wished suddenly that he had been able to see Janus again. He needed Janus now. He badly needed someone he could trust—and who better than Janus? He would come, of course, for Bethsheba had promised to send him as soon as he got back from a turtling trip—but with the way the weather had been that might not be for another week or two.

He poured himself a second cup of coffee and carried it to the south window and stood sipping it while he studied the far turn of the road through the pines. The sun—the first touch of real sun since the wind had started—was slanting in bright shafts through the trees and making little spots of white on the sandy road. From a pond he saw three egrets fly up into a shaft of sunlight over the road and vanish above the treetops. Was someone coming?

Then he heard a bluejay scolding in the distance. Someone must be coming.

While he watched the road he groped for something Cassius had told him when they'd been talking about the gold. It was one of those off-the-track comments that Cassius had a way of making when he wanted you to think about a matter. This concerned the verities. How had he put it—that a man had to discover them for himself? True enough, no doubt—but how did it apply to a ship that had been driven for a half mile over the island, pounding over the hard sand and spewing her armament and gear all along the route with every lurch and roll? He'd found the rotting prow of that vessel wedged in the pocket where Cassius had found it, with some of the timbers—what was left of them—right on the surface of the sand. No doubt many a man out hunting, probably even Branch Clabo, had scuffed his boots on one of those timbers and thought it no more than a piece of half-buried driftwood or perhaps the rotting trunk of a fallen tree.

Had Cassius, when he found those rotting timbers long

ago, been able to view them from such a philosophical height that he had not permitted himself to go farther? Wouldn't any man have gone on and dug? Cassius wasn't any man—but treasure is treasure, and Cassius was only human.

There was something Cassius hadn't told him . . . something Cassius wanted him to find out for himself.

The bluejay was scolding again, shrilly.

He turned and, cup in hand, went outside for a better look at the road.

II

Emily Lassaphene glanced up at the tower. Something, she thought, looked wrong. She finished sweeping the sand from the front steps, then glanced up again.

Charlotte, coming around the side of the cottage with a watering can, said, "Now what do you see?"

"It's the lantern curtains," said Emily. "They haven't been lowered."

"*Oh!*"

Charlotte dropped the watering can and ran out on the tower walk.

Emily said, "It's *her* place. *I'll* tell her."

"We'll settle that later," said Charlotte, hurrying. If a house were afire, she thought, you wouldn't argue about whose duty it was to throw water on it. Maybe a little sunlight wouldn't hurt the lenses—but the sun had come out strong again this morning and it was high enough now for the direct rays to crack a lens belt, if left uncovered.

She climbed to the lantern and hastily lowered the east curtains. Then she saw the smashed lamp chimney and the exposed lamp with the lens belt swinging wide. It wasn't just an accident—she could tell that at a glance. The chimney had been thrown, not dropped. She felt a sudden vestal wrath at this desecration, but because the light came first and must always be ready, she filled the lamp and brought a new shade for it. But she did not clean up the broken glass.

She lowered the remaining curtains, then paused by the gallery door for a hopeful glance across the island.

Instantly she saw the dark streamer of smoke coming from the cabin. For a moment she forgot the lamp. She wanted to sing.

She went almost gaily down the stairs and outside, then she stopped abruptly at the fork in the boardwalk and frowned at the Haik cottage. She bit her lip, but all at once she gave a little jerk of her head and, for the first time since coming to the island, crossed the Haik yard and went up to the door and knocked.

When there was no answer she called, "Mrs. Haik?" Then, louder: "Mr. Haik? Is anyone home?"

Finally she went around the side between the two cottages, and up on the back porch. Again she knocked and called. She sensed the emptiness of the place and a little prickling went over her scalp. The kitchen door was open and she could see smoke rising from the frying pan and smell bacon burning. She turned and peered through the door of the hallway. A spilled powder box was on the floor, and scattered near the foot of the stairs were several articles of clothing—a woman's shoe, a roll of what seemed to be underthings and a bit of ribbon.

Charlotte went into the kitchen and thrust the frying pan over on the far side of the stove, then hurried outside and around to the front of her own cottage where Emily waited.

"Is Uncle Simon awake?" she asked.

Emily looked at her sharply and shook her head.

"That's good," said Charlotte. "Now we'll have a chance to find out—I think there's something wrong next door." She told about the clothes and the frying pan.

Emily said, "I heard them out back before breakfast, near the barn. Sounded like they . . ." She began walking slowly around the house.

Charlotte followed. They went out through the gate and around to the barn. Under the open part they stopped and stood silently in the shade by the spring wagon while they glanced around at the shop, the woodpile, the long sand drift, and finally at the corral across the road where the mule watched them by the watering trough.

Emily said, "Sounded like they were having an argument, but I didn't pay much attention. I couldn't see them around on this side of the barn. I saw him come out of the house, wearing that new peg leg he made. Then in a little while she came, and I heard him swearing. . . ."

"The woman was in a temper," said Charlotte. "She broke a lamp chimney; just threw it on the lantern floor."

They were silent a moment.

Emily looked at the woodpile. Near it on the sand were several rolls of tarpaulins and old sails, partially opened.

"Well," she said, "at least he was working for a change. Simon told him a month ago to take that canvas out and air it before the mildew ate it up. He must have been doing that when she came out. I don't know where they could have gone except down the road—but why would they do that?"

Charlotte gripped her hands, then said quietly, "Mr. Call is back."

"How do you know that?"

"I saw smoke over at that cabin the guards built."

"Then that's the answer," Emily said in relief. "For a minute I, well—I had the queerest feeling. I was just sure something had happened. But of course that's the answer. She must have seen the smoke and wanted to go over there—and likely they got into an argument about it, and she went on down the road and he followed."

She stopped and turned her head, listening. "Did you hear Simon call?"

"I didn't notice."

"That sounded like Simon. He's probably awake and wants something. I'd better go."

Emily went back through the gate, but Charlotte stood motionless, still gripping her hands. She looked off where the road vanished in the pines, and took a few hesitant steps away from the bed. She passed the half-opened bundles of old canvas and saw something near them on the sand. It looked like Ben Haik's cane.

She stopped abruptly and stared at the pile of canvas.

In the next instant she saw the protruding peg leg, and near it the ax. Her eyes widened and she put her hand to her mouth, then backed away. She looked down the road again. Beyond the sand drift, in the fresh whiteness of the wind-scoured road, a single set of woman's footprints followed the wheel track toward the pines.

"That devil!" Charlotte whispered. *"She's gone to him. God knows what she'll tell him!"*

She glanced back at the house, then started swiftly down the road.

III

Bella was a shadow when he saw her, leaning in movement against the light like a figure running; she was not running but he gained that instant impression of flight from her forward-leaning body, so that the thought of flight stayed with him even after she had left the road and was coming up the slope toward him. She was wearing a green dress and carried a carpetbag. As she reached the top of the knoll she stopped and leaned against a pine, dropped the bag and closed her eyes a moment. Her bonnet had fallen back over her shoulders and he could see the bruise under her eye and the bright beads of moisture on her forehead. She was out of breath, and her face was oddly pale. Suddenly she opened her eyes and looked at him, and he was startled by their paleness in the sunlight. She seemed to be looking at him with little sharp points of steel.

"I've left Ben," she said. "You've got to take me away."

There was no color even in her voice. It was flat, without inflection.

He stared at her, suddenly wondering what he had ever seen in this woman, amazed that his imagination had been able to create such a powerful illusion from her. Now here she was, appearing abruptly at a time like this, announcing that she had left her husband and practically demanding that he take her away.

"Good Lord!" he burst out. "What's the matter with you?"

"I just told you—I've left him! And I'm not going back!" A metallic edge had crept into her voice.

"This is a hell of a time to do that! What happened?"

"We—we had a fight. He—he accused me of all kinds of things. He hit me." All at once her chin quivered, and she became plaintive, almost tearful, but the steely points of her eyes never left him. "He beat me!" she wailed. "See?" She touched the bruise under her eye, and then pulled the top of her dress down over one shoulder to show him the long deep scratches running from her neck to her arm. "Oh, Max, it was awful! So the minute I saw the smoke coming from here I packed and ran out of the house. I won't go back! I'll never go back!"

He stood there scowling at her, still holding the tin cup of coffee he had brought outside when he heard the bluejay scolding.

"And what am I supposed to do?" he said finally.

"You promised you'd take me away! You promised it! You—you can't go back on me now when I need help!" She came over to him and caught his arm. "Please, Max—if you care anything at all about me you'll take me away from here right now. I—I can't stand it if I have to stay on this dreadful island any longer!"

His jaws knotted. "I didn't promise I'd take you away on demand. I said I'd see that you got away when the right time came. This isn't the time for it. I spent two days fighting the wind trying to get back here, and I've hardly had a chance to clean up and eat breakfast. What's more, I haven't got a copper. How d'you ex-pect——"

"I've got money! I've got more than three hundred dollars——"

"Then you don't need me. If you refuse to stay on the reservation, I'll take you over to the city and leave you."

"I don't want to go over to the city," she said instantly. "I—I want to get as far away from it as I can. I want to go to Mobile—or even New Orleans." Her voice began to rise. "And I don't want to wait. I want to go now—right now!"

He turned from her and placed his coffee cup carefully on the block of wood by the door.

"Don't be a fool," he said, looking at her intently. "You ought to know my little vessel isn't able to go outside now. Hear that surf! It'll be that way for another day or two. We'd never get over the bar—let alone make it to Mobile."

"The lighthouse boat could make it," she said.

"The tiller and all the gear are locked in the cabin. Anyway——"

"Oh, dear—I forgot the Lassaphenes have the key. But what's to stop us from breaking the lock?"

"I'm to stop it! What makes you think I'd steal a vessel just to give you a pleasure cruise away from Ben?"

"Oh, you!" she said furiously. "You weren't too good to steal your boat when you were getting away!"

"That was different. I was fleeing for my life. Anyway I stole it from a pair of drunken soldiers in Key West who had no business with a boat."

Her face seemed to contract. "I'm fleeing for my life, too."

He snorted. "Running away from that fool Ben. The sooner you wake up and go back——"

"Ben's dead," she said stonily. "I can't go back."

"He's *what?*"

"He's dead. I—I killed him."

"I don't believe it!"

"You'd better believe it! You're in it too! He found
out about us and tried to kill me, so I—I had to do it!
Now you've got to help me! You—you owe it to me!"

Suddenly he felt an almost irresistible urge to strike
her and tell her that he owed her nothing whatever. But
he turned from her and pounded his fists slowly together
and tried to see his way through the mental storm she
had loosened in him. He was caught again in the maelstrom that had whirled him under on the morning of his
arrival here. It blocked reason and made a nightmare
of reality.

"Let me think," he muttered, and the words might
have been a prayer. Suddenly he turned and looked at
her again. She had betrayed him before, and she would
not stop now. He could see it in her eyes.

"Where is he?" he asked.

"Out by the—the woodpile."

"How did you do it?"

For a moment he thought she was not going to answer.
Then she spat it at him: "With the ax—and I'd do it
again!"

"God!"

After a moment he said, "You left him there—right
there in the sand?"

"I—I piled those old tarpaulins over him."

He turned away and started down the knoll.

She said quickly, "Where are you going?"

"To have a look at things."

"That won't do any good. I want you to take me
away."

He stopped and looked back at her. "I'm not going to take you away—not now, or ever. Get that in your head. And don't you try running the pass now—because you'll never get over the bar alone. I'll do what I can for you. But I've got to look things over—and I've got to think."

CHAPTER *18*

━━━━━━━━━━━━━━━

I

HE WENT down the knoll to the road and started toward
the reservation. There was little or nothing he could do
there, and he knew it. What was done, was done. But
he had to clear his mind. He had to put Bella and the
cabin out of his sight before he could view anything in its
proper relationship.

He reached the little pond where he had seen the
egrets, and his tortured eyes took in the quiet water
and the lily pads and the shadows of the great cypress
trees that filled the pond and raised their tops high into
the wind. He could hear the steady singing of the wind
through the branches, and far off across the island he

could hear the mighty shuddering pounding of the surf. Bethsheba's war drums. Violence had come and gone, and this was the aftermath. The island was used to that. Long before his time the island had known the violence of both nature and man, and it would continue to know them long after he was gone. What was the murder of a man of no importance by a woman who had suddenly become important only because she had killed? In the days of the island's years it made no difference. It would pass and be forgotten. It did not really matter. Not, at least, to the island and the great scheme of things.

But at this moment it mattered. It mattered to him, now. And it might matter greatly to others. It upset every calculated plan. . . .

He went on, slowly, clenching his hands.

He was not aware of Charlotte until he heard his name spoken, and he raised his head abruptly and found her hurrying toward him, bareheaded and breathless.

At the sudden and unexpected sight of her he stopped for a moment; then profoundly grateful for her presence he went quickly on to meet her. He had not even hoped for the chance of talking to her so soon.

Deep concern had heightened the sensitiveness of her face. "Max, I—you've seen her?"

"Aye," he ground out. "She's at the cabin."

"Then you know what—what she did?"

"She told me. I got it out of her. How did you find out? Did you . . . see it?"

"No, I—I found Ben. And she forgot to hide the ax."

"God!"

He stared down at her; and she, seeing the storm in his eyes, reached forth and took his hand as if to steady him.

"I knew you must be back," she said. "I saw the smoke. And when I realized she'd come this way, I—I was terribly worried. You see, this is going to involve you. It's bound to—unless we can think of something. I thought maybe I . . . "

"I'm glad you came. I had to get away from her . . . try to think it out. She wanted me to take her away. I won't do that. Of all the . . . "

She said quietly, "She doesn't mean anything to you any more, does she?"

"How did you know she ever did?"

"Women just know some things—how isn't important."

"Well, she did mean something to me once, during the war. I don't know why, unless she was different then—or unless it was just the times. I thought about her a lot while in prison, and when I came back and found she'd . . . Anyway, she doesn't mean a thing to me now—and I don't say that just because of what happened today."

She shook her head. "I see how you must have felt."

They were at the edge of the pines and there were trees here along the road that had fallen during the last hurricane. She moved over to one of the trees and sat down, and peered up at him silently a moment.

"I'm glad you told me what you did. Now we can talk about her frankly. You see, this will have to be reported, just as soon as possible. Uncle Simon——"

"Does he know about it?" he interrupted.

"Not yet. Aunt Emily finally managed to give him sedatives after you left, so he's been in bed for the past two days. I'm the only one who knows. I'm just trying to think. Someone will have to go to the city—and if

Uncle Simon isn't able, then I'll have to go. I've never handled the boat alone, but I suppose I can. You see, the Customs Office will have to be notified—and of course they'll send men over immediately, and there'll be an inquiry. As I understand it, the army is running everything now, so I expect they'll send soldiers over."

She stopped and looked up at him again, and bit her lip. "Do you see what I'm getting at?"

He nodded and fumbled for his pipe. She watched him silently while he filled it and went through the ritual of lighting it. The pipe went out almost immediately, but he was unaware of it.

He said, "Even if I had been willing to go away with her, I'd hate to attempt the pass now. But I did offer to take her over to the city and leave her."

Charlotte did not seem surprised. "But what good would that do her?"

"She's got some money. She could buy passage inland on one of the river boats. I don't know how conditions are now, but one or two boats must still be running."

"Where could she go on a river boat?"

"Connect with a stage or a railroad and go any-where—Tallahassee, Jacksonville, Atlanta—but travel these days might be pretty bad for a lone woman. Maybe that's why she didn't want to try it."

"Max, if you were in her place, what would you do?"

"I—I don't know. It would depend on how I felt. As for me, I'm tired of running. I've had to run and hide, but I'd rather fight than be a fugitive."

"This isn't a question of fighting—it's a matter of how you're going to face something. She's having to face something now, and so are you."

Charlotte traced patterns in the sand with her finger.

"I don't care about her," she said. "I—I won't judge her. Let God do that. I'm going to sit right here and wait as long as I can, and not do anything about her until I'm forced to. Because, as soon as she's reported, there'll be people over here . . . and if there's a trace of you around——"

He moved restlessly about on the narrow road, then stopped and frowned down at her.

"I hate like fury to go away from here now," he said. "Even for a few days. And it isn't just because of this." He drew out his gold piece and turned it in his hand, then put it away. He said, troubled, "There are so many things. . . . "

"Max, you've *got* to leave!"

"I don't like it. I don't like going away at a time like this and leaving everything on your shoulders."

"What difference does that make?"

"It makes a lot of difference. If your uncle is sick, it'll be putting the whole ugly mess right in your lap. For one thing, there's Ben——"

Her lips firmed. It was odd to see the sudden strength in a face so sensitive. "Ben will just have to lie there until the time comes to move him."

"Why do you do this for me?"

"It isn't much."

"I'd say it was a lot."

"But you helped me. And it was the cause of your being sent away. I—I felt awfully bad about that."

"Oh, that didn't matter. You shouldn't have worried about it. You knew I'd be back, didn't you?"

"Yes, of course. And it's because I believe in certain things that I—I want to do all I can for you."

"But you don't believe in the things I believe in."

"Perhaps not, but I believe in you."

He frowned. "How can you believe in me if you don't believe in the things I believe in?"

"Because I—I know how you feel, and why. Because I've been thinking a great deal about all you told me that night when we went after Uncle Simon. I can see I've been as one-sided in my thinking as you've been in yours. I believe in time, when you realize it's all one country——"

"It isn't one country," he interrupted. "It's two countries, with one devouring the other to make it one."

"No, Max. It's one country blindly devouring part of itself. If you can realize that——"

"It doesn't matter how you state it. Nothing on earth will ever change how I feel."

"I realize that—now that I know you better. You'll always have to fight. And with the way things are, I expect you'll always be needed. But I—I just want you to see it clearly, so that you'll fight the right thing."

He looked down at her, strangely agitated. "Why should all this matter to you?"

"It just does." She looked away. "There are some things you can't explain."

He touched her hair. It was neither gold nor red, but here in the flecked sunlight and shadow of the pines it was gold. She turned and looked up at him suddenly, and the way she moved her head made him think of the sea birds on the beach, the white circling terns that had followed her as if she were one of them.

Suddenly he was aware of the deep scratches on her cheek and neck.

"Something clawed you," he said.

Charlotte said nothing.

"Good Lord, did she do it?"

"Yes."

"She looked as though she'd been through something. She told me Ben had beaten her."

"Ben didn't beat her, so far as I know. We had a fight. Don't ask me to explain it; those things just happen. I'm glad no one saw it."

"But she's bigger than you! She might have killed you!"

"Hardly—though she tried to. But let's forget it."

She stood up. "If we went down by that pond, do you think we could see——" She stopped abruptly and caught his arm, whispering, "There's someone coming."

A man was coming. A Negro. They saw him stumble into view fifty yards away where the road curved at the end of the pond. He was just another Negro at first, a stocky bareheaded man in white pantaloons and shirt, moving drunkenly in the shadow of the trees, his bare feet dragging in the sandy wheel track. Then suddenly they both realized there was something wrong; they could see it in him and feel it about him, and it seemed to be repeated in the high thin sound of the wind and the heavy rumbling of the surf, and it was in the air and the heat and the sudden shrill singing of the locusts, and in the sharper smell of the pines.

There was something wrong. The man wasn't drunk. He was hurt. One sleeve had been torn from his shirt to make a crude bandage for his arm. There was a splash of scarlet on his clothes.

They both began running toward him at the same time, for the man was Janus.

When he saw them Janus stopped and leaned against a pine. They thought he would fall before they reached him, but he did not.

"I'm all right," he told them. "Just tired. Come to

tell you, Cap'n. It's happened, like I said it would. It's happened." His eyes were very bright and feverish and full of pain, and his brown face had the grayness of earth, but he was not excited. There was in him instead the sort of sickness that gets into a man when he has been forced to view something abhorrent to his nature. It showed in his eyes.

"*What* happened, Janus? Where've you been? I thought you were down the coast fishing!"

"No, Cap'n. Not at a time like this." Janus ran his tongue over his gray lips. "I made like I was going off, but I didn't. I ran up in East Bay, back of Clabo's. Been fishin' there, so I could be close to things, so I could get back to the city quick. I just come from Clabo's. Don't you go there, Cap'n. Don't *any* of you folks go there. That's what I came to tell you: *Don't any of you leave the island.*"

Max looked incredulously at Janus. "If I ever get my hands on Branch I'll kill him for turning those rifles over to the Bureau! But go on—what's happening now?"

"You don't have to kill 'im, Cap'n. He's dead. They've got his head stuck on a pole outside the door."

Charlotte gasped, "No—oh, no!"

Janus closed his eyes and slid suddenly down to the foot of the pine and sat there as if he had gone to sleep. "He's fainted," said Charlotte. "He's lost so much blood. We've got to take him to the reservation." But Janus opened his eyes and said weakly, "I'm all right, ma'am. I'm just tired. Just let me rest."

Max said, "You've got a bad knife cut—it's still bleeding. Go on and talk, Janus, while I tie it up better. Try to tell us what happened." He tore off his shirt and ripped it in strips, and began whipping a bandage around the long slash that Janus' torn sleeve had hardly covered.

Janus said, "When the wind came I ran in back of the point behind Clabo's, and that boy o' mine went ashore to get drunk. Early this morning I walked across the point to get that boy, 'n' I heard Lily Bright screaming. First thing I saw at the tavern was Mr. Branch's head on the pole. Then I saw that Pinchy 'n' some o' his friends. They'd gone wild, Cap'n. A boatload of 'em had sailed over from the city last night to get more whisky—seems like they'd run out o' whisky in the city—an' they'd gone drunk 'n' wild. That boy o' mine had joined 'em, 'n' he was wild too. I tried to take 'im away 'n' he turned on me quick with a knife 'n' cut me 'n' said he was serving the king—not me. You hear that, Cap'n—the *king!* That crazy boy. They were all crazy, drunk 'n' wild. I don't know all that happened before I got there, but I think Mr. Branch had talked gold to 'em an' tried to buy 'em off. Anyhow, they were talking about gold, 'n' they'd torn the place apart 'n' couldn't find it . . . 'n' I saw 'em take a knife to that little Hermes. . . ."

Janus closed his eyes, and Max said grimly, "Why didn't you go to the city and get help? Tell those soldiers——"

"Cap'n, the soldiers have gone. An' those rascals, they've taken the city. That's what I've been tryin' to tell you."

Max gaped at him, utterly dumfounded.

"But that can't be!" he cried. "Janus, you must be wrong! Why, that troopship is still there!"

Janus looked up at him miserably. "I know, Cap'n. That fooled me too. But I learned the truth before I left Clabo's. The politicians wanted those soldiers out

of there, 'n' when they couldn't get 'em out on the troopship, they sent 'em upcountry on a river boat."

"Oh, God! When did that happen?"

"Monday afternoon. Then things broke loose right
away."

"Monday—and this is *Wednesday!* Oh, hell and
heaven!" Max stood up, suddenly white, shaken. "I've
got to get over there! Right now! Charlotte, can you
manage——"

Janus, in quick alarm, said, "No—no! You keep away
from there! You can't do anything!"

"I can try!" Max cried. "I've got to! I can't let
Cassius——"

Janus struggled to his feet. "Cap'n—*please*, Cap'n—
listen to me! You can't help him now. You can't help
anybody over there. Before I came here I cut across the
upper bay 'n' sailed down through the harbor. All along
the docks there were Bureau men with rifles. They shot
at me just to be shooting at something. An' there are
bodies in the water. I saw three in the channel when I
headed over here. Cap'n, if Mr. Cassius is alive, he's
locked up in his house like all the other good people are,
an' he's prayin'. That's all he can do now. Just pray."

Max clenched his fists and stood looking desperately
into space.

Charlotte said earnestly, "Janus is right. Can't you
see? You'd be risking all for nothing. There must be
some other way, something . . ."

Max thrust his hands into his pockets. The hollows in
his face deepened. They were right, of course. He'd
been thinking with his heart, and refusing to see the
utter imbecility of even attempting to enter the city
during the day. If he waited till night it might be pos-

sible to get Cassius and his mother out of there—if they were still alive—but it wouldn't help the hundreds of others or change what had happened. Oh, why hadn't he kept his eyes open around Branch and realized how the man had been dealing? Why hadn't he listened to Cassius and watched Branch from the first? But it was too late now. It was too late. If he had all the gold on the island it wouldn't help. . . .

"That damned gold!" he spat out.

What could he do? What could he possibly do?

He strode across the road and turned, and stopped suddenly in his tracks. There *was* something he could do. Probably, at this moment, he was the only person available who could do it.

But preparations would have to be made. He would have to see Lassaphene and make peace with him, and see that Janus was taken care of. And there was Bella. He'd forgotten all about Bella. He would have to let her know what had happened.

"Janus," he said, "do you think you can make it to the lighthouse?"

"If we take it easy, Cap'n, I can get there."

Charlotte said, "I could go ahead and get the mule and wagon."

"No, that would take too long. I'll carry Janus if he gets tired. I want your uncle to sew up his arm, and I've——"

"Max, what are you going to do?"

"I'll tell you later. You two start walking. I'll catch up with you in a few minutes. I've got to let that woman know. . . ."

He turned and began running in the direction of the cabin.

II

As he ran he wondered what a man like Branch Clabo, in his extremity, might have said to Pinchy about gold. Not that it would have stopped Pinchy—especially a drunken Pinchy who had hateful memories of Branch's father and who had probably been waiting for years for the chance to draw Clabo blood. But if Branch had mentioned gold, then he must have mentioned the island. How long would it take Pinchy's twisted whisky-crazed brain to focus its attention on the lighthouse? But maybe that wouldn't happen. Maybe, with enough whisky in him, the "king" would just go to sleep.

At first he thought Bella was gone. Then he saw her sitting on the bench in the shadow beyond the fireplace. An empty coffee cup sagged in her hand. Her shoulders drooped and she looked up at him dejectedly and opened her mouth as if to speak, but said nothing. All at once he felt an overwhelming pity for her. After all, he thought, we inherit our natures. If the vessel sails poorly, is it the fault of the vessel, or the hand of the shipwright that shaped it? Aye, let God be the judge.

He said, "There's trouble over in the city. Whatever you do, don't attempt to go over there. The troops have pulled out and a bunch of renegade blacks from the Bureau have taken things over."

"I saw that colored man go by," she said in a low voice. "I wondered."

"The devils are over at Clabo's, too. Some of them may take it into their heads to come over here. To be on the safe side, I think you'd better go back to the reservation."

"No. I'll not do that. I'll never go back there!"

"Suit yourself."

He opened his bag and jerked out a shirt and his case of pistols. "Bella, are you armed?"

"Yes. There's a pistol in my bag." Suddenly she said, "Why won't you take me away? Is it because of that Mrs. Maynard?"

"Not entirely that, no."

"But you do love her, don't you?"

Faced with the fact of it, he nodded slowly. "Yes." He was a little astounded that such a truth should now be apparent. Then he shrugged and started for the door. "But a lot of good it does either of us now."

"Max—what am I going to do?"

He stopped and looked back at her. She was standing up now, and in the shadow the hardness seemed to have gone out of her pale eyes and her face was tragic.

"I'm sorry, Bella, but that's up to you. We have to make our own decisions. I've just had to make one, and it's come damned hard." Then suddenly he thought: I can't go off and leave her like this. I've got to help her somehow. He said, "Bella, take my boat and get under way. There are provisions on board, and there's more stuff here—take all of it you want. Go on down the bay and anchor at the other end of St. Vincent until the weather clears. If you watch the weather you'll have no trouble reaching Mobile."

He strode out, stopped briefly at the corner of the cabin to study the bay in the direction of Clabo's, then ran down to the road, struggling into the gray shirt as he ran.

He passed the cypress pond and again the distant familiar thunder of the surf seemed to come to him louder, and the high shrilling of the locusts seemed to reach a pitch of madness in the heat. He wondered if everyone, with the awareness of danger, felt this heightened perception of all things in nature.

Charlotte and Janus were halfway through the pines, waiting, when he came up with them. Now, approaching, he saw the reservation's mule and wagon. Captain Lassaphene was driving.

CHAPTER *19*

1

LASSAPHENE backed the wagon across the road and stood up, holding the reins with one hand while he braced himself a little unsteadily against the seat. His eyes were sunken, and a gray stubble ran down his gaunt jaws and merged with his goatee. He had the look of a tired baffled man swaying on a delicate balance between curiosity and anger. His protruding lower lip was working soundlessly as he turned on them, a flame and a question in his eyes.

"What's going on here?" he demanded, before anyone could speak. "Mr. Call, I was under the impression that

I ordered you off the island. What are you doing back here?"

Max said patiently, "Captain, let us be friends. You've no right to order a man off his own property—but that's of no importance now. Something very bad has happened. This is a time when we need each other's help."

"Eh?" Lassaphene stared at him, and looked sharply at Janus. He sat down slowly and peered at Charlotte. "You tell me, Charlotte."

She told him about the Haiks, then wisely she waited while his mind grappled with the problem of them.

He swore, and muttered darkly, "What a thing to have happen here!" He shook his head and added, "Now we'll have to go to the city. This will have to be reported."

Charlotte looked at Max, and he said, "Captain, unfortunately that's out of the question. The soldiers have left the city and there's been an insurrection. The Freedmen—or rather a certain faction in the Freedmen's Bureau—have taken over. There's an armed mob on the loose over there, and the citizens are defenseless. Some of the mob went over to Clabo's to get more whisky, and they've killed Clabo. Janus here has just come from there. He's got a bad knife cut, Captain, and it'll have to be stitched. If you can take care of him, I'll ride over to the reservation with you while we talk over what to do. And, Captain, we must hurry. I realize this is a lot to thrust on you all at once, but there are people's lives at stake. Every hour we delay . . ."

It was, Max saw, almost too much for a man in Lassaphene's condition to grasp in a moment. To make it worse, he was not only almost totally ignorant of conditions on the mainland, but he had the natural prejudice of one who, in his abhorrence of slavery, could feel sympathy only for the Freedmen.

As he urged the balky mule toward the lighthouse, Lassaphene said, "Whatever is happening in the city, Mr. Call, seems rather out of our province. It's too bad, but I fail to see that there's anything we can do about it. That's a matter for the government to handle."

"But there's no government to handle it!" Max exclaimed. "There's no law! Those people over there are completely at the mercy——"

"Mr. Call, I deplore violence, but I must say that it speaks ill of a people when their former slaves must resort to arms to maintain their rights. I heard some time ago there was to be an election, and that the rights of the Freedmen might be contested. But you must realize that they *are* free, and that they must be permitted to vote and hold office and take their rightful place as citizens. It's too bad about Clabo—but that's only an incident. I've no doubt that all this will blow over in a few days and that order will be restored."

It came to Max with a sudden terrible clarity that Lassaphene's view would undoubtedly be the general view of the South's problems that would prevail in other sections of the country for years. The thought horrified him.

"For God's sake," he cried, suddenly exasperated, "no one's trying to take away the rights of the Freedmen! How can we? We can't vote! We've no rights ourselves! We haven't even got the right of self-defense! You don't realize the country down here is full of Northern opportunists who are perverting the Freedmen's rights for their own ends! They started this trouble!"

"I don't believe it," Lassaphene said flatly.

In the back of the wagon Janus raised his head and said weakly, "Cap'n Lassaphene, he's telling you the truth. I'm a Freedman, Cap'n, but I have no rights. An' do you know why, Cap'n? It's because I can read and write. Men like that Mr. Dau in the city don't want an educated Freedman in the Bureau who can tell other Freedmen what's going on and how they're being cheated. But Dau's a fool, Cap'n. He's started something he can't stop. If he could have stopped it, I think he would have. So I think he must be dead. I know some of the devils in that mob, Cap'n, and I know what they'll do."

Lassaphene was suddenly bewildered. He shook his head. "But surely, a thing like this—why, it's out of our hands. Anyway, order will be restored as soon as——"

"Who's going to restore order?" Max interrupted grimly. "It's going to be hell over in the city until I can get help. You won't even be safe over here!"

Lassaphene straightened. "That's ridiculous! Why would anyone bother us over here?"

"That depends on what Clabo told those devils. He said something to them about gold, apparently trying to buy them off. If he so much as mentioned the lighthouse, they'll be over here."

"They sure will," said Janus. "I know Mr. Branch has been looking for gold over here, an' if I know it then Pinchy knows it. An' those fellows were wild. Really wild."

They were at the reservation now. Lassaphene was silent. He turned in under the shed, got out and hitched the mule to a post, and stood a moment looking darkly at the pile of old tarpaulins over beyond the chopping block. Then his lips compressed and he moved unsteadily through the gate and across the yard to the kitchen where a startled Emily was ordered to put water on to boil and to bring the surgical kit.

Charlotte gave him whisky to steady him, and poured some for Janus. But when the needles were scalded and ready, Lassaphene was unable to go on.

He fumbled with the forceps holding the needle, and dropped it. "I'm sorry," he mumbled. "I've been ill. I've no control over my fingers today. Charlotte, do you think—?"

"Let me try it," said Max. "I've seen enough of it done. I think Mrs. Maynard had better go up in the tower and keep watch, just in case."

With Lassaphene directing and Emily helping, he took eleven fairly neat stitches in Janus' arm while Janus sat looking out the window without a murmur. When it was over, Emily poured whisky and Lassaphene asked how many had been in the raid on Clabo's.

Janus said maybe eight or ten. He wasn't sure.

"How were they armed?"

"Rifles," said Max. "Enfields."

"Oh, those muzzle-loaders with paper cartridges. We've got better than that." Lassaphene looked at Janus. "How're you feeling now?"

"All right, sir," Janus told him weakly. He was lying back in the kitchen rocker with his arm in a sling.

Max said, "What have you got in the way of arms, Captain?"

"A Colt revolver, a Sharps carbine and a shotgun for geese." Lassaphene went into the front of the house and came back presently with his weapons and a bag of ammunition. He placed them on the kitchen table.

Though he was unsteady on his feet, he seemed fully in possession of himself. Nor did he appear alarmed. Max thought, He doesn't believe they'll come over to the reservation. Pray to God they don't! I've got to get away from here soon. Every hour . . .

Lassaphene said, "Just how do you propose to get help for the city—that is, if you feel it rests on you to get help, which I fail to see? There's a telegraph office there. Surely, if it's as serious as you say, someone's already——"

Janus grunted. "Cap'n Lassaphene, the Bureau had charge of the telegraph office. Anybody that tried to send a message would have just been crazy. Anyhow, Mr. Cassius——"

"Who is Mr. Cassius?"

"Cassius Drew," said Max. "He's the leading lawyer in this area. He's been trying for months to keep the soldiers there. He's appealed to the military governor, to everybody he can think of, but they paid no attention to him. So the other night when I was over there I asked him to try to telegraph the commanding officer at the Pensacola garrison to send more troops—but, as Janus says, the Bureau had charge of the telegraph office, so it's a question whether anyone was able to sneak the message out. Even if the Pensacola garrison did get the message, I'm not sure they'd act on it, things being as they are. You see, Captain, it's useless to appeal to the political element. And others, who have no ax to grind, look at it the same way you do. They don't understand. It has to be explained to them." He stopped, and added, "The only way to get to Pensacola from here is by water. I want to take the best boat—either yours or Janus'——"

"You can't get through the pass today," Lassaphene said instantly. "Not in a small vessel. Hear that surf, Mr. Call? It'll be pouring straight across the channel for the whole length of it."

"I know. But if I get under way in the next two hours I'll have the tide to help me out—providing you tell me how the channel has shifted in the past three years. I—I haven't seen it in three years, but it's your place to know——"

He stopped, suddenly aware of Charlotte standing in the doorway, looking at him. She was pale, and for the first time he thought he saw fear in her eyes.

"What's the matter?" he said.

"Max, what are you planning to do?"

"Go to the garrison at Pensacola for help," he said.

"But you can't do that. You—you know why. You just *can't!*"

"I've got to. The captain here isn't able to try it, and neither is Janus. There's no one else——"

Janus was sitting up. "You can't keep me from trying it. I'm not going to let *you* go!"

Lassaphene said, "All this argument is beside the point. Mr. Call, what gives you the impression that anyone in Pensacola would pay any attention to you? If they've ignored a man like Drew and other leading figures——"

"They'll listen to me. They'll know all about me in Pensacola. Captain, my name isn't Call—it's Ewing. It's a name that was once well respected in shipping circles on this coast, but even though that fact may be forgotten, they'll remember some other things. I'm—I'm an escaped prisoner, Captain. One of those privateersmen they wanted so badly to hang. My sentence has a long time to run, so in the circumstances . . ." He shrugged. "At least they can't ignore my appeal."

All were silent. He could feel them staring at him—Emily with her red-knuckled hands bunched in her apron, Janus sitting up with a look of ineffable melancholy on his gray face and Lassaphene rigid except that his lower lip worked without sound. Charlotte was still in the doorway. She had not moved save to bring the back of her hand across her mouth as if to stifle a cry. Her eyes were tragic and eloquent.

Suddenly Lassaphene said, "They'll not ignore you—not if they're human! I—I wish I could spare you this. With all my heart, sir, I wish I could." He stood up unsteadily. "The least I can do is ask your forgiveness for a complete lack of understanding. And next, please take my advice about the pass. The channel has shifted close in to the other island, and these seas pouring across it will drive any small craft ashore. But there's a bar to windward, and if you'll wait till just before sundown when the tide is low . . ."

Charlotte said, "He'll have to wait, Uncle Simon. There are some men coming down the beach." Her voice had that odd clear faraway quality, and she might merely have been announcing the chance sighting of some fishermen. "They ran their boat up into the marsh this side of the palm grove, and I saw them crossing the sand. There are eight of them."

II

He did not realize it was long past noon until he saw the men turn in the white glare of the beach and start up the slope of hot dry sand toward the cottages, still trotting as they had been when he first sighted them but moving slower as they struggled to reach the shadow cast by the lighthouse. Only when they touched the shadow and became upright parts of it in motion did he notice the shadow's length. He stood by the parlor window with Lassaphene's pistol in his hand, suddenly aware of the passage of time and thinking: *I must get this over with.* But he could hear Lassaphene just beyond him whispering, "Wait! Let them come closer!"

Now the wind brought their high quick excited voices to him over the sound of the surf, and he could feel the taut driving wildness in them. They were drunk. They had that weaving gait of men who have been drunk a long time, as drunk on excitement as with whisky, drunk to a sort of pagan madness that drove them beyond any conception of what they were doing. When he had first seen them they had been trotting slowly, tirelessly, in a straggling group along the edge of the surf, their bodies bent forward a little and their rifles hanging loosely at their sides. They had made him think of a wild-dog pack, yapping blindly after their leader. But now all at once as they crossed the shadow of the tower and burst into the glare of sunlight again and he caught the gleam of dark tight-drawn faces, sweat-polished, and the shine of lean torsos under unbuttoned shirts, and saw their leader with his red shirt and sash and his gold-braided cocked hat that had once belonged to a naval officer, he thought of Haiti and black murder.

His name, Max thought, shouldn't be Pinchy. There is no dignity in the name, and the man isn't funny in spite of his cocked hat and his sash and his cavalryman's sword he carries like a scepter. His face is pinched, but the name is wrong because the face is evil, and there is in him at least the perverted dignity of evil. Then suddenly Max raised the pistol, thinking, It's time to put an end to you, King Pinchy.

But again he waited, for the corner post on the veranda was in the line of fire. And the king had turned. The king had reached the little walk beyond the retaining wall and was now swinging toward the tower. And all the others, oblivious of possible danger and ignoring the cottages as if they were already in complete possession of the place, swung with him and converged on the tower. It was as if the tower were a glittering objective that had driven every other thought completely out of their minds.

He could hear their quick feral voices, sudden cries coming in staccato bursts of excitement. They might have been schoolboys in the heat of a game.

They flung themselves upon the tower door that Charlotte, before coming back to the house, had carefully padlocked.

"Hit's locked!"

"Bus' hit down! Hit's full o' money! Bus' hit down!"

"Goddammit, lemme at it!"

"Git out'n de way! I wants to roll in dat money!"

"We all wants to roll in it! Lemme at it!"

"Bus' hit down!"

They kicked the door. They screamed at it in sudden rage and pounded it with their rifle butts. Then they shot at it.

Charlotte ran to the side window, crying, "Oh, those fools! What could that man have told them? If they break into the tower they'll wreck the lamp!"

Suddenly Lassaphene, with Janus protesting, darted out on the veranda. Lassaphene shouted.

"Avast there! Get away from that tower! That's government property! You've no right to trespass here!"

He was answered by a yell and a laugh and a wild shot. He raised his carbine and discharged it, but apparently without effect. The man with the pinched black face under the cocked hat whirled away from the tower door and started for the cottage, whirling his sword and pointing it in quick fury.

"Go git 'im!" he yelled to those behind him. "Burn de man down! Dis heah's Freedmen's property! All de gold belongs to de Freedmen!"

Max leaped through the window to the veranda, but Janus darted ahead of him. Janus had one of the old pistols that had belonged to the elder Ewing; he raised it and braced it against the veranda post, and fired. The man with the cocked hat and the sword came on for three more paces, then abruptly pitched forward on his face. The sword, falling free, stuck upright in the sand on one side of the walk. But the hat remained in place on the head, and something about the angle of it made the sprawled figure seem a little ridiculous in death.

The men coming from the tower stopped as if lightning had struck in front of them. Janus slid over the veranda railing, ran out to the walk, snatched up the sword and cried, "There's no gold here! An' you've no right to anything here! All this belongs to the Government that freed you! Shame! Shame to you! You don't act like Freedmen!"

Most of them were youths, and rank with whisky. Max could smell them as he ran to help Janus. He saw one of them raise his rifle, and he fired quickly. The heavy bullet knocked the youth in a heap with a broken arm, but he bounded up with a yell of pain and fear and ran off toward the beach.

"Drop your guns!" Max ordered. "Lively—or I'll shoot every damned one of you!"

They stared at him, weaving a little, comprehending slowly. Their weapons, he decided, must be empty, for they had hardly had time to reload them after shooting at the tower door. Perhaps they all deserved to die, considering what they'd done; and in his present mood it was hard not to empty Lassaphene's revolver at them—but they were young, ignorant, drunk and mis-led, and nothing was to be gained by taking out his wrath upon them. Possibly, when they sobered, they might remember a little of this incident and recall what Janus had said to them; possibly the germ of what Janus had said would be imparted to others and bear distant fruit.

One by one they let their rifles fall to the sand.

"Now go!" he ordered. "Go back to your boat! Go on to the city and tell them that your king is dead!"

That, too, might possibly bear distant fruit, though for the time being it would alter nothing. On the main-land any man with a rifle was a law unto himself, and it would be unholy hell in the city until help came.

He stood a moment watching the retreating figures, then again he noticed the creeping shadow of the tower and was reminded of the passage of time. It seemed in-credible that it was still Wednesday.

"I've got to get under way," he said, as Lassaphene came down the steps. "It'll take an hour to reach the pier and get the boat ready, and it'll be another hour before I'm squared away outside. . . ."

"Yes," Lassaphene replied, nodding, his eyes on the sprawled body with the cocked hat. "Yes . . ."

Max looked down at Pinchy. "I hate to go off and leave you with two of those on your hands."

"Two?" Lassaphene looked vague a moment, then his face sharpened. "Oh! I'd quite forgotten. It is so easy to forget a matter when it ceases to be important. But that's our worry. You've far greater worries of your own. Come—I'll drive you over to the pier in the wagon."

Charlotte, coming down the steps, said, "I—I'd better go with you, Uncle Simon. You haven't got your strength back yet."

"I assure you that I'm quite all right," he said a trifle testily, and not in the least comprehending.

As he put the helm over and the sloop came about, heeled and gathered way, he looked back at them and saw them standing close together on the pier, one tired and stooped a little and seeming older than he was, the other straight and slim as a young girl, with something about her that made him think of a bird poised for flight. It seemed that he had only to beckon and she would fly toward him and never leave him. On the way across the island they had spoken little, but he had tried to store all of her in his memory—every precious and familiar quality of her, every small silver tone of her voice, every movement of her head and body. Even the play of sunlight on her hair and the light quick touch of her fingers were matters to be treasured.

But neither of them had needed to voice the thoughts unspoken. What they'd felt was there between them, almost a tangible part of them, and each had understood the other without the medium of words. Had either weakened and spoken from the heart, the moment would have been unbearable.

It was better this way. When you've ceased to believe in life—or destiny or fate—you can no longer allow yourself to expect much of it. You have to accept it as it comes, and do your best to forget about it. You cannot hope. To hope you must be able to look forward.

At the moment he could look no farther forward than a destination a hundred and twenty-five miles away. With luck, and if the wind held, he should be able to reach it and find audience before noon tomorrow. Some time might be saved, perhaps, if he should encounter the supply vessel that made more-or-less regular runs along the coast, from the Pensacola garrison east to St. Marks. Sometimes, Lassaphene had said, there were troops aboard. He could watch for it, and it might save precious time . . . but the final summing up would be the same.

He continued to glance back until he could no longer see the pier, then suddenly he thought of something he had forgotten. He had left his sloop anchored near the beach. It had not been there when he reached the pier.

Bella, then, was gone.

As he ran through the pass toward the white seething water of the bar, he knew he could put her out of his mind forever.

CHAPTER 20

_I_

THE wind hauled that night and came offshore, bringing a sudden spattering of rain; then it died altogether and for hours the sloop rolled with bare steerageway. By dawn, instead of being near his destination, his journey was little more than begun. He was in despair.

Yet it is out of despair and chance that hope is often born again.

With dawn a little breeze sprang up in the west. He tacked into it grimly, seeing himself spending the day beating to windward, and his despair had deepened when he made out a sail approaching on his weather bow. He

changed course and placed himself almost in the path of
it, and jogged along close-hauled, not daring to hope that
this could be the supply vessel.

A steam brig, Lassaphene had said. There was presently no doubt that it was a steam brig approaching. As
the sun slid up molten from the sea astern, stabbing his
back with a sudden forge heat, he saw her clearly in detail. She was running easily under courses and lower
topsails, and seemed in no great hurry, for her paddle
wheels were barely turning in their housings. From her
stack a thin streamer of smoke drifted forward over her
sooty canvas. There were tarpaulins over her fore and
spar decks, spread there to shelter the men she was
carrying.

Aye, this was the supply ship—and there were troops
aboard. Men suddenly lined the rail as he came about
and ran in close and hailed the quarter-deck.

A little hunch-shouldered man in a sagging vest leaned
over the taffrail and eyed him sourly a moment. "Brig
Tupelo," he rasped. "Pensacola for St. Marks—an' what
in the hell d'ye want?"

"I'm from St. George Light, on a matter of extreme
urgency! Give me a line!"

Had the wind not hauled during the night, so that the
Gulf was now almost like a millpond, the business of
boarding would have been quite another thing; in fact,
but for the calm and the wind change, all of it would
have been different and he might have missed the
Tupelo entirely. But fate seemed to have turned a leaf.

The sloop, with sails furled, was presently riding
astern on a towline, and he was on the quarter-deck
wearily asking for the troop commander.

"Ye'll find 'im below," the captain told him sourly.

"Mebbe he's up an' mebbe he ain't. Who are ye, an' what's your business?"

"Call—Captain Call, sir. And I want to request that you turn in at West Pass and help put down an insurrection. The city——"

"Ha!" The captain dribbled tobacco juice over the rail. "Insurrection. Thought that was put down in sixty-five. I'll tell ye right now the Major's got something more important to think about than any piddlin'——" He stopped, finding himself addressing only thin air, for Max had spun away from him and was hurrying down the companionway.

In the small salon below, an officer with his blouse unbuttoned and sleep still in his eyes was being served coffee by a colored mess boy.

"I'm looking for the officer in charge of these troops," Max thrust at him. "Where can I find him?"

"I'm Major Gaines," the man at the table said irritably, looking up. "Who are you, and what do you——"

Sound died on the major's lips. His mouth remained round and open for a moment, then it went tight shut as the sleep left his eyes and they widened and then narrowed with recognition. Max Ewing was suddenly motionless as he looked down at the fiery sun-bitten face with its spattering of freckles. Neither man in all his life was ever likely to forget the other and the circumstances of their last meeting. Each had delivered opinions that the other could recall almost verbatim, and one had slapped the other's face, hard on both cheeks. Even now, long after one had escaped and the other had received his prayed-for transfer to a better billet, each could recall that slap and his feelings at the moment as if it had happened only an hour ago instead of many weeks ago high on the terreplein at Garden Key.

"Well!" said the major, in a voice as brittle as ice. *"Well!"*

For a moment longer they looked at each other in silence. Then Max said, hoarsely, "Major, I was on my way to Pensacola to get help. There's trouble in my city. The troops stationed there have been removed and a group of renegades have taken over and armed the Freedmen and all hell has broken loose! The citizens are entirely without protection and since Monday they've been locked up in their homes——"

"Sit down," the major interrupted. "Let's get the straight of this."

Max had known that he would have to explain it, just as he had had to explain it to Lassaphene. But he had not expected an audience who listened with such cold imperturbability and indifference. Major Gaines might have been listening to a plea for clemency by a disorderly private. He shrugged. He drank his coffee. Occasionally he eyed his visitor as if to say: Well, what of it? Why do you come to me?

But Major Roland Gaines said nothing at all until Lieutenant Maximilian Ewing, formerly of the privateer *St. George* and lately of Garden Key, had finished his speech.

Finally he thrust his coffee cup aside and said, "Now let's hear about you. What name do you use, and where have you been—and just what is your connection with all this?"

"I've been going under the name of Call. I've been hiding, of course, and working part of the time at the lighthouse." He told briefly of the attack on the reservation.

"I see. And what, Mr. *Call*, did you expect to gain by appealing to the garrison at Pensacola?"

"Gain!" Max cried. "Help, of course! My God, surely they'd listen to a man who was willing to give himself up!"

"Possibly." The major shrugged. "But what makes you think I can do anything about all this? After all, I'm only a——"

Max grasped the table with suddenly trembling hands. "Are you going to order this vessel to turn in at West Pass or not?"

"And suppose I don't?"

"By the Almighty God, I'll kill you if you don't! D'you think I care what happens to me at this point? All I care about is getting help for people who are desperate! Even if I didn't have a pistol in my pocket, I'd kill you with my bare hands! What kind of a man are you?"

The major sat back and looked curiously at his visitor. "I believe you would kill me," he said quietly. "But calm down, Mr. *Call*——"

"You may as well use my real name. You know what it is!"

"No, let us forget a certain name for the time being. In the first place, I'm traveling under orders. I've no authority to stop off at a certain port and concern myself with that port's troubles. I am to proceed directly to St. Marks with my command, and take the train for Tallahassee—which I understand is only a few miles from there. In Tallahassee I am to present myself to the military governor who has a fondness for parades and military display——"

"Parades!" Max rasped.

The major sighed. "They serve their purpose, sir. Though it seems unreasonable that they should all be held in one place. I should admit that a great many things have seemed unreasonable to me—but I am only an army man, Mr. Call, and I must obey orders." He looked away. "It happens, however, that this vessel is in very poor condition, and I expect any minute that something can happen—say a leak, or engine trouble or the like. The captain is a sour old wart, but he's not unreasonable. If we are forced to put in at the nearest port for repairs, then it's not my fault. And if there happens to be an infractious element at that port, well, I'll just have to take control. It'll be my duty. And when I telegraph the circumstances back to Pensacola, I rather expect I'll be ordered to remain in control."

"Major, forgive me——"

"Please, let's forget about some things," Roland Gaines said a little stiffly. "For one, there's that detail of a name. Some time ago when I was on duty at Fort Jefferson, two prisoners tried to escape. I remember the matter very clearly. One of the prisoners was named Meriwether, and the other Ewing. They were both shot while trying to swim the channel to Bird Key. Meriwether's body was eventually recovered, but Ewing's was never found. Anyway, the report went out that both men were killed." He shrugged. "Of course, that doesn't solve matters exactly. Probably only time can do that."

Max clutched the table and stared at him.

"Major, I—I don't understand," he said hoarsely. "You—why in God's name are you doing such a thing as this for me?"

Roland Gaines frowned. He looked at his hand and

absently touched his cheek, then stood up and suddenly thrust his hand into his pocket as if he had remembered something he preferred not to think about. "Oh, hell," he muttered. "I expect all of us have been guilty of acts we'd rather forget. If our situations were reversed . . ." He looked hard at Max and added, "Anyway, I just wanted you to know, *Mr. Call,* that we're not all vindictive. Now, if you'll excuse me, I'll have a talk with the captain."

II

The *Tupelo* steamed up the channel and swung slowly in to the docks. A small crowd had gathered at the main landing, and Max could see the restless uncertain movement of it, as if those in it felt the strength of numbers but had no individual strength to guide or hold them. But men were coming through the streets to join them and with every minute the crowd was becoming more like a mob, armed, threatening, defiant, and suddenly loud as several drunken members ran out in front, screaming at the top of their lungs and leaping like maddened witch doctors while they shook their rifles at the oncoming ship. The water front and every building in sight showed the mark of ignorant force that had gone wild with the removal of restraint. There were broken windows, the streets were cluttered with the debris of looting, and the brick shell of a warehouse was still belching smoke from burning cotton bales. It seemed a wonder to Max that the whole city had not burned.

The shouting on the dock abruptly died as the first

staccato notes of the bugle rose in warning from the
Tupelo's quarter-deck. The soldiers crouching a little
nervously on the hatches sprang to attention at the rail.
The morning sun gleamed on fixed bayonets. All at once
the drum began to roll ominously and the bugle sounded
again. The mob ashore was suddenly still. And now as
the vessel swung closer to them, an order rose loudly
from the quarter-deck. The order quite ignored the
established military wording set forth in Casey's Infantry Tactics, and was delivered solely for its psycho-
logical effect ashore:

*"Don't fire till you see the whites of their eyes—and
then kill every man in sight!"*

The mob fell back on the instant, broke and began to
scatter, and rifles for which ammunition had long since
been expended were tossed aside. In five minutes the
docks and the streets were empty. Not a shot had been
fired.

The incident was beginning to seem a little funny to
the young men in blue as they tumbled ashore; but to
Max, showing Gaines to the telegraph office before hurrying to find Cassius, there was only a sickening awareness
of the years of uncertainties stretching ahead.

III

The Drew house had been broken into while Bethsheba
was out, but the occupants, hiding in the attic, had escaped harm. "Bethsheba was down on the pier trying to
catch a meal when they came," said Cassius. "They were
only some strays, around looting. I'd got Mother to the

attic, and was trying to decide what to do about them when Bethsheba suddenly came back. You should have heard her turn on those rascals!"

They sat that afternoon on the veranda, talking over what had happened and speculating on the future.

"I hear Dau is missing," Cassius said. "He may be dead, though it hardly matters. There'll be more like him along. We can't keep them out."

"Is there any chance of getting my house back?"

"I doubt it, Maximilian. It was confiscated, so there's little chance now. Perhaps later, if we can get your name cleared . . ."

Cassius poured wine from a precious bottle of prewar scuppernong. "Here's to Fight and Fortitude!" he said quietly. "From now on we'll have to fight when and how we can, and endure the rest of it the best way we can."

Max sipped his wine and looked thoughtfully out over the blue and bronze sweep of the bay. His attention centered on the island, a vague line on the far horizon. He closed his eyes, suddenly thankful for this moment of peace. Far more than the wine, he was relishing the miracle of being able to hope again.

"Do you believe you can get my name cleared?" he asked.

"I'm sure of it. But it'll take time, Maximilian."

"I'll be patient."

"That's a strange word from you."

"Oh, I haven't changed. I've merely adjusted a point of view." He stopped a moment, then said, "Those young fellows on the *Tupelo*. Why, they were just boys. They've never seen combat. They must have been in school during the war."

The realization had been a little shattering. Something he might have felt against seasoned men had suddenly evaporated in the face of their youth. They didn't know what it was all about. Probably they'd never know. In time they'd go home from here as from a foreign land, and they'd soon forget. They'd never quite understand. Those others who had done the fighting were already at home, forgetting and hardly caring about the fate of the vanquished because they'd been thrown into something they'd never fully understood in the first place. The sincere ones had seen themselves fighting to preserve the Union—but how many had realized that the struggle was economic? Now the Union was preserved and they were long out of it, and you couldn't fight them again.

As if he had spoken his thoughts aloud, he heard Cassius say, "You see now how it has to be, Maximilian?"

"Aye, I see."

"And your friends on Garden Key. They'll have to wait, just as you and others are having to wait."

His lips thinned and the knuckles of his clenched hands showed white a moment. This was the worst of it, this having to give up a mission he would have given his life to complete. But it had to be. There was no other way. What would it profit to save a few if it only added to the burden of the many?

He nodded, silent.

Cassius said, "When you first returned, you remember you asked about the money you had left with your mother? Well, when I said I didn't know what had happened to it, I was telling a half-truth. There is a little left—how much I don't know, but it's probably under two thousand. Bethsheba has it, hidden away somewhere. We thought it would be safer with her than with me. As you may recall, I went out and spoke to her that night before I let you see her. The way you were feeling then, I was afraid of what might happen if you got your hands on that money. I knew you'd need it badly later to make a small start in life." Cassius paused, and added, "Especially when you discovered—as perhaps you have—that the gold on the island is not quite available."

He looked quickly at Cassius. "I'd been wondering about that. I found only the vessel's prow. If the hull was badly battered and broke open, when it was driven over the island . . ."

Cassius nodded. "That's what happened."

They were silent a moment, and each sipped his wine slowly, making it last while they gazed seaward at the thin line beyond the silky brightness of the bay.

Finally Cassius said, "What we were, what we had, can be likened to that Spanish vessel whose remains are hidden over there. We've been wrecked in a hurricane, broken to bits, and our treasure scattered—just as that treasure is scattered. It isn't entirely lost, for you'll always be able to find bits of it if you look. But we'll find more by looking ahead rather than backward."

"There you go, speaking in parables again."

"I'm afraid that's a sign of age, Maximilian. On that matter I can't help myself. But fortune is a curious thing, and the older one becomes the more he ponders it. Cicero said that man's life is ruled by fortune, not by wisdom—but I'm still young enough to take issue with him. Certainly man has choice—and as long as he can choose he'll have something to say about his destiny."

They finished their wine. Max stood up.

Cassius said, "You're not leaving?"

"Aye, I'd better. The tide has turned, and they'll be wondering about me over at the island. They may need me. But I'll be back soon. I've much to talk over with you, but I'll have to think about it first."

As always, when he was alone on the water, his thoughts came clearer and all things seemed to fall into their proper place. He looked back once at the town dwindling astern, and saw it blending into the coast, the houses becoming dots of white among the somber oaks. A smudge of smoke from the smoldering cotton in the ruined warehouse grayed the harbor. In the still afternoon he could hear faintly, like a memory, the tolling of a church bell, and a few quick notes from a bugle. The breeze had shifted a little, coming now offshore so that for a moment he could smell the acrid smoke mingling with the forest fragrance from the troubled land. Then he was out and beyond the channel with illimitable blue distance on either side, and there were only the clean smells of tarred cordage and salt sea.

The weights and the cares of the land suddenly vanished. Ahead, sharper now, a band of darker blue on the horizon, lay the promise of his destination. His eyes centered on it as he thought of Charlotte, and again there came to him the memory of her voice and the way it had seemed to reach out to him across dark chasms that day in the tower. He thought of her on the beach, spirit to the circling terns as she came to meet him, spirit to the island itself as if she had always belonged to it, as if she were an inseparable part of it. Aye, she was part of it; she was the very spirit of it. As long as he lived she would be the spirit and the beauty of it, and the refuge of it, and all things that a woman can ever mean to a man.

With the bright vision of her everything was suddenly clear in his mind. There was no need to ask what he wanted to do, how he wanted to shape his life. It lay before him with the clarity of a course marked on a chart. Janus, the island, the money Bethsheba had saved for him—all these were segments of the course. The future was Charlotte's, for her hand would be in the shaping of it.

For the time being, while his status was in doubt, he would have to remain on the island. And perhaps he had better safeguard it by having it transferred to Charlotte. Surely Cassius could arrange that. As for the money Bethsheba had saved, it was precious little to begin the building of a fleet—but with Janus to help they could buy a small schooner of sorts for the coastal trade. Aye, that would be a start.

A tern crossed his bow and circled on slim white wings. It might have been a messenger sent to greet him, to assure him of his course.

The rest, he knew, was patience. The fleet would come in time. All things would come in time, including the power to fight for the rights that were being denied.

Patience.

Afterword

Publisher's Note: It has been more than 60 years since the first publication of Alexander Key's Island Light and nearly 150 years since the time period in which the novel was set. This Afterword provides a brief overview of the novel's historical context and the changes which have occurred since that period to shape the Forgotten Coast of today.

The Forgotten Coast Then and Now: A Brief History of Apalachicola, St. George Island and the Cape St. George Light

Today's visitor to the Florida Panhandle and its popular Gulf Coast may find it hard to believe that huge portions of the region remained inaccessible and undeveloped well into the twentieth century. During the time period in which *Island Light* is set, immediately following the War Between the States, access to settlements and trading posts in the region was primarily by water, either from local creeks and rivers or from the Gulf of Mexico.

The City of Apalachicola

Historic Apalachicola, first settled in 1820 as a customs collection outpost, adopted its current name in 1831, and by the mid-1800s was the third largest port on the Gulf. Commercial goods, including 80% of the river basin's cotton production, were transported from Alabama, Georgia and Northern Florida down the Chattahoochee, Flint and Apalachicola rivers to Apalachicola, then shipped by sea to other port cities along the United States Eastern Coast, to England and other European destinations. Due to the challenges of navigating the shallow Apalachicola Bay, local ships' captains were often hired to pilot goods in and out of the busy port.

Franklin County was formed in 1832, with Apalachicola as its county seat. A year later, the first lighthouse on St. George Island was built at the western entrance to Apalachicola Bay. Florida became a state in 1845, but in 1861 became the third state to secede from the Union following the election of Abraham Lincoln to the United States Presidency.

The Port of Apalachicola, during and after the War Between the States

Early in the Civil War, Union warships blockaded Apalachicola's port. Max Ewing, *Island Light*'s central character, commanded the fictitious privateer St. George of the Confederate States Navy, a blockade runner and a target for Union forces. Confederate ships, when seized while attempting to thwart the blockade, had their crews imprisoned and vessels and cargo sold for profit. When Ewing's fictional ship was captured in 1864, according to Key's narrative, Ewing was charged with piracy and treason and received a harsh sentence of 20 years in prison.

The years following the war were difficult for Apalachicola residents, although the port enjoyed a brief resurgence in trade by 1869. Under Reconstruction, the city was governed from a distance by Union Forces based in Pensacola, and the 82nd Colored Infantry, stationed in the city to maintain order.

St. George Island

St. George Island, setting of Key's *Island Light*, is the largest of the barrier islands separating Apalachicola Bay from the Gulf of Mexico. The area has a long history of human habitation, going back more than 12,000 years. Spanish and French explorers established outposts during Florida's later history, but many of Florida's Indian tribes had permanent settlements, including the dominant Apalachees.

In 1804, at the suggestion of the Spanish government, over a million acres of land between the St. Marks and Apalachicola Rivers, including St. George Island, were ceded to Englishman John Forbes and Company, in settlement of Indian land debts. This transaction was later contested and remained in dispute until resolved by the U.S. Supreme Court in 1835. In that year the Apalachicola Land Company was formed, and land in the region was sold piecemeal until the company became insolvent in 1858. Along with other barrier islands along the Apalachicola Bay, portions of St. George Island were sold and resold over the years. Key's character, Max Ewing, was to have purchased a portion of St. George Island prior to the Civil War. At the time of Key's novel, St. George Island was remote and largely uninhabited, covered by sand dunes and stunted scrub brush, and accessible only by boat. The Lighthouse Keeper, his family and his staff would have lived a primitive and isolated existence.

Changes to St. George Island In the 20th Century

During World War II, St. George Island was occupied by U.S. Forces for B-24 bombing and amphibious assault practice. German U-Boats were known to prowl the Gulf waters along the coast. Some foreign vessels were apprehended and prisoners captured in the area during this period.

St. George Island has been breached many times over the years due to storms and erosion. In 1954, the Army Corps of Engineers dredged a channel, Bob Sikes Cut, across the island. Bob Sikes was an influential congressman from Florida's panhandle. The Cut provided a fast alternate route between the bay and the gulf, benefitting Apalachicola's commercial fishing fleet. Today, the site attracts recreational fishermen as well.

Dr. Julian G. Bruce St. George Island State Park stretches along nine miles of the island's eastern tip. Its 2000+ acres retain a relatively wild nature although the park offers full service camping sites, hiking trails, boardwalks and observation platforms. A popular destination for bird watchers, the park is also popular with recreational fishermen, offering two boat launches and miles of undeveloped beaches for fishing, swimming and sunning.

*The Founding of Eastpoint

The relationship between Apalachicola and its neighbors across Apalachicola Bay changed little until around 1900. In 1898, the community of Eastpoint was settled in approximately the location of Key's fictitious "Clabo's Tavern." Families from Nebraska established Eastpoint as an experimental community, with profits from farming, lumbering, seafood and manufacturing to be shared by its inhabitants. Although the experimental community eventually disbanded, the settlement of Eastpoint remained.

*Connecting the Communities

Until 1935, Eastpoint was accessible from Apalachicola only by ferry. In 1935, the 6.5 mile John Gorrie Bridge was completed, named after a local doctor, who in the 1840s pioneered the development of refrigeration and cooling techniques to treat victims of yellow fever. The Gorrie Bridge and its causeway made automobile traffic possible between Apalachicola and Eastpoint.

A causeway and bridge linked Eastpoint to St. George Island in 1965. Named the Bryant Grady Patton Bridge, the structure was replaced by a new bridge in 2004. The third longest bridge in Florida and the longest in Florida's Panhandle, it contains a span 72 feet in height providing clearance for tall ships navigating the Intracoastal Waterway.

Today, with its connection to the mainland, St. George Island contains a small, but thriving community, including a vibrant commercial district and both permanent residential and resort properties.

*St. George's Lighthouses

St. George Island's lighthouses have a tempestuous and compelling history, marked by hurricanes, erosion and human determination. Lighthouses have played a critical role in the Gulf Coast's navigational history, which includes numerous stories of piracy and shipwrecks. The Cape St. George Light was one of several lighthouses established in the early 1800s to improve navigational safety along the Gulf coast.

The first St. George Island Lighthouse, built in 1833 on the westernmost point of St. George Island, marked the West Pass shipping entrance into Apalachicola Bay. Its location was problematic, partially hidden by the island, which made the light difficult to see for ships approaching from the East. Vulnerable to storm surge, this first light was destroyed in 1846.

The second light was built in 1848, relocated farther east at the southernmost point of Cape St. George. Salvaged materials from the first light were used to build the second light, known as the Cape St. George Light. This lighthouse stood ten feet taller than the original. At 75 feet, it was easier to spot by sailors from the east. Three years later, this second lighthouse was toppled in a hurricane which also destroyed neighboring lights at Cape San Blas and Dog Island.

The third lighthouse was rebuilt nearby, but farther inland. "Built to last," the new structure was supported by seven-foot pine pilings driven into the sand to provide the foundation. This would be the lighthouse described in Island Light. The light was turned off during the Civil War, to discourage the entrance of Union vessels into Apalachicola Bay, but was relit following the war, on August 1, 1866. Its damaged lens, removed and hidden during the war, was replaced in 1889. In 1949, the light was automated and operated until 1994 when it was deactivated by the U.S. Coast Guard.

*Preserving Island History

Already ravaged by storms and natural erosion, this third lighthouse was washed from its foundations in 1995 by tidal surges following Hurricane Opal. Though still standing following that storm, the structure tilted seven degrees.

That year, committed citizens of the region formed the Cape St. George Lighthouse Society in an attempt to save their historic lighthouse. More than $200,000 in grants and donations were used to stabilize the structure. By 2002, the lighthouse was deemed restored and the group disbanded.

Gulf storms continued their assaults. By spring 2005, ground around the lighthouse had eroded, leaving the light standing 20 feet from the shoreline. On October 21, 2005 the Cape St. George Light collapsed into the Gulf of Mexico.

Again, local citizens rallied. The St. George Lighthouse Association, established in 2004, worked with the State of Florida Department of Environmental Protection to salvage materials from the destroyed light. Building plans for the 1852 Lighthouse were obtained from the National Archives in Washington, D.C. and reconstruction began in 2007. Twenty-two thousand bricks reclaimed from the previous structure were used to surface the interior walls, floor and ceiling of the new tower. This fourth lighthouse is located on St. George Island in St. George Lighthouse Park. It was completed in December of 2008. The site includes a replica of the original Lighthouse Keeper's House, which serves as a museum dedicated to telling the story of the historic lighthouse.

The Cape St. George Lighthouse is listed in the National Registry of Historic Places.

Today's "Forgotten Coast," Remembered

Today the Lighthouse and St. George Island State Park are just a few of the many attractions which draw thousands of visitors to St. George Island's famous beaches and a variety of accommodations, restaurants and shops.

Apalachicola remains a charming and historic community, offering four state museums, a new Maritime Museum, and a variety of accommodations, both historic and modern. Its world-class restaurants take full advantage of the strong local seafood industry, serving up along with many other choices, the best oysters in the world.

Today's Gulf Coast offers the best of the modern and traditional worlds. Each year lovers of the outdoors flock to Apalachicola and the Forgotten Coast, to explore its natural beauty, including its rivers and creeks and many federal and state forests, gamelands and parks, where it is possible to catch glimpses of the region's untamed past. Here it is still possible to experience the setting of Alexander Key's Island Light.

Susan Nosco Wolfe

Sources for this article:

A variety of websites were used to gather the information for this article, including websites for Apalachicola, Carrabelle and Franklin County history. One of the best included information provided by the Apalachicola Historical Society. The Florida Department of State Division of Library and Information Services maintains its State Archives of Florida Online Catalog, which proved useful. Historical sites often have their own information website. It is also possible to search by name or topic. As with many queries, one often leads to another. In the age of "point and click," with a computer and a bit of time, it's possible to find answers to most questions, and often, in the process, find something unexpected. Many thanks to the persons who develop and maintain these sites and to the historical societies and other groups which support them. If asked, they will be glad to guide you through the discovery process.

CPSIA information can be obtained at www.ICGtesting.com

232117LV00001B/3/P

9 780967 591766